"What are you afraid of?"

"I'm not afraid." She glanced away, and then, with an effort, she met his gaze again. "No, that's not true. I am afraid. It's just not right for us now. Not for Katie *or* me. I want you to leave us alone. Please."

Alan sighed. Removing his hat, he shoved a hand through his hair and turned to stare off in the distance. Maura held her breath.

"Sorry," he finally said. "I can't do it. Not this time." Looking back at her, he resettled his hat on his head. "You see, this isn't exactly what I wanted, either. But it happened. And I have no intention of leaving you alone."

He grinned that cocky, little-boy grin of his and her heart melted.

"In fact, I plan to spend a lot of time with you and that little girl of yours. You might as well get used to the idea."

Patricia Keelyn

Keeping Katie

Harlequin Books

TORONTO • NEW YORK • LONDON
AMSTERDAM • PARIS • SYDNEY • HAMBURG
STOCKHOLM • ATHENS • TOKYO • MILAN
MADRID • WARSAW • BUDAPEST • AUCKLAND

ISBN 0-373-70590-5

KEEPING KATIE

This edition published by arrangement with Harlequin Enterprises B. V.

Printed in U.S.A.

ABOUT THE AUTHOR

"I've always loved a book that could make me cry," confides Patricia Keelyn. "So when I set out to write *Keeping Katie*, I kept that in mind. What could be more heartbreaking than to see a child taken away from its mother?"

Patricia makes her home in Georgia, with her husband and daughter. She has several other stories in the works and will undoubtedly become a popular romance novelist.

To Andrea and Jeff,
for their love, faith and patience

PROLOGUE

MAURA WAITED.

Sitting in the dark, a single backpack at her feet, she watched the clock as its hands inched forward. Still, when the soft chimes declared the hour, she flinched.

Midnight. Time to go . . . or stay.

Pushing the last thought aside, she rose from the couch and moved toward the back of the house, to Katie. As she slipped into the child's bedroom, emotion collided with purpose. The room was cozy and warm, softly lighted by a Mickey Mouse night-light. She took a moment to absorb the familiarity of the room, recognizing in the shadows the things Katie loved: her picture books, her dolls, the Fisher-Price kitchen set and the dancing ponies painted on the wall.

Moving toward the bed, Maura stooped to pick up a stuffed kitten and return it to its proper place on a nearby shelf. She stood there for a time, arranging, straightening, cherishing these last few minutes in this room. She hated what she had to do, and wondered how Katie would react. How would she feel in the morning when no army of soft toys greeted her awakening? Sighing, Maura turned away and went to her daughter's bed.

Katie, beautiful Katie. Maura sat down beside her and thought how wonderful it must be to sleep so soundly. But then, three-year-olds were usually oblivious to the dangers the world held. She reached out and brushed a stray curl away from Katie's cheek, feeling the soft baby skin with the backs of her fingers. Even Dave's death last year went almost unnoticed by the child. So innocent, so precious.

Absently, she reached up and touched her own unfamiliar crop of short hair. Would Katie notice?

Enough, Maura, she silently chastised herself. *Get on with it.* Reaching for the clothes she'd left lying on the end of the bed, she began to dress the sleeping child. Katie barely stirred, murmuring and occasionally turning away from her mother's ministrations. It was only as she lifted the child onto her lap, slipping a warm winter jacket around her shoulders, that Katie woke up enough to recognize her mother.

"It's okay, sweetie," Maura whispered. "Mommy and Katie are going on a trip." She kissed the top of the child's head while slipping first one tiny arm, then the other, into the jacket. "Like last summer. Remember?"

Katie nodded sleepily and snuggled closer against her mother. "Here, let me zip you up." Maura shifted the child so she could get at the front of the jacket.

"Not cold," Katie mumbled, twisting herself against Maura's chest.

"I know, sweetie," she said. "But it's cold outside."

"Davey coming, too?"

Maura smiled and reached behind her to pick up a stuffed dog. Putting the toy into Katie's hands, she said, "Of course Davey can come."

The drive to the railway station was short, and Katie slept the whole way. From there, Maura planned to leave her car and walk the seven blocks to the Greyhound bus station. Under normal circumstances it would have been a short, pleasant walk. But not tonight. Even Miami was chilly in January, especially at 1:00 a.m. Carrying a backpack and a sleeping toddler would be no picnic.

Reaching over to undo the safety belt of Katie's car seat, Maura hesitated. Katie slept so peacefully, unaware that her world was about to change. Maura pulled away, letting her head fall back against the seat.

How could she go through with this?

Everything she knew and loved was here. Nursing, the career she'd paid dearly to pursue and still loved after ten years. Her friends, those who had stood by her these last months. Her home. A small three-bedroom house that she and Dave had bought the day they found out about Katie. It sat silent and empty now. And David? Buried, but still here, where they'd lived and loved and hoped and cried until the day Katie had come into their lives. He was still here.

How could she leave all this?

The iridescent numbers on the car clock caught her eye. One o'clock. It was now or never. Maura looked back at Katie again.

How could she *not?*

This time she didn't hesitate. Maura Anderson was dead. From now on, she'd be Maureen Adams. Unlatching Katie's safety belt, she thought, *It doesn't matter. The only thing that matters is Katie. And no one is going to take her away from me.*

CHAPTER ONE

ALAN PARKS STEPPED off the curb and planted his five-foot-eleven-inch frame squarely in front of two hundred and twenty pounds of oversize teenager. "Where do you think you're going, Joe?"

Startled, Joey Simmons barely avoided a head-on collision. "Damn, Sheriff, where'd you come from?"

"The important question here is, Where do *you* think you're going?"

For a moment Joey met Alan's gaze, then glanced at the truck he'd been heading for. Alan watched the play of emotion that crossed the boy's face—first surprise, then anger and the urge to challenge, before he turned away guiltily. In truth, Alan felt sorry for the boy, but this was the third time this month he'd been warned. Things were getting out of hand.

"I was just gonna get something out of the truck, Sheriff," Joey said. "I wasn't gonna drive it."

"Don't lie to me, boy."

Joey dropped his gaze again, sliding his hands into the pockets of his overalls.

"This is your last warning."

"But, Sheriff..."

"No buts." Alan moved in closer. "Next time I catch you driving that truck, I'm going to land your butt in the state juvenile home. Then I'm going to throw your daddy in jail for contributing to the delinquency of a minor."

Joey took a step back, but Alan followed him. "So, you tell that old cuss he either runs his own errands into town or finds someone of age to drive his truck."

"Sheriff, you know Daddy ain't fit to drive."

"I know your daddy spends most of his time inside a bottle. Now, he needs to sober up or get someone else to do his driving."

"But there ain't no one else, Sheriff. And I'm gonna be sixteen in a few months."

Alan was sympathetic to this man-child caught between his daddy and the law. But the law was the law. "You aren't sixteen yet, and you can't drive that truck without a license. Now, go on." Alan motioned toward one of his deputies, who'd been watching from across the street. "Ray there will drive you home. Tell your daddy to get Widow Cellar to bring him in if he wants his truck back.

"And by the way..." Alan turned and reached into the cab of the pickup truck behind him. Pulling the rifle off the rack, he opened the gun and emptied the cartridges into his hand. "Remind your daddy that hunting season's six months away yet."

"Come on, Joey." Ray laid a hand on the boy's arm and motioned toward the police cruiser. Joey glared at the deputy and shook the man's hand from his arm, then turned back toward Alan. Once again, Alan braced himself, watching the boy's raw emotions rip across his features. And once again, he breathed a sigh of relief as Joey's anger died and was replaced with frustration. Then he turned and followed Ray to the waiting car.

"Wonder how much longer before that boy realizes he outweighs you by a good thirty pounds." The comment came from Jake, another of Alan's deputies.

Alan grinned to hear his own thoughts spoken aloud. "Well, let's hope not for a while."

"I wouldn't count on it." Jake crossed his arms and rested a hip against the truck's fender. "You ask *me,* he's got a mean streak like his old man, just waiting to explode."

Alan threw a surprised glance toward his deputy. Jake wasn't one to make snap judgments. "Has Joe been throwing his weight around with the other boys?"

"Caught him the other day. Had Judge Perrill's kid pinned up against a wall."

Alan snorted. "Young Bradley probably deserved it."

"Yup, he probably did, but I hate to see it. Joey's too big, and he ain't had an easy life."

"Yeah." There was no doubt about it, life had been tough on the Simmons boys. Ever since their mama up and ran off some five years ago, old man Simmons had been living in a bottle. Lord only knew how much of his anger ended up on those boys' backsides.

"Yeah," he repeated more to himself than to Jake. "I guess it's time I take a drive out there to see just what's going on." With a sigh, he walked away from the truck. "For now, though, I'm going over to Jill's to catch something to eat."

Jake nodded. "Gonna check out our newest resident?"

"Yeah. Hopefully she'll be easier to deal with than young Joe."

"Probably didn't have bus fare to Seattle."

"You're probably right. But I'm just going to make sure."

SIX DAYS IN WAITEVILLE, and life had already settled into a routine. Every morning Maureen rose at five, kissed her sleeping daughter goodbye and headed downtown to Jill's Café, where she worked the breakfast and lunch shift.

The mornings passed quickly. A slow but steady stream of customers kept both Maureen and Jill busy. By nine the rush ended, and Maureen would take a few minutes to call Katie. Usually she would be finishing breakfast while Rita fussed over her. Then, after Maureen's call, Rita would deliver Katie to the babysitter across the street, where she would stay until her mother got off work at two.

For the hundredth time since arriving in Waiteville, Maureen thanked God for Rita Ember. The woman was a saint. Just renting them a room would have been enough to earn Maureen's eternal gratitude, but Rita's generosity didn't stop there. She even found a neighbor eager to watch Katie while Maureen worked. Then she helped them settle into their room, finding this and that to make the small space more comfortable.

Maureen closed her eyes and let herself hope—for just a moment—that maybe she'd found a place where she and Katie could stay. It was so quiet here, so remote. Who would ever think to look for her in this place; a little speck of a town on the eastern slopes of the Washington Cascade mountains?

"Hey, Jill, what have you got for a hungry man this morning?"

The rough male voice, followed by the slam of the front door, shattered Maureen's thoughts. She looked toward the commotion and her stomach took a sudden turn.

Jill grinned and slipped an arm around a trim male waist in a law enforcement uniform. "Well now," she said, "that depends on just what that man was hungry for."

The man's smile broadened, and he gave Jill a quick squeeze. "How about a couple eggs, over easy, and a plateful of that ham you keep back there. And plenty of coffee."

Jill reached up and pinched his cheek. "You got it, handsome." Laughing, she released him and headed for the kitchen.

Only then could Maureen move. With trembling hands, she turned back to her work, telling herself there was nothing to worry about. So the man was a police officer. Towns everywhere had them. She had to stop panicking every time she saw one.

Alan lowered himself onto the stool closest to the door and dropped his hat on the counter. He idly passed a hand through his hair while glancing around. With a nod or a wave, he acknowledged the other people in the café. Friends or neighbors all, he knew every face but one. Jill returned, and he gratefully accepted the coffee she set in front of him.

"Thanks, gorgeous," he said with a wink. As always, she returned his smile with one of her own before moving on to other things.

Relishing his first sip, he let his gaze wander to the booths lining the back wall of the restaurant. The woman he'd come to see—the one unfamiliar face in the place—cleared dirty dishes from an empty booth.

He watched as she loaded the plastic tray and then leaned over to wipe off the table.

Not much to look at was his first thought. Too skinny. Her jeans looked at least a size too big, and an oversize T-shirt hid whatever other feminine attributes she might possess. She looked as though she could use a good meal or two.

Jill interrupted his thoughts with a plate of ham and eggs, cooked just the way he liked them. He smiled in appreciation, not only at the breakfast but at Jill's lush curves. Now that was the way a woman should be built, he thought. Soft and round.

He'd explored Jill's curves a time or two—years ago. For a while, when they were in high school, the two of them had been an item. Lots of people had assumed they'd eventually marry. Then he'd gone off to Seattle, and when he'd come back, well, things just weren't the same. Still, between Jill and him there would always be something special.

As soon as Jill left, Alan's gaze roamed back to the other woman. She was a drifter, all right. She wore her dark hair short, and her skin was pale as snow. He wondered why she'd decided to stop in Waiteville. Probably, as Jake suggested, she'd run out of money. It was just like Rita Ember to take in a stray, especially one with a child.

Yet, as he watched her, something didn't fit. He couldn't quite put his finger on it, but something was wrong. The answer was there, just out of reach, nudging at his mind. *What was it?* With an inward shrug he pushed the thought aside. He knew better than to try to force it. The answer would come to him—eventually.

Maureen felt his gaze on her. For the past half-hour, as he'd finished off the huge breakfast Jill brought him, he'd watched her. He spoke to everyone else in the place, flirting with the women, talking crops or hunting with the men. But he *watched* her.

She avoided him, taking care of other customers, wishing she could fade into the surroundings.

Maybe she'd made a mistake stopping in a small town. It would be easier to disappear in a place where no one knew or cared who their neighbors were. She should have gone on to Seattle, the way she'd planned. If only it hadn't been so pretty the day she and Katie got off the bus here, with all the apple trees in bloom. They'd been traveling for more than three months, never staying anywhere for more than a couple of weeks. Maureen was tired and Katie cranky. They ate lunch at Jill's, and Maureen saw the Help Wanted sign. It seemed like fate. Now she wasn't so sure.

The morning crowd began to thin out, but not him. Maureen wanted to call Rita and talk to Katie. She needed to hear Katie's voice. She needed to hear it desperately. Not yet, she told herself. Another fifteen minutes.

Why didn't he leave?

Then he lifted his empty coffee cup in her direction, and there was no escape. Fighting the urge to turn and look for Jill, Maureen picked up a full pot of coffee and headed toward him.

"New in town," he said, watching the steaming black coffee she poured into his cup.

"Yes," she answered, willing an unfelt calmness to her voice.

He picked up the sugar dispenser and sweetened his coffee. "Planning to stay awhile?"

Maureen shrugged, remembering the carefully practiced script she'd worked out for questions such as this. "That depends."

He looked at her closely then, straight and hard, his fathomless dark eyes seeking answers. She knew then she'd made a mistake. No, two mistakes. The first was thinking she and Katie would be safe in Waiteville. The second was in her evaluation of this man. This was no small-town, bumbling idiot of a sheriff—although why she'd ever thought this would be true escaped her. Nor was he the vacuous pretty boy she'd suspected when he'd waltzed into the diner, winking and flirting with Jill. Intelligence lurked in his eyes. And danger. A danger that went far beyond what his badge threatened.

A needle of fear pricked her spine, chilling her. She wanted to run, but she knew that would be a mistake. She held firm, instinct telling her that the worst thing to do when confronted with a predator was to flee.

Then he smiled and lifted his cup to his lips. "Where are you from, sweet thing?"

Maureen couldn't answer. Not at first. As quickly as she'd been struck by the cunning in his eyes, it had vanished. With a smile, a wink and a chauvinistic endearment, he'd hidden it. Oh, the threat still lingered. She wouldn't allow herself to think she'd imagined it. She suspected he didn't like people to see too much.

"Chicago," she answered finally, easily, knowing she, too, wasn't what she seemed. And she had far better reasons than this man to keep her identity hidden. Still, she couldn't keep the irritation out of her voice as she added, "And my name's Maureen." She paused, smiling to soften her words. "Maureen Adams. And you, Officer?"

He returned the coffee cup to its saucer, and his smile broadened. "Alan Parks, Waiteville sheriff, at your service."

"Nice to meet you, Sheriff." Nodding, she started to turn away.

"Hear you rented a room from Rita Ember."

Maureen stopped and turned, trying out a carefully constructed smile, though her stomach churned. "I guess news really does travel fast in a small town."

"Yup."

"Mrs. Ember is a very nice lady. It was kind of her to rent one of her rooms to my daughter and me."

"Your daughter?"

"Yes." Maureen held her smile with an effort. "Katie. She's three."

He picked up his cup again and took another sip. "Depends on what?"

"I'm sorry, Sheriff. What?" she said, feigning ignorance.

"You said how long you stay depends. Depends on what?"

"Oh." Maureen shrugged again and lowered her eyes to the coffeepot she still held in her hands. "Well, you know, on how things work out."

When she raised her gaze back to his, she saw the danger again. At that moment, she would have sworn he knew everything about her. She mentally shook herself. She was being foolish. This was just a small-town sheriff checking out a stranger.

She launched into the script she'd prepared. "I lost my husband recently..." *The truth,* she told herself. *Stick to the truth as much as possible.* "I just needed to get away." She shrugged again, feeling more confident. "I was headed for Seattle, but your town charmed me." She smiled shyly, realizing she could pull this off. After all, everything she'd said so far was true.

Alan heard her answers but paid little attention to the words. It was her eyes he watched. A person could say anything, but their eyes, well, they seldom lied.

Besides, this woman had the loveliest eyes he'd ever seen. They were soft blue, the color of spring wildflowers. They seemed out of place with the rest of her—the dark, lifeless hair, the...no, just the hair was wrong. Her skin was pale, flawlessly pale, like fine porcelain, while her thinness added an air of delicacy. Just the hair was wrong, and something else he couldn't quite get a handle on. Something...

"Sorry about your husband," he said, watching her more closely, trying to make all the pieces fit.

He saw her pain briefly before she looked away. She acknowledged his sympathy with a nod but said nothing. An awkward moment passed, and Alan knew she'd spoken the truth, at least about this.

"So," he said, breaking the silence, "it sounds like you're looking for a place to settle down."

She shifted uneasily. "I can't say, Sheriff. Maybe."

"Well..." Alan leaned back on his stool and pushed his empty coffee cup away. "Waiteville's nothing like Chicago, but it's a nice town. Quiet. You know what I mean."

"Yes, I do." She met his gaze. "That's one of the things I like about it."

"Good." Alan searched for something else to say, something to keep her talking.

"Well, it was nice talking with you, Sheriff," she said, "but I need to get back to work."

"Sure. Go ahead. I'm sure we'll get a chance to talk again." He nodded and let her go.

As she walked away, it hit him. The way she moved. That was the other piece that didn't fit, the point nipping at the edge of his mind since he'd first seen her. Her movements were graceful, almost elegant, like a dancer's. Every gesture, every step indicated this woman knew how to handle herself. There was nothing lost or downtrodden about her. Instead, she possessed an understated confidence. Drifters didn't move like that.

Things were not what they seemed with Maureen Adams. And instead of all the pieces falling into place the way they should, they seemed more scattered than ever. It looked as if he needed to get to know her a little better. She was running from something, and he wanted to know what. After all, the woman was a puzzle, and he didn't like puzzles—at least not in his town.

JACOB ANDERSON'S OFFICE was cold. Like the frigid Chicago wind. Like the man. Cooper hated the office and figured he probably felt the same way about the man. If he had to guess, he'd say Anderson wasn't too crazy about him, either. Still, the money was good, and he, Sam Cooper, was the best at what he did. So they tolerated each other.

Cooper stepped into Anderson's inner sanctum and closed the door behind him. Anderson stood, staring out the windows at a panoramic view of downtown Chicago. "Good of you to come on such short notice," he said without turning around.

Cooper moved further into the plush office. He knew Anderson didn't expect a response, so he offered none.

"I want you to find someone for me," Anderson continued a moment later.

"Of coursc." Cooper lowered himself into a chair of chrome and leather. "Who is it this time?"

Anderson turned slowly away from the windows and fixed him with an icy stare. Cooper suppressed the urge to stand back up and wondered—not for the first time—how this man had ever become such a successful trial lawyer. How could a jury ever look into those chilly gray eyes and not shudder?

"Take a look at the contents of that folder," Anderson said, motioning toward his desk. "Tell me what you see."

Cooper leaned forward and picked up the manila folder. Flipping it open, he found two sets of large glossy photographs and several neatly typed pages of what he assumed was background information. First he studied the pictures. He liked to make his own assumptions before reading what someone else had to say about a situation.

"The woman's a looker." He took his time, studying the face, memorizing details. "Great eyes. Great hair. Not many woman have hair that color." He studied her a moment longer, going through picture after picture, before adding, "Looks natural."

"It is."

Cooper raised his eyes at Anderson's unexpected comment, but the other man had returned to the windows. "Should be easy to spot."

"She's probably dyed it. Cut it, too."

Cooper hesitated, wondering if he'd actually heard a tremor in Jacob Anderson's voice. Could this woman mean something to him? Shaking his head, Cooper decided he was imagining things. Anderson didn't care about anything or anyone, except maybe the law. Or power.

Cooper pulled out the second set of photos. "Cute kid. Not related to the woman. Looks Latin." He stole a glance at Anderson again, watching for the slightest reaction. But the other man offered up nothing more than his stiff back.

Then Cooper pulled out the written report, not bothering to read aloud the typed material. He had no doubt that Anderson already knew every word in it.

"I want them found," Anderson said, just as Sam finished reading the report. "Before the authorities find them."

"They've been missing for three months." Cooper shook his head. "That's a pretty cold trail."

"Yes."

"It's not going to be easy."

"If it was easy, I wouldn't need you."

Cooper let out a short laugh. "Yeah. I guess you wouldn't."

Anderson turned back around, pulled a plain white envelope from his pocket, and dropped it on the desk. "There's fifty thousand. That should take care of your immediate expenses. There will be fifty more when you find them."

Standing, Cooper picked up the envelope and shoved it in his jacket pocket without looking at it. "I'll be in touch." He turned to leave but only got halfway across the room.

"I expect to hear from you once a week."

Cooper stopped and turned, wondering what was really going on here. He and Anderson might not be the best of buddies, but they had an understanding. He never questioned who or why Anderson wanted someone, and in return, Anderson never told Cooper how to do his job.

"When you find them," Anderson said, "don't make contact. Just let me know where they are. Immediately."

Anderson had just stepped over the line. Cooper crossed his arms and faced the other man. "So, who's this woman, anyway?"

He saw the quick flare of heat in Anderson's eyes before they turned frigid again. Then he smiled, that beatific smile that jurors always fell for, but Cooper knew to be false, and said, "She's my daughter."

CHAPTER TWO

IT FELT GOOD to have something fit again, even if it was only a pair of jeans. She'd lost so much weight in the last year that everything she owned hung on her. Stepping in front of the mirror, Maureen turned sideways to get a better look at herself. Well, she thought with a wry smile, I always wanted to lose a few pounds. I guess I finally succeeded.

Then she caught sight of her hair. Reaching up, she brushed her fingers through the unfamiliar crop of dark waves. David had loved her hair. Pale blond and falling in soft curls to her shoulders, it had been her one claim to beauty. It had made her memorable... and too easy to spot. So the night she fled from Miami, she'd cut it short and colored it dark brown. And now she was compelled to watch closely for the first signs of blond roots.

With a sigh, she turned away from the mirror. What did it matter? It was only hair. The important thing was that Katie was with her and they were safe.

The question of safety brought her thoughts back to Alan Parks—a subject that had plagued her from the moment he'd walked into the restaurant yesterday morning. At the time she'd felt certain he suspected something. He seemed more than casually interested in her. She kept telling herself she was imagining things. It was her "city girl" reaction to the small-town attitude—everyone knowing everybody else's business. Still, every instinct she possessed screamed a warning, and she couldn't get him off her mind.

"Mommy, I'm hungry."

Katie's words snapped Maureen back to the present. Scooping the child into her arms, she nuzzled the soft baby cheek. "You are?"

Katie giggled and shook her head. "Uh-huh."

"Do you think I should let you eat in that pretty new outfit?"

Katie nodded her head again.

"No, I don't think so," Maureen teased. "It's too pretty."

"Yes, Mama." Katie grabbed her mother's chin and forced her head to move up and down.

Laughing, Maureen tumbled the child on the bed, finding every ticklish spot on her three-year-old body. "No, no, no," she insisted as Katie surrendered to a fit of high giggly shrieks, with an occasional "yes" thrown in for good measure.

Finally Maureen collapsed, feigning exhaustion. "Okay, you win. You can wear the outfit."

Sporting a triumphant smile, Katie climbed to her knees and planted her chubby little fists on her hips. "Good," she said with a decisive nod of her head. "I win!"

Maureen smiled at her daughter and drew her into her arms. Katie's need for clothes had spurred their buying trip today. They'd found a consignment shop, where she'd bought Katie several nearly new outfits, plus the pair of jeans for herself. She felt a little guilty about spending the money, but they both needed clothes.

"Let's go down and eat," she said, pulling herself and Katie off the bed.

All the way down the stairs, she teased her daughter with tickling fingers and a bouncy rhythm. Laughing, she pushed through the kitchen door and came to an abrupt halt. Alan Parks leaned casually against the counter, one booted foot draped over the other, arms crossed, listening intently to Mrs. Jamison, Rita's only other boarder.

He looked different without his uniform. Less civilized. More dangerous. Something stirred inside her, bringing an unwelcome warmth to the room. She tried to shake the feeling, telling herself there was nothing unusual in what he wore—just a pair of jeans and a soft chambray shirt open at the throat. Nothing unusual, except maybe the way the jeans fit, as if he'd been born in them, or the way the soft beige of his shirt emphasized the coppery darkness of his skin. He looked barely tame. Suddenly she ached in places she had thought long dead.

Her gaze drifted to his face, and she saw the amusement in his eyes, the knowledge of his effect on women. The arrogance of it annoyed her, clearing her stunned senses. Why were good-looking men always so damn cocky?

"There you two are," Rita said.

Maureen pulled her gaze away from Alan, and the sights and smells of the kitchen rushed in on her all at once. Rita stood over a stove laden with food. Mrs. Jamison sat cutting raw vegetables at the kitchen table, and the room smelled of roasting turkey and rich, spicy apples.

"Are we late?" Careful to avoid looking Alan's way again, Maureen carried Katie across the room and sat her on one of the counter stools.

"No, dear. You're just in time." Rita finished stirring something on the stove and, after wiping her hands on her apron, reached for Katie. "Come here, sweetie. Don't you look nice."

"It smells wonderful in here," Maureen said, handing Katie to the older woman. "What's the occasion?"

"No occasion." Rita fussed with the new top Katie wore, winning a smile from the little girl. "I like making a big dinner on Sunday, and I've always felt turkey was too good to save for Thanksgiving." Motioning toward Alan, she added, "Maureen, this is my nephew Alan. He eats with us on Sunday."

"We met at Jill's yesterday." Alan's smile never faltered as his eyes scanned her from head to toe, once again stirring that unfamiliar warmth. "Nice to see you again, Maureen."

Annoyed as much with her own reaction as with him, she merely nodded. Fortunately, Rita wasn't finished with the introductions. "And this," she said to Alan, "is Katie."

"Hello, Katie." Alan reached out to touch Katie's hand, but she shied away, burying her head in Rita's chest.

"Alan won't bite, honey," Rita soothed. "You know, he used to be a little boy just your size, and I'd take care of him. Just like I take care of you."

Katie seemed to consider this while studying him from the safety of familiar arms. Then she squirmed sideways, reaching for her mother.

Maureen took Katie from Rita, but she could tell Katie wasn't really frightened—she was just toying with the adults. "It's okay," she said. "Mr. Parks is the sheriff here."

"What's that?" Katie asked.

"It's like a policeman," Maureen answered. Then, when Katie didn't respond, she added, "He doesn't look like a policeman because he's not wearing his uniform."

"Oh." Katie didn't look convinced.

Laughing, Rita scowled playfully at Alan. "Maybe if you got yourself a haircut, the child might not be afraid of you."

"Don't worry yourself, Aunt Rita." Alan planted a kiss on the older woman's cheek. "She'll come around." Then, with a wink and a grin at Maureen, he added, "They all do."

His grin caught her, rendering Maureen breathless for a moment. Why hadn't she noticed yesterday how captivating this man was? How could she have missed the burnished copper in his dark brown hair? Or the color of his eyes? Not dark, but not light, either. They looked as if they'd been painted with the same brush that touched his hair.

Feeling foolish, she could do nothing but smile in return. She thought herself immune to handsome men—especially those who so obviously knew it. But she couldn't lie to herself. Alan Parks made her extremely uncomfortable. Her body fairly hummed in anticipation of the things his eyes suggested.

Then Katie laughed, jarring Maureen, and she was abruptly reminded of who she was, and who he was: a man she couldn't risk having thoughts about. It was time to put a little distance between herself and Alan Parks.

"We'll be right back, Rita," she said, turning and heading for the kitchen door. "Katie and I need to wash our hands."

Alan smiled as Maureen fled the room. He liked the way she looked tonight—fresh, young and undoubtedly female. She'd been laughing when she entered the kitchen, a light, carefree laugh filled with warmth, while the child in her arms giggled and squirmed. He could see how the pair of them would add a homey texture to this big old house.

Then she had spotted him, and he'd recognized her reaction. It was all woman. That, too, warmed him. The only surprise had been how much it pleased him.

Tucking that insight aside for later, he let his thoughts drift to the other differences in her. For instance, the jeans she wore fit snugly, revealing a very feminine posterior—something she'd hidden yesterday beneath oversize denim. Her face, uncomplicated by makeup, nearly glowed, and her startling blue eyes reflected her every thought. In the few minutes she'd been in the room, he'd seen joy, hunger and annoyance in those eyes. No, she was nothing like the wary woman he'd met at Jill's yesterday. Nothing at all.

"What're you standing there grinning about?" It was Mrs. Jamison who interrupted his thoughts. "Ain't like you never saw a pretty girl before."

"That doesn't make it any less pleasant to see another one," Alan said, directing his most charming smile in Millie Jamison's direction. "However," he added with a wink, "I like my women more mature."

"Get on with you." Color rose in Millie's cheeks as she brushed his comment aside. "You're such a flatterer, Alan Parks. Always have been."

Alan laughed and reached down to help the older woman from her chair. "Whatever works, Millie. Whatever works."

"If you two are done flirting," Rita said good-naturedly, "I could use some help."

With a final smile at Millie, Alan went to Rita's aid, lifting the huge turkey from the oven. Meanwhile, Millie began carrying platters of food into the dining room.

A few minutes later, when Maureen and Katie returned to the kitchen, Alan stood at the counter, carving the turkey. She pointedly ignored him and took Katie into the dining room. Once again he smiled. Yes sir, he had her attention now. And finding out about her was going to be a lot more interesting than he'd expected.

Once they sat down to eat, no one spoke as they filled their plates with the sumptuous meal. Rita had outdone herself. Alan was used to Rita's Sunday dinners, but tonight could have been Thanksgiving and Christmas combined, considering all the food she'd made. He knew it was because of the woman and child sitting across the table from him. Rita loved having family around, and she'd evidently taken these two in as if they were her own. He was beginning to understand why.

He watched Maureen as she tended her daughter. Her role as a mother suited her. Her devotion to the child was obvious in her every move. Every graceful, *confident* move, he reminded himself. Once again he wondered what circumstance had brought them to

Waiteville. The thought shook him, reminding him that things weren't cxactly as they seemed with this woman.

"Maureen and Katie are from Chicago," Rita said, breaking into his thoughts and giving him the perfect opening.

"Yes. She told me." Alan caught Maureen's quick glance in his direction. She didn't like talking about herself. He could read it in her eyes. "What part of Chicago?"

She didn't answer immediately but finished cutting Katie's turkey into small bites, then turned and smiled. "Are you familiar with Chicago, Sheriff?"

"Alan."

"Pardon mc?"

"Call me Alan." He smiled, wondering how hard it would bc to brcak down all those walls she kept throwing up. The question intrigued him. Though, he told himself, it was only because he wanted to know who Maureen Adams really was. "And no, I've never been to Chicago."

"Oh." She seemed nonplussed for a moment, glancing quickly at Katic bcfore continuing. "Well, I grew up in a neighborhood on the north shore of Lake Michigan. Later, my husband and I moved to Champagne, near the university."

"Were you in school there?"

"Yes." She took a bite of her own dinner and turned back to Katie. She fussed over the child for a moment, though it seemed to Alan that Katie was doing fine all by herself.

"Alan went to college, too," interjected Rita.

"Now, Aunt Rita..." He didn't want to change the subject. He wanted to keep Maureen talking.

"He graduated at the top of his class," Rita continued.

"Really." Maureen turned questioning eyes toward him. "What did you study?"

He frowned at Rita—who only smiled in return—before answering. "Criminology."

Maureen's face registered her surprise. "Criminology? How interesting." She reached for her water glass and took a sip. "Was that a job requirement for becoming sheriff?" Before he could answer, Rita answered for him. "Of course not. He planned on going to law school."

"Rita..." Alan put a gentle warning in his voice, knowing as he did that Rita would ignore it. They'd been through this before, countless times.

"You should have gone." Rita reached across the table and patted his hand. "You would have made a good lawyer."

He smiled warmly at her and took her small, birdlike hand in his own. "I'm happy here. Besides, I'm a good *sheriff.*"

"If you ask me, you're too hard-nosed," interjected Millie.

"Hard-nosed?" Alan released Rita's hand and turned toward Millie.

"I'm talking about that Simmons boy, and how you ousted him from town yesterday."

"I didn't *oust* him from town..." How had the conversation taken such a sharp turn? It seemed to Alan they'd been talking about Maureen. He'd been trying to find out something about her. Now here they were, suddenly talking about his choice of careers and Joey Simmons.

"Sure looked that way to me," Millie said, addressing Rita. "Took Joey's keys and had one of the deputies drive the boy home."

Alan sighed. "Millie, he was driving without a license, and this is not the first time."

"From what I hear, that boy keeps his family afloat." Millie still wasn't talking directly to Alan. "Raising young Tom with no help from his pa. They'd probably all starve otherwise."

"They wouldn't starve."

"I feel so sorry for those boys," said Rita. "I never did care for their father. And then he married that young girl, well, I don't blame her for running off like she did. But leaving those two babies..."

"Everyone feels sorry for them," said Alan, turning back to his aunt. "But that still doesn't make it right for Joe to break the law."

"No, but something should be done," Rita insisted.

Alan understood his aunt's concern. He'd thought the same thing himself. He wanted to help those boys, especially Joey, before it was too late. But he didn't know how. Shifting his gaze to Maureen, he realized she'd been following the conversation with interest.

He sighed. "Okay, Rita. If it will make you feel better, I'll go out and talk to old man Simmons. Other than that, there's not much I can do. Meanwhile, I doubt if Maureen is interested in Joey and his father."

"Oh, but I am." In fact she looked very pleased to be talking about something other than herself.

Alan ignored her statement. "What about you? What did you study in college?"

She shrugged and once again turned to her daughter. "This and that."

She was a cool number, Alan thought, hiding behind her daughter and vague answers. He couldn't remember the last woman he'd met who didn't welcome the chance to talk about herself. And here he was, trying to get the most insignificant pieces of information from her and getting nowhere. It made him even more determined than ever to find out about her.

Maureen couldn't wait for dinner to be over. Except for the detour the conversation had taken concerning the Simmons boy, no one would let up on her. Even Rita—in the nicest way possible—seemed intent on knowing her life history.

She kept telling herself that excess curiosity was normal in small towns. Still, it wasn't what she was used to, and it grated on her nerves. It took every ounce of willpower she possessed to keep smiling and answering their questions politely.

The whole ordeal of questions and answers would have been much easier to deal with, however, if it hadn't been for Alan. Every time she glanced his way, she found him watching her. He made no attempt to hide his interest—he just smiled that lady-killer smile of his and asked another question.

At last everyone finished eating and escape seemed imminent. Rita was the first to rise, picking up her plate. "Maureen," she said, "would you mind helping me?"

"Of course not." Maureen rose and reached to pull Katie from her chair. "Come on, Sweetie. You can play with your blocks in the kitchen while I help Rita clean up."

"Oh, Alan can watch her," said Rita. "You don't mind, do you, Alan?"

"No problem." Alan circled the table and held out his arms. "Come on, princess. Let's go into the living room."

Tension gripped Maureen's stomach. "Do you want to go with him, Katie?" She didn't want Alan around her daughter, but unless Katie objected, there was no graceful way out of this situation.

Katie hesitated only a moment before opening her arms to the man in front of her. In one smooth movement, Alan lifted her to his shoulders and headed for the other room. "Okay, princess. I'm going to teach you how to be a real cowgirl."

Katie squealed with delight as they bounced out of the room.

Maureen stood for a moment, fighting the urge to go after them. Finally, winning the battle with herself, she turned to clear the table of dirty dishes. It never used to be this way, she thought. When had her obsessive fear of letting Katie out of her sight started? With an armload of dishes, she joined Rita in the kitchen.

"Thank you," Rita said. "Would you bring in the rest of the dishes while I start washing?"

Maureen nodded and returned to clear the remaining dishes from the table. Of course she knew when the fear had started. It was the day her lawyer called.

Closing her eyes, she forcefully pushed the memory aside. It was over. She wasn't going to dwell on it. Gathering up the remaining dishes from the table, she went back into the kitchen.

"That was a wonderful meal," Maureen said, trying to dispel her somber mood.

Rita smiled in answer. "Thank you, dear. I do so love Sunday dinners—especially with family around."

Maureen smiled to herself, understanding the implication of Rita's words. She considered Maureen and Katie part of her family. Maureen herself felt closer to Rita than she had any right to. After all, they'd only known each other a week.

"What do you think of Alan?" Rita asked after a few moments of silence.

Maureen handed Rita the dishes she carried and picked up a towel to start drying. "He's nice."

"Handsome, too. Don't you think?" Rita's words were said in an offhand manner, but Maureen knew better.

"Are you matchmaking, Rita?"

Rita glanced sideways at her. "No, I just..." Then she laughed. "You can't blame me for trying."

"He's very good-looking," Maureen agreed, thinking of how his smile had affected her. "And no, I can't blame you for trying, but..."

"But?"

"It's too soon for me."

"Oh." Rita smiled in understanding. "Because of your husband."

Maureen nodded. "And other things." *Like Katie, and the fact he's a lawman who studied criminology.*

They worked together in silence for a while, Rita washing and rinsing, Maureen drying and stacking. They were a good team, Maureen thought. There was an easy camaraderie between them, as if they'd known each other for years.

"He's not really my nephew, you know," Rita said, breaking the silence.

"No?" Her announcement didn't completely surprise Maureen, but she hadn't expected it, either.

"His mother and I were best friends all our lives. I couldn't have children and, well, when Alan was born, he was the next best thing to having my own."

Her own troubles forgotten for the moment, Maureen lifted her gaze to Rita and saw wistfulness in the other woman's eyes. It was a longing she herself knew well. "I can understand that."

Rita blushed and turned back to her sinkful of dishes. "Then his father died, and Renee—his mother—fell apart. After that, Alan spent more time here than he spent at home. He was only ten, and I think it was too much for him to handle."

Silence fell again, leaving Maureen feeling burdened with this unsolicited glimpse at Alan's past. She saw him through Rita's eyes, and her heart softened toward the child he once was. A child with one parent dead and the other wishing she was. Maureen tried to steel herself against the boy by remembering the man, but her thoughts remained with the boy.

"Some people think it's strange," Rita said, breaking the silence once again and pulling Maureen from her thoughts. "But I've always loved Alan like he was my own."

Maureen returned to her own task, trying to hide the swell of emotion threatening to overwhelm her. "I don't think it's strange at all." Her voice strained at the edges. With a flash of irritation, she wished Rita had kept this all to herself. For Maureen, this subject was too close to home. Yet she couldn't deny Rita the reassurance she sought. She felt she owed the other woman that much. "I believe it's love that makes a family, not blood."

"Do you?" Rita met her gaze, and Maureen saw gratitude in her eyes.

"Yes," she said, a little ashamed of her momentary irritation with this woman who had been so good to her. "I do."

Rita smiled, and Maureen felt warmed all over. What had she done to deserve finding Rita Ember?

"Mommy!" Katie's voice brought them both back to the moment. "Come see!"

Maureen glanced in the direction of her daughter's voice, then looked back at Rita.

"Go ahead, dear," said Rita. "We're almost done here."

Nodding, Maureen took the opportunity to escape the strong emotions unleashed by Rita's revelation. Later she would pull out Rita's words and sort through them. For now, she put the conversation aside and headed out of the kitchen.

When she entered the living room, however, another emotion struck her. Dread.

Katie clung to Alan's broad back as he bounced around the living room in imitation of a bucking bronco. Alan nickered and neighed, while Katie squealed in delight, yelling, "Down boy! Down!"

Maureen bit her bottom lip to keep her tears at bay. What was this man doing to her? To them? He crept into her thoughts and heart at every turn. First the chemistry that flickered between them, arousing a part of her she didn't dare unleash. Then the image Rita described of the lost little boy, tugging at her heart. And now here he was, playing with her daughter, winning her over. It was too much. He was too much. She couldn't afford to want this man. *They* couldn't afford it.

"Katie, it's time for bed." Her words sounded harsher than she'd planned, and Alan stopped midway across the room.

"Go, horsey," Katie insisted, ignoring her mother.

"Now, Katie."

Katie started to object, but Alan moved to the couch, helping the little girl to slide off his back. "You wore the horsey out," he said, settling himself on the couch while running a hand across his brow.

"No!" Katie insisted, jumping onto his lap.

Maureen crossed the room to claim her daughter. "Katie..."

"That's enough for tonight," Alan said, maneuvering the child into a sitting position.

Katie's face clouded, and Maureen thought they were in for a tantrum. But Alan reached up and brushed the child's dark curls away from her face, smoothing the pending storm. "Do what your mother says, princess. We'll play another time."

Katie looked at him solemnly for a moment. "Promise?"

"Promise." Alan crossed his heart and held up his hand.

"You won't be too busy, will you?" Maureen caught her breath at Katie's question. She hadn't thought Katie remembered. There had been so many broken promises.

Alan smiled while tapping Katie on the nose. "Sheriffs always keep their promises. And we're never too busy for princesses."

Katie seemed to consider this a moment, then nodded, evidently accepting Alan's word. She gave him a quick hug before he stood and handed her back to her mother.

Maureen took her daughter, amazed at how easily he'd controlled her. "Thank you," she said, while inside she felt like screaming. He'd made Katie a promise, and Katie believed him. One more reason to avoid this man.

She took a deep breath and braced herself against the sudden rush of tears once again threatening to fall. Without another word, she turned and headed upstairs. Not only could she and Katie not afford to want him, they couldn't afford to have him making promises he wouldn't or couldn't keep. Promises for a future that could never be. Promises that would break their hearts. Again.

CHAPTER THREE

KATIE WENT DOWN EASILY. Within minutes of playing horsey with Alan, she'd snuggled into the big four-poster bed and fallen fast asleep. Maureen watched her for a moment, amazed as always at how quickly she switched gears. One minute she would be wild and rowdy, then the next she would be sleeping like an angel. Maureen guessed it was just part of being three years old.

She pulled a chair over to the open window and sighed. She wasn't as fortunate as her daughter. She couldn't shift gears so easily. Turning on a small lamp, she hoped a good book would take her mind off the evening's events. Maybe then, she, too, would be able to sleep.

Unfortunately, she found no solace in reading. The book didn't hold her interest, and she ended up staring out the window, unable to make sense of the thoughts scurrying through her head.

So much had happened in the last year. Starting with David's death, her life had moved steadily from orderly and predictable to chaotic. She had tried to put things right, but everything she attempted backfired. Now here she was, a thousand miles from home, drawn to a man who could only make matters worse.

Leaning her head against the back of the chair, she tried pushing the confusion aside. She needed to understand and deal with things in a logical manner. All her life she'd been strong, a woman who took control, a woman used to being able to handle things. Others looked up to her. She was calm, collected and sturdy.

A lone tear slid down her face, and she brushed it aside, irritated at her own weakness. She was none of those things any longer. Her strength was gone, depleted by the events of the last year. There was nothing calm or collected about her. There was no control left.

Suddenly the walls pressed in on her, and she needed to get out of the room before she suffocated. Abandoning the chair, she grabbed a sweater and fled. She left the bedroom door slightly ajar and headed down the back stairs. Maybe the night air would clear her head.

As she stepped out onto the back porch, her hopes of being able to think clearly vanished. She was not alone. Alan sat on the top step, his back against the rail, one leg bent, the other stretched out to rest on a lower step.

Her first reaction was to turn and run back upstairs, back to the safety of her room. After all, she'd come outside to escape her disturbing thoughts of this man. Just as she turned to go, something stopped her. Whether it was her survival instinct or just curiosity, she didn't know, but a surge of resentment sliced through her, making her bold.

She and Katie had been through enough. Now this man, this small-town lawman with his questions and cocky smile, threatened to make things worse. Well, she wasn't going to let that happen. She wanted to know just how much Alan Parks knew or suspected about her and Katie. And if he suspected nothing, then it was time he left them alone.

At least that's what she told herself as she moved to the railing opposite the one he leaned against.

"Nice night," he said. "Summer's come early this year."

"Mmm." Maureen nodded and pulled her sweater tight around her. To her it seemed a bit chilly, like a cool winter evening in south Florida.

"I don't know how May is where you're from—Chicago, isn't it?"

"That's right."

"But..." Looking up at her, he shifted sideways and patted the step. "Come on, sit down."

She hesitated, thinking this wasn't such a good idea after all. Where was all her bravado of a few minutes ago? "I'm really tired, Sheriff. I just needed a little fresh air."

Reaching up, Alan took her hand and coaxed her down next to him. "Just for a few minutes. And I thought we'd dispensed with that 'sheriff' stuff."

Maureen sat, keeping herself as far from him as possible on the narrow steps. Still, he was too close. She could feel the heat from his body like a tangible thing, while the smell of his after-shave, subtle and all male, assaulted her senses.

"I don't bite, you know."

She turned to look at him, and he smiled, a slow, lazy smile. In the dark his face was all shadows and angles, his eyes dark and unreadable, but his smile... she would have recognized the predator in that smile with her eyes closed.

"Don't you?"

The smile faded. "Only when provoked."

"I see." She shifted again, moving closer to the rail, away from the heat of his leg, away from the threat of that smile. "Then I'll be sure not to provoke you."

Alan chuckled and leaned back, resting his elbows on the porch. "Your daughter's a charmer."

Maureen's thoughts shifted to Katie and she smiled despite herself. "Yes, she is."

"A real cutie."

"Mmm." She relaxed a bit. It was true, Katie charmed everyone around her.

"Kids have so much energy. It always amazes me."

Maureen chuckled, thinking how well she understood. "It was nice of you to entertain her."

They sat quietly for a moment, the night enfolding them. Maureen let her thoughts drift, the sweet silence soothing her. She'd never lived in a place like this, where you could smell the rich scent of pine while gazing at a million stars overhead. How strange that fate had brought her here under these circumstances. Why had she never thought to come somewhere like this before, where you could sit on a porch in the evening and be content?

"She must resemble her father."

"What?" His words cut into her thoughts, bringing her sharply back to the present—and the man sitting next to her.

"Katie." Alan pulled his legs up and leaned forward to rest his elbows on his knees. "Her coloring is nothing like yours. I thought she must take after her father."

Irritation replaced her momentary feelings of contentment. Probing. He constantly probed. Why couldn't he leave her alone? And what could she tell him that would appease his curiosity? She thought of

David and his blond, all-American good looks. No. Katie didn't look like David. She didn't look like either of them. But it wasn't a question she could refuse to answer. Not without arousing Alan's curiosity even further.

"Yes," she finally answered, her first real lie bitter on her tongue. "A lot of people thought she looked like David."

"Was he Latin?"

An image appeared in Maureen's mind of a small dark woman-child with great brown eyes—so like Katie's—and a soft melodic voice. "Yes," she said, the words like ashes in her mouth. "Her father was Latin."

Alan nodded as if satisfied, for the moment anyway, and went back to studying the darkness. Then he asked, "How did he die?"

With a sigh, Maureen hesitated. Strange that the memory of David's death brought no pain, merely sadness, like an old wound properly healed.

"If you'd rather not talk about it..."

"No, that's okay." David was a safe subject. She could talk about him. It would keep Alan from asking other questions that she'd find more difficult to answer. "It was a car accident. He'd been out with clients. It was late..."

"Drinking?"

"Yes, but it wasn't the alcohol. We were having problems." She hesitated again, wondering how much to tell him. "He got home late. We argued, and he stormed out of the house. I think he was sober by then, but angry. Too angry to be driving."

She stopped, thinking about that night and the way she'd lashed out at David. "Anyway, the next thing I knew, the police were at my door, and David was dead. He drove his car into a canal."

"I'm sorry."

"Yes, me too." She'd been so angry with David, not just that night, but with what he'd become, what he'd been doing to their marriage. Still, she had loved him. "I should have tried to stop him. I knew he shouldn't be driving, but..."

"You didn't."

"No. It wouldn't have done any good, but I should have tried. Actually, at the time, I was glad he left. I was afraid our arguing would wake Katie." She looked away, feeling the same flush of guilt she always felt when she thought of those last moments with her husband.

"You can't blame yourself."

She looked at him and saw the sincerity in his eyes, the concern. "I don't really."

Sighing again, she pushed her hair away from her face and leaned back against the porch. Why was she telling him all this? She thought of Katie and reminded herself it was easier to speak of David than of other things. Besides, it felt good to finally talk to someone about it.

They sat quietly for a moment, Maureen thinking how strange it was that she had chosen Alan to tell about David's death. She'd never told anyone before. Oh, she'd given the police the facts, but she had never told anyone the things she'd just revealed.

"What about Katie?" Alan asked after a few minutes. "How did she take it?"

This, too, saddened her. Katie hardly missed David. At least that's what Maureen had thought. Until tonight. When Katie had made Alan promise, and it reminded Maureen of all the times David had broken his promises to the two of them.

"She asked about him for a while. She named her favorite stuffed animal after him. But she was only two, and she didn't know him very well. He was very busy."

"Too busy for his own daughter?"

She thought she heard anger in his voice, and it surprised her. "Yes, well, that's part of what we argued about."

"I see."

Maureen closed her eyes and nodded, thinking that maybe he did understand—at least about what she'd told him. Of course, she couldn't tell him about the money, the debts she'd known nothing about until after David's death. Nor could she tell him about Katie, and the people who wanted to take her away. No, she couldn't tempt fate by expecting him to understand about that.

Alan watched her as she sat lost in her own thoughts. He hadn't expected to find so many layers to this woman. Now there was this new side to her. This courage. The whole time she'd talked about her husband, there was a strength in her voice. Her husband's death, and the circumstances surrounding it, saddened her. But she had dealt with it. She was not the type of woman to fall apart when left without a man.

Once again, he knew this woman was no drifter. So why was she here? What would make her pick up her daughter and leave home, only to end up waiting tables in a town like Waiteville?

"You intrigue me," he said, shocking himself by saying the words aloud.

She opened her eyes and looked at him, surprised. Then he saw the slight tightening around her mouth, the stiffening of her shoulders.

"I'm just a novelty," she said, her voice hard and cold. "Someone you haven't known all your life."

He thought about that. There might be something in what she said. He'd been back in Waiteville for ten years, and none of the women in town had sparked his interest. Hell, he *had* known most of them all his life. Maybe there was something in the fact she was new in town, but he thought there was more to it. She wasn't the first unattached stranger to visit Waiteville.

"No," he said, turning to get a clearer view of her face. "I don't think that's it."

She met his gaze head-on. "It must be my raving beauty, then," she said, sarcasm lacing her voice.

He reached up and brushed the hair away from her face. It was all wrong. Her hair, short and lifeless, took away from her beauty. His fingers strayed to her temple, the softness of her skin drawing him, pulling him toward her. She trembled ever so slightly, while her eyes softened. "You are lovely, you know." He realized only as he said it that it was true.

Her eyes widened, making her look even younger, more vulnerable. Then they shut down, closing him out. "I'm not interested," she said, her voice sounding far-off, shaky.

"Liar." He whispered the word, but she flinched as if he'd hit her.

Something undefinable sparked in her eyes. "How dare you." But there was no potency in her words, no conviction.

He shifted on the step, moving closer, one hand slipping behind her while the other wove itself into her hair. He planned to kiss her. When the idea had first entered his mind, he couldn't say. He told himself he wanted to comfort her, but he knew in a flash that comfort had nothing to do with what he wanted to give her. He only knew he wanted to taste her, to feel her lips under his.

He lowered his mouth to hers, anticipation sparking a deeper yearning . . . and stopped cold. Her eyes spoke volumes. She desired him, and she was angry about it. But more than anything else, she feared it. Taking a deep breath, he removed his hand from her hair and eased away from her.

"I'm sorry," he said after a moment.

She didn't answer, and he turned back to look at her. She sat coiled within herself, lost in her own thoughts.

"I guess it's too soon," he said, although he didn't believe that was the problem.

"Yes." She nodded without looking at him.

"Well, we have plenty of time." She glanced at him quickly then, and he knew he'd said the wrong thing. "I mean . . ." He meant to say something to reassure her, but he didn't know what.

"No, *Sheriff,*" she said, and there was steel in her voice once again. "There is no *we.* Not now. Not ever." She rose from the steps. "And I'd appreciate it if you'd remember that." Reentering the house, she closed the door firmly behind her.

As he watched her go, Alan wondered what she was running from. But the question that truly nagged at him was, What did he plan to do about it? Too many things about this woman didn't add up, and he'd had every intention of finding out the truth about her. Now there was this other feeling, this attraction, creeping up on him, and he didn't quite know how he was going to deal with it, either. For the moment, he would put it aside. But something told him he wouldn't be able to ignore it for long.

Shaking his head, he turned back to the silence of the night. "You're wrong, Ms. Maureen Adams," he said quietly. "It's just a matter of time."

MAUREEN LAY AWAKE listening. Through her open window she could hear all types of sounds: the chatter of insects, the rustle of the breeze through the trees, and Alan Parks. He was still down there, on the back porch where she had left him an hour ago.

What was she going to do?

It was bad enough yesterday, when he seemed curious about her from a policeman's point of view. It was even worse tonight when he'd exerted his masculine charm to find out all he could about her. But the real killer, the thing making her long to bury her tear-streaked face in her pillow, was that she'd almost succumbed. She'd wanted him to kiss her. Lord, how she'd wanted it. And more.

Rolling onto her back, she gave up trying to keep her eyes closed. She stared at the ceiling, watching the shadows of dancing branches illuminated by the moon.

She never should have stopped in Waiteville. How often had she said that to herself in the last twenty-four hours? She wondered how many times she'd say it again before she found a way to leave.

She and Katie should have gone on to Seattle. That's what she'd planned to do. But she'd been low on money, and Waiteville was so peaceful, so tempting. She should have resisted. One more short bus ride and they'd have been in a city. A place Maureen understood, a place where they could hide.

Now that was behind them. She'd used almost all of her remaining funds to get them settled here. She'd insisted on paying Rita two months' rent in advance. *Damn, why had she done that?* Of course, she could ask for it back, and no doubt Rita would comply. But she'd also want to know why.

Maureen still had a little money left, but settling in Seattle would be more expensive than it had been in Waiteville. There would be first and last months' rent. And what kind of place could she afford? She knew her chances of finding another Rita Ember were pretty slim. Then there was day-care for Katie. Maureen would have to find a job. Someplace that wasn't too quick to check references or social security numbers. That, too, would be more difficult to find in a city.

She flipped back over on her side, and Katie murmured something in her sleep. Maureen reached over to her daughter and pulled the covers around her. She brushed her fingers along the child's cheek. *Oh, Katie,* she thought, *sometimes I just don't know if I've done the right thing.* Katie let out a soft, baby sigh and snuggled closer to her mother. Maureen's heart constricted and fresh tears fell from her eyes.

For several minutes she let the tears flow, allowing her mind to shut down. Then she shook herself. Reaching over to the small nightstand next to the bed, she grabbed a handful of tissues. She had no time for self-pity. It wouldn't help her or Katie.

Think, Maureen, she said to herself. *What are your options?*

First, she and Katie needed to get out of Waiteville. She had no idea how she was going to manage that without money. But there had to be a way, she told herself. There were always alternatives.

She thought of her father.

Would he help her this time? A phone call was all it would take to find out. One call and she'd know. Would he come to her? She knew he would enjoy watching her squirm, making her admit she'd been wrong. Maybe he would help her if she begged. But then again, maybe not. He might do what he'd done the last time she asked for help—he might refuse her.

Closing her eyes, she held back a resurgence of tears. No. She couldn't ask him for help, and she refused to cry over him again. He was dead to her as surely as David. Besides, the authorities would be waiting for her to contact him.

Or would they?

Gladly she let her thoughts shift away from her father. She really didn't know if anyone *was* looking for her. Maybe that was something she needed to find out. If she could get a look at some back issues of the *Miami Herald,* maybe there would be an article or something. It was doubtful that Waiteville's small public library would carry the *Herald,* but the one in Seattle should. She could take the bus into the city and find out, once and for all.

As for getting out of Waiteville, that would take time and money. Meanwhile she'd just have to deal with things. It was her only reasonable alternative. She couldn't let a man she barely knew threaten what she'd come so far to achieve.

She would have to learn how to avoid Alan Parks until she could find a way out of Waiteville—not an easy task, but a necessary one.

JACOB ANDERSON SAT in the dark, needing nothing to illuminate his thoughts. The lack of light fitted his mood, suited the way his guilt settled about him like a shroud.

He'd betrayed her.

His own daughter. The only person he'd ever truly loved, ever needed, and he'd turned his back on her. Now she was out there somewhere, alone with her child, running from the law.

It was ironic that she was fleeing from the very force he knew and understood so well. The very thing he'd put above everything in his life, including Maura and her desires. The force he could bend to his will so easily.

If she'd only come to him.

But he was being honest with himself and he knew why she hadn't called on him. She had come to him once before, and he had refused her. She meant the world to him. Yet in his arrogance, in his confidence that he knew what was best for her, he had let her down. How could he expect her to come to him this time? There was too much of himself in the girl.

Now he waited.

Cooper wouldn't fail him. He would find Maura and her bright-eyed child. Jacob had no doubts about that. But would it do any good? Would she accept his help? Would she even speak to him after the way he'd treated her? He didn't know.

The phone rang, shattering the stillness. Jacob hesitated a second, his heart suddenly pounding, his hands trembling as he reached for the receiver.

"Yes."

The voice on the other end started without preamble. "She left Miami on a Greyhound bus around 1:00 a.m., January fifth. The night clerk ID'd both her and the kid from pictures the cops had shown him in January."

"What about the authorities?"

"She'd been gone four days before anyone realized it. The cops put out a state-wide bulletin, even though they figured she was already out of the state by that time. It seems they have better things to do than look for your daughter."

Jacob thought he'd reached the limits of his pain. But Cooper's words sliced through his soul.

"Anderson?"

The question in the other man's voice forced Jacob to pull himself together. "Where did they go from there?"

"I was able to trace them to Georgia. A waitress at one of the truck stops thought she remembered the two of them."

"And from there?"

"Don't know yet."

"Find them."

"They could have gone in any direction. It's going to cost a lot . . ."

"Money's not a problem." Jacob felt his strength returning. He wouldn't let this thing beat him. He would have his daughter back. "Find her," he said again, this time with more force.

"Sure. I'll find them." He heard Cooper's hesitation on the other end.

"What else?"

"You were right about the hair. She dyed it and cut it short. The cops found evidence in her house, and the night clerk at the bus station in Miami recognized a computer mock-up of her altered appearance."

Anderson closed his eyes and took a deep breath. "Find her," he repeated. "I don't care how you do it, or what it takes. Just find her." He returned the receiver to its cradle, calling on all his strength to keep from slamming it down. Then he was alone again in the dark with his memories. And his guilt.

CHAPTER FOUR

ALAN SAT BEHIND his desk, feet propped up on an open drawer. He was supposed to be doing paperwork, filling out any one of the endless forms that crossed his desk. Instead, he stared out the wide windows overlooking Main Street.

One of the first things he'd done when he took this job was have those windows installed in his office. He wanted to feel the sunlight and be able to look out and see what was going on in his town. One thing he'd never envisioned, however, was sitting here, idly watching for a particular woman and her three-year-old daughter to walk by.

Alan dropped his feet to the floor, rose and crossed the room to pour himself a cup of coffee. The pot was almost empty and its remaining contents looked strong enough to walk, but he poured some into his cup anyway. Then he added a substantial helping of sugar and headed back to his desk.

Since Sunday he'd been unable to get Maureen off his mind. Something kept drawing his thoughts back to her. It didn't seem to matter where he was or what he was doing—he couldn't shake his ever present awareness of her. He didn't understand it, and that in itself preyed on him.

He glanced at his watch and turned back to the paper littering his desk. She'd be getting off work at the diner about now, and then she'd pick up Katie and head this way. It would be another fifteen or twenty minutes before they passed his office on their way to the playground. He knew, because he'd timed it every day this week.

He took another stab at going through the reports for the previous month. There were a dozen or so speeding tickets, a few arrests for disorderly conduct, an attempted robbery at one of the gas stations, and a couple of warnings to local teens for shoplifting and the like. Nothing very serious. Nothing like what he would be dealing with if he'd taken a job with the force in Seattle. But he had no complaints. He liked Waiteville and the peace it offered him.

That is, until recently, when Maureen Adams had arrived in town and shattered his serenity. Now he would have given anything for some all-absorbing case to take his mind off her.

She'd looked pretty good Sunday night, with those tight-fitting jeans hugging her slender body. Not to mention her eyes. They were something else again—enough to snag any man's attention. But he knew lots of pretty women. He even knew a few he'd classify as beautiful. Hell, Jill was a knockout. But it wasn't those other women who hovered in his mind.

He reconsidered her comment about being a new face, someone he hadn't known all his life. That must be it, he thought. She was just someone different. And, of course, there was the mystery surrounding her, so thick he could feel it. Maybe it was because she was a challenge. Wasn't there a saying that you always want what you can't have.

His mind drifted to the strength he'd seen in her Sunday night. He liked that about her. He'd never had any use for clinging vines, no matter how beautiful or unfamiliar the flower.

With a sigh, he tossed his pen on the desk and once again turned toward the windows. What was the use of trying to figure something like this out? Maybe if he just let it alone, eventually...

Then he caught sight of them: Maureen, with Katie skipping along beside her. Just like every other day this week. Only today, there was an extra child gripping one of her hands. Alan recognized the boy as Josh Winters, one of the neighborhood children, maybe a year older than Katie.

They came abreast of his office, and Maureen glanced in his direction, but quickly turned away. That didn't surprise him. She'd stated her position clearly Sunday night, and without speaking a word, she repeated it every time she saw him. At the diner she barely acknowledged his presence, freezing up when he spoke to her. But he didn't buy it. And he was nothing if not persistent.

With a smile, he rose from his chair. Maybe he'd wander down to the playground himself and pay Maureen and Katie a visit. After all, it was Saturday and a great day to spend a little time outside.

Grabbing his hat, he headed for the door.

As he approached the playground, he could hear Katie's high-pitched giggles and Maureen's light and lovely laugh filtering through the air. The sounds brought a smile to his lips, and he quickened his pace.

When he saw them a warmth stole through him. The children were on the swings, side by side, while Maureen scrambled behind, alternately pushing one laughing child, then the other. She looked almost like a kid herself, dressed once again in baggy jeans, obviously enjoying catering to the children's whims.

"Higher, higher," called Katie.

Maureen laughed as she gave the swing another push, then stepped sideways to do the same for Josh. They were going to wear her out, she thought, but the afternoon was clear and warm, and she loved having both children with her. It seemed like nothing could go wrong on a day like this.

Then she spotted Alan.

He stood watching them, smiling, his arms crossed, one broad shoulder propped against an old oak that stood at the edge of the playground. Apprehension coiled inside her.

He acknowledged her with a slight nod of his head and a brief touch to the brim of his hat. Then he pushed away from the tree and walked toward her. She kept her gaze on him, unable to look away as he approached.

Why was he here?

Over the last few days she'd maintained her resolve to avoid him as much as possible. He came into the diner every day, but she barely spoke to him. She was polite but reserved. It didn't seem to do any good. The man had a stubborn streak a mile wide. He smiled and flirted with her, ignoring the distance she tried to put between them. And now here he was, showing up in the last place she expected to see him.

"Afternoon," he said.

"Hello, Sheriff." Maureen nodded and gave Josh's swing a sturdy push.

Alan shoved his hat to the back of his head and tilted his head to admire the perfect spring sky. "Great day."

"Yes, it is." She tried to concentrate on the children, to ignore the strange, disturbing effect he had on her. Then, because she needed to put a little distance between them, she put ice into her voice and asked, "Isn't this a little off your beat?"

Alan chuckled, and the sound trickled down her spine. "The whole town's my beat."

"Mommy," Katie interrupted. "Push me."

Thankful for the distraction, Maureen moved to do as her daughter asked, but Alan stopped her with a hand on her arm. "Here, let me."

Her gaze fell to the spot where he touched her, to the hand sending ribbons of heat through her system. As if burned, she pulled her arm from his grasp and took a step backward.

Alan grinned, and she could have sworn she saw laughter in his eyes before he shifted his attention to Katie. Grabbing hold of her swing, he said, "You don't mind if I push, do you, princess?" The little girl giggled, and Alan released the swing, sending her soaring into the air.

Maureen moved over behind Josh, trying not to think about the feel of Alan's hand on her arm. It was only a touch, she told herself. A light, friendly gesture. Nothing more. But it had felt like something else.

Lust, she decided.

No woman in her right mind would deny the attractiveness of this man. Why should she be any different? Now that she'd seen him in skin-tight jeans, not even the loose-fitting sheriff's uniform could hide his physical attributes. With broad shoulders, a flat stomach, narrow hips and long legs, the sight of his body would melt any woman.

But she wasn't any woman. And he wasn't just any man. She was on the run, and he was a lawman. It was a distinction she couldn't afford to forget.

"So, how did you end up with two kids today?" Alan asked, breaking into her thoughts.

Maureen closed her eyes briefly and took a deep breath. She couldn't allow him to get to her, to make her forget herself. "It's part of the arrangement I have with Josh's mother." To her surprise, her voice sounded normal. "She watches Katie while I'm working, and as partial payment, I take Josh two afternoons a week."

"Sounds like a good deal."

"Yes."

"You seem to enjoy the kids," he said after a moment's pause. "Almost like you'd rather be one yourself."

Maureen laughed lightly, nervously. This man saw too much. "Yes, well, I guess there are times when we all wish we didn't have to grow up."

For a few moments neither spoke. Maureen pushed Josh. Alan tickled and teased Katie. The children laughed and called to each other, oblivious to the wall of tension between the two adults.

"Seems to me," Alan said, shattering the silence between them, "that a woman who loves children as much as you do should have more than one."

The statement startled her, and she turned to meet his gaze. There was a glint in his eyes she couldn't read. Was he teasing her? She had no intention of answering his unspoken question. Yet she heard herself saying, "Actually, I've always wanted about a dozen."

He didn't look away as she'd hoped, but let his gaze linger on her. "You're still young." His smile disappeared, and his eyes seemed to bore into her soul. "You might have more yet."

"No." She shook her head, and her thoughts flew to the endless tests that she and David had endured. The years they'd waited and hoped for a baby, only to be told in the end that it wasn't possible. She would never carry a child, never hold her own son or daughter in her arms. Then Katie had come into her life, and Maureen had loved her more than life itself.

Turning away, she added, "It wasn't meant to be."

Alan remained silent, and she thanked whatever powers were listening. She couldn't predict what she would tell him if he probed further. He had a way of luring her where she didn't want to go, making her remember things she'd rather forget. He asked questions and she answered, giving away pieces of herself she would have preferred kept hidden.

"Okay, kids," she said when she'd regained her composure. "How about giving us old folks a rest. Go on over and play on the ponies for a while."

"Yeah!" Josh answered, and was off the swing in a flash, with Katie close behind.

"Good move," Alan said.

Maureen nodded and lowered herself onto one of the now vacant swings. "I figured you could use a break."

Alan laughed and moved to lean against one of the swing set's metal supports. "What about you?"

"I'm used to it."

An uneasy silence fell between them.

Maureen felt Alan's gaze on her, but she kept her eyes on the children. She watched them climb onto painted wooden ponies set on large springs. Josh immediately set his in motion, forcing the red-and-white reproduction to rock back and forth with a vengeance. Katie was slower, electing to sway gently and watch Josh.

Maureen's thoughts shifted to the man standing a few feet away. He made her uncomfortable. She didn't know what to say to him, and she was afraid she'd already said too much. But whatever he was here for, whatever he wanted, she felt herself more capable of handling it without two sets of tiny ears listening.

"So," he said finally. "How do you like Waiteville so far?"

Maureen wrapped her arms around the metal chains and idly rocked the swing. "I like it a lot. As you said the other day, it's peaceful here."

"Some people would say it's boring. Especially coming from a big city."

"I'm not looking for excitement." She kept her eyes on the children. The small talk was a reprieve, but she was becoming impatient with it. "Just a place to raise my daughter."

"Well, you've come to the right place then." His voice was smooth, confident. "This is definitely a family town."

Her impatience grew.

What did he want from her? Why was he here? Was he still looking for answers? Or was there something else? She thought of their conversation on the porch Sunday night, and how close she'd come to letting him kiss her. Just the memory warmed her. But she didn't want to think about that. She didn't want to be attracted to Alan Parks.

Turning to look at him, she asked her question aloud. "Is there something in particular you wanted, Sheriff?"

He smiled, a slow, guarded smile. "When are you going to start calling me Alan?"

She lifted her chin a bit. "I didn't realize we were on a first-name basis."

"Everyone in Waiteville is on a first-name basis." His smile faded. "It's not a very formal place."

"I see." She steadied herself, trying desperately not to show the effort it took to meet his gaze.

"My name is Alan." He kept his voice low, but there was an underlying command to his words.

"Yes. I know." She hesitated, not wanting to say his name, not wanting to pass over the invisible boundary between thinking of him as the sheriff and thinking of him as a man. But something told her he wasn't going to let it go.

"Well?"

"Okay," she said, and dropped her gaze. "Alan."

"That's better." He let out his breath, unaware till that moment that he'd been holding it, waiting for her to speak. Now that she had, the sound of his name on her lips stirred him more than he would have thought possible.

Shaking the feeling, he moved over to lean against one of the other metal supports, once more in her line of vision. "Now that that's settled, I want to apologize for the other night at Rita's."

She looked up at him again, and he saw her surprise. Then she looked away and shrugged. "It was nothing."

"Oh, I don't know about that." He chuckled, thinking that if it had been nothing, they wouldn't be having this conversation.

She looked at him again, but now she was irritated. He couldn't be exactly sure what was bothering her, but he had a pretty good idea. She didn't want to admit how close she'd come to enjoying what had almost happened on Rita's porch. The lady was fooling herself if she thought either of them would forget.

Suddenly he knew what he planned to do about it. "I was out of line Sunday night," he said.

Wariness crept into her eyes, and he suppressed a grin.

"We don't get many new faces around here," he continued. "And, well, I know you've just suffered a loss..."

She nodded but remained silent.

"Anyway, I'm sorry about Sunday."

Still she didn't answer. Finally, she said, "Apology accepted."

"Good." He pushed away from the swings with a smile. "So, I guess I'll just stay out of your way."

"Thank you...Alan," she said, but the uncertainty returned to her eyes.

She didn't trust him, but that was okay. He imagined she would think a lot about him over the next few weeks. And that was exactly what he wanted.

CHAPTER FIVE

"REALLY, JILL, I'd rather not." Maureen refilled the last of the catsup bottles and put the lid back on. She wished she could finish her conversation with Jill as easily. The last four weeks had taught her otherwise. Once Jill got her teeth into something, she didn't let go.

"You need to get out more," Jill insisted.

Maureen picked up the tray of plastic bottles and slid it into the small refrigerator behind the counter. "I need to go home, put my feet up and spend time with Katie."

"That's what you do every night." Jill settled on the stool opposite Maureen and began removing lids from mustard bottles. "What about getting out, having a good time, meeting people in town?"

"I have a good time with Katie, and I meet someone new in here every day."

"That's not the same."

"Jill—"

"'Afternoon, ladies." Maureen and Jill both turned at the familiar voice. Closing the door behind him, Alan strolled into the diner and made his way to the stool next to Jill. Dropping his hat on the counter, he ran his hand through his hair.

Maureen suppressed the urge to turn and leave the room—just as she did every time she saw Alan. It was difficult being around him. Since the day he'd shown up at the playground, her emotions rode a roller coaster of annoyance, fear and desire whenever he was around.

Logic told her things should be easier. After all, he'd been true to his word. He'd left her alone. In fact, he hardly seemed to notice her anymore. At the diner, Jill took care of him. On Sundays he was cordial but nothing more.

She told herself to be glad his interest in her had been so short-lived. She should be grateful—and she was. She had begun to feel safe again. Still, logic couldn't account for everything in life, and it certainly had nothing to do with her reaction to Alan Parks.

"You're late today," Jill said, slipping an arm around his. "Busy day fighting crime in greater Waiteville?"

Alan chuckled. "Nothing more than a couple of farmers arguing over a stray dog in a chicken coop. However," he said, glancing from Jill to Maureen, "sounds like the two of you could use a little policing. Was that an argument I heard when I walked in?"

"Don't be ridiculous," Jill insisted.

Alan winked at Maureen. "What's she trying to con you into?"

"I wasn't trying to *con* her into anything," Jill stated. "I simply suggested that she come with me to the festival planning meeting this evening. Not that it's any of your business."

"Sounds like a rousing evening to me." Alan's voice dripped with sarcasm. "I wouldn't pass it up if I were you, Maureen."

"You're no help." Jill gave him a playful punch in the arm. "For your information, we have a good time." Sliding off her stool, she walked around the counter. "Now, what do you want to eat? Not that you deserve anything."

"Ouch." Alan grimaced. "Even after I've spent all morning making the streets safe for you women?"

Jill rolled her eyes skyward and refused to comment. Then she dropped her hands to her hips and managed to look incredibly bored.

"Can I get a hamburger?" he asked, giving her his best lady-killer smile. "With everything on it."

"I don't know," she answered with a shrug. "Can you?" Turning on her heels, she retreated to the kitchen.

"And fries!" Alan called after her.

Maureen laughed at their antics. She couldn't help herself. Not when Alan sat there grinning like a schoolboy, his eyes dancing as though he'd never had a serious thought in his life.

Then he turned those eyes on her, and for a moment she lost herself. What would it be like to let go with this man? To know those wonderful caramel eyes saw nothing but her. To run her fingers through the hair tickling the back of his collar. To taste his lips on hers . . .

"You should smile more often." Alan's voice, no longer laughing, penetrated her thoughts. "You have a great smile."

Maureen blushed. She wanted to turn away, but it was too late. He held her with eyes shades darker than they'd been moments earlier. Thought fled her mind, and she felt the heat. It radiated from him, scorching her, promising her things she shouldn't want. Then he released her, and she turned away quickly, back to cleaning up.

For a while, neither spoke. Maureen fumbled with mustard bottles, chiding herself for letting her guard down, for thinking—even for a while—that she was safe around this man. Alan sat motionless, his gaze intent on the sugar dispenser he rolled between his palms.

"I don't blame you for not wanting to go to Jill's meeting tonight," he said, breaking the silence. "Sounds like a real yawner. Especially with you being new in town."

Maureen shrugged, refusing to look at him again. "It's not that." If he could pretend nothing had happened, then so could she. But it annoyed her how quickly he switched back to light chatter. "I just don't like leaving Katie in the evening after working most of the day."

Alan nodded as if he understood. "Hard on kids, having a working mother."

"Yes, well, we all have to eat." She meant to sound casual. Instead, her words came out flippant, showing her irritation. At herself. At him. At the situation. Turning away, she grabbed the large mustard jar from the refrigerator and set it on the counter.

"Did you work when your husband was alive?"

Maureen sighed. "Yes, Alan, I worked." She was almost used to all the questions. Almost. "This is the nineties, you know. More than fifty percent of the female population works outside the home."

"Whoa!" Alan raised his hands in a defensive gesture. "I didn't mean to step on toes here."

Maureen took a deep breath and curbed the sharp retort that sprang to her lips. *Get a hold of yourself.*

Showing Alan just how much he got under her skin wouldn't do her, or Katie, any good.

"Sorry," she said after a moment's pause to regain her equilibrium. "I shouldn't have jumped on you. I guess I'm just a little tired today. Katie kept me up most of the night."

"Is she all right?"

"Fine. You know how kids are. They wear you out being sick in the middle of the night. Then the next morning, when you're dead on your feet, they're perfectly healthy."

Alan chuckled. "Well, I don't know much about other kids, but I know Katie can certainly wear you out."

"Yes, well, she loves the way you romp with her on Sunday nights." Another fiasco, trying to keep Katie from attaching herself to Alan. It made no difference how much distance Maureen kept between them, every Sunday he and Katie spent the evening tumbling around Rita's living room.

"We'll have to get her on a real horse soon," he said.

Maureen started to object but stopped herself. She didn't plan on being in Waiteville long enough for Alan to get Katie on a horse.

"Here you are, traitor." Jill emerged from the kitchen and placed a platter of food in front of Alan. "It's on the house, if you can convince Maureen to go with me tonight."

He laughed. "Not a chance. I know better than to get between two stubborn females."

"Jill," Maureen said, her voice sharper than she intended. "I don't *want* to go."

"Okay." Jill lifted her hands in surrender. "I know when I'm licked. You don't want to come tonight." She moved over to the counter and began replacing yellow lids on the bottles Maureen had just filled. "But what about tomorrow? It's your day off, and we're going to start gathering everything in the school gym. You can bring Katie."

"I can't," Maureen said. "I've got plans for tomorrow." She regretted the words the minute they were out of her mouth. She kept forgetting where she was. This wasn't Miami but Waiteville, Washington, where everyone knew what everybody else was up to. Now she'd have to come up with something pretty quick.

"Plans?" Jill crossed her arms suspiciously. "What plans?"

Maureen looked from Jill to Alan and back again. "I'm going to Seattle tomorrow."

"Seattle!"

"Yes, Seattle." Now that she'd said it, she thought it was an excellent idea. She'd planned to go for weeks now, and this was the perfect opportunity. It would get her out of the festival preparations, plus allow her to check back issues of the *Miami Herald.*

"Whatever for?" Jill asked.

Maureen hedged. Forgetting the mustard bottles, she slipped from behind the counter and started gathering salt and pepper shakers from the tables. "I have some personal business to take care of."

"What kind—"

"Jill," interrupted Alan, "she said it was personal. Don't you think you're being a little nosy?"

"I'm not being nosy..."

"Yes, you are," Maureen said, suddenly very tired of this town and all its good intentions. She just wanted to be left alone.

"I tell you what, Maureen," Alan said. "I need to go that way myself tomorrow. I'd be glad to give you a lift. It'll save you the bus fare."

Maureen's hand froze as she started to grab a salt shaker. "Thanks, Alan, but I couldn't..."

"Why not?"

She turned to look at him, meeting his gaze as steadily as her sudden attack of nerves would allow. "I couldn't impose on you like that."

"Don't be silly." His mouth smiled while his eyes challenged. "I'd enjoy the company."

"Well..." Maureen hesitated, feeling the trap close around her. She threw a glance at Jill, who watched the exchange with interest. Looking back at Alan, she saw determination written across his features. "I might take a while," she said, making one last attempt to get out of this. "Hours."

"No problem." His smile broadened. "I'll need several hours myself."

Maureen knew she'd lost. She couldn't refuse Alan's offer without arousing his and Jill's curiosity. Yet how could she let him drive her to Seattle? Even if he gave her the time she needed to search for articles in the library, how was she going to handle spending hours alone with him in a car? She took a deep breath and told herself she'd just have to deal with it. She had no choice. Besides, there *was* the added benefit of saving the bus fare.

"Sure," she finally said, "that would be great."

Alan caught the frustration in Maureen's eyes and couldn't help but smile. She no more wanted to accept a ride from him than she wanted to jump off the nearest cliff.

That was just too bad.

He'd avoided her for weeks, hoping time and distance would bring her around, make her more receptive to the attraction between them. It hadn't worked. She still avoided him, turning cold and bristly whenever he entered the room.

Of course, he would have left her alone altogether if not for the moments she'd let her guard down. The times when he'd looked into her eyes and seen the heat. The woman wanted him as much as he wanted her.

Getting her away from Waiteville might be the answer.

ALAN SHOWED UP at Rita's house at eight o'clock the next morning as promised. Maureen opened the door for him, looking soft and vulnerable, as if she'd just crawled out of bed. Her gaze drifted down the length of him, her cheeks flushing prettily in the morning light.

"'Morning," he drawled, letting his own gaze linger at a point just above the opening of her blouse, before moving on to her mouth. "You look ready to me."

He heard her sharp intake of breath and saw the slight quiver of her lips. Taking a step closer, he looked into her eyes. "What do you say? Ready?"

"No." She took a step backward and her hand sprang forward as if to stop him. "Yes. I mean, just about."

Grinning, he moved in a little closer, capturing her wayward hand in his and bringing it to his lips. "It's a great day for a ride."

That did it. She jerked her hand from his grasp and visibly pulled herself together, closing herself off to him. "Is it?" She raised a questioning eyebrow to him while taking another, larger step backward.

Alan suppressed a chuckle. "Sure looks that way to me."

He wanted nothing more than to press her up against the nearest wall and kiss her senseless. Sooner or later he would do it, too. He'd just about run out of patience. But for now he would let her stiffen her spine and put ice in her voice if it made her feel safer. But he wouldn't wait forever.

Removing his hat, he decided it was best to change the subject. "Are you going to make me wait out here?"

Maureen hesitated a moment longer before stepping back from the door, allowing him to enter. "Rita made us coffee and sandwiches to take along. And I need to tell Katie goodbye."

"I thought she was coming with us."

"Rita offered to watch her." He saw uncertainty flicker across her features. "I thought it would be better than dragging her along."

That surprised him—not that Rita had offered, but that Maureen had agreed. He'd never met a more protective mother. But he was glad Katie was staying home. She was a real sweetheart, but he wanted a little time alone with her mother. Maureen Adams remained a puzzle he wanted solved.

A half hour later, laden with a thermos and basket of food, Alan led the way outside.

"I hope you don't mind the Jeep," he said, storing the food under a blanket in the back. "It's a little windy, but I prefer it to driving one of the department's cruisers into Seattle."

"That's fine." Maureen climbed in without looking at him. "The breeze will feel good."

Alan nodded and slid into the driver's seat. "Let's go, then." He started the engine and headed west, toward the mountains. As the town fell away behind them, he picked up speed.

Taking a deep breath, he marveled at the perfection of the morning. Maureen was right. The breeze did feel good: clean and exhilarating. Behind them, the sun climbed toward midmorning, casting rays of rose-colored light on the mountains. On a morning like this, everything seemed right with the world.

Stealing a glance at Maureen, he thought how fresh she looked with the wind whipping through her hair. It reminded him of the day in the playground when he'd watched her with Katie. She'd had the same look about her, the same glow.

She caught him looking at her and blushed slightly before turning away. "How long will it take?" she asked.

Alan shifted his attention back to the road. "About three hours to Seattle. But I need to make a stop first."

"Oh?" She turned sideways on the seat, grabbing her hair in one hand to keep it out of her face.

"Sorry," he said. "I should have warned you to bring a scarf or something."

"It's okay. I like it."

He believed her. The smile on her lips flickered gaily in her eyes, and she seemed more relaxed than he'd ever seen her.

"So," she said, interrupting his thoughts, "where do you have to stop?"

"The Simmons ranch." He probably should have warned her about his little side trip. Of course, then she might have used it as an excuse to turn down his offer of a ride. And he liked having her with him.

"That's the boy Millie and Rita talked about a few weeks ago? The one you kicked out of town?"

So she remembered. "I believe the word Millie used was *ousted.*"

"Yes, ousted. Same boy?"

"Yep. His name's Joey Simmons." Alan stole another glance at her. "Thought I better have a word with his father."

Maureen sat quietly for a few moments. "Is what Millie said true? Does the boy keep his family fed?"

"Maybe."

Alan thought about the rifle in the back of Bud's pickup. He was sure Joey had more than a passing familiarity with the weapon. After all, generations had lived off the wild game in these parts long before there was a hunting season. Someone like Bud Simmons would simply ignore the fact that times had changed. He wouldn't think twice about sending his son out to bring home dinner—no matter what time of year.

"Boys grow up fast out here," he said aloud. "Especially with a man like Bud Simmons for a father."

She didn't say anything to that but turned away, lost in her own thoughts.

"The thing is," Alan continued, wanting her to understand, "nothing justifies Joe breaking the law. It isn't right, and it will get a lot worse than his driving without a license."

"But surely if he has no choice..."

"He has a choice, and so does his old man."

He felt her gaze on him. Glancing her way, he saw she watched him intently, frowning, as if trying to see through him. It made him uncomfortable. He couldn't read the expression in her eyes. Did she understand about Joey? Then she looked away, back to the scenery, without a word.

He considered saying something else to try to explain how he saw things. Then he changed his mind. What did he care if she understood or not? This was his town.

About forty-five minutes later, he pulled off the highway onto a service road. After a few miles, he turned onto the route leading to the Simmons ranch. It was little more than a dirt track, twisting and turning beneath a forest of huge conifers.

Alan loved this country—the quiet, the rich smell of earth and evergreen. He glanced at Maureen and realized she, too, was absorbed in their surroundings. He wondered how she saw it. She was a city girl, but that didn't mean she was immune to the beauty around her. For reasons he refused to dissect, he wanted her to see it as he did.

The trees parted, and they drove into a clearing that was the Simmons place. Alan pulled up and stopped the Jeep in front of the house. He sat for a moment, his thoughts drawn back to his reason for being here.

"Wait here," he said, never taking his eyes off the house. "I'll only be but a few minutes."

He caught Maureen's nod out of the corner of his eye. Climbing out of the Jeep, he headed for the house. At the door, he hesitated. The place looked worse than he'd anticipated. But then, what had he expected? He hadn't been out here for years, not since the day Simmons reported his wife missing. It hadn't exactly been a showplace then, but it had been a working ranch, well-tended and in good shape. Now it looked like a dump.

Remembering that Maureen waited for him, he pushed his thoughts aside and knocked. For a moment it seemed no one would answer. Maybe no one was home. He knew better. Word was, Simmons hardly left his house anymore. Besides, his battered old pickup was parked out front.

Alan knocked again. Louder. He heard movement inside, nothing definite, more like a shuffling.

"Bud," he called out. "It's me. Alan Parks." More movement from inside. "Open up, Bud. I need to talk with you." Silence. "Come on, Bud. I know you're in—"

The door flew open. "What the hell ya want, Parks?"

Bud Simmons stood before him, a shadow of the man Alan remembered. He had always been a big man, six-four if he was an inch. The last time Alan had seen him, he'd been a combination of hard muscle and gut. Not a trim man, but powerful. Someone you wouldn't want to go up against. Now Simmons seemed shorter, shrunk into himself, and all stomach. His face was a white pasty mask, his eyes bloodshot and his nose bulbous and red-veined. A wreck of a man. If his ranch had fallen into disrepair, then Bud himself had totally decayed.

Forcing a smile past his shock, Alan nodded a greeting. "Bud. Long time."

"Yeah, not long enough." Simmons seemed to gather himself, pulling up to his full height.

Noticing the gesture, Alan braced himself. "Need to talk to you, Bud."

"What about?"

"About your boy, Joey."

"He ain't here."

Alan took off his hat and glanced around the yard before returning his gaze to Simmons. "Can I come in?"

Simmons didn't budge. This was going to be harder than he'd anticipated, Alan thought. He wished he hadn't brought Maureen along. If things got out of hand, he didn't want her around.

"It'll only take a few minutes," Alan insisted.

Finally Simmons shrugged and moved away from the door, back into the house. Alan stepped inside. He took a moment to accustom his eyes to the dim light before proceeding in the direction Simmons had headed.

He found the older man sprawled in a recliner, surrounded by empty beer cans, the television blaring. A quick survey of the room showed the place to be in decent shape—better than the outside. The room was clean, or nearly so. It occurred to Alan that Bud's closest neighbor, Widow Cellar, must have paid a recent visit. There had been a time when people thought Jean Cellar would be Bud's salvation, but that was a while back.

Walking over to the television, Alan shut it off.

"Hey," said Simmons, "you ain't got no right—"

"I need to talk to you." Alan drifted around the room, taking in its contents. Stopping before a handbuilt wooden shelf, he picked up a framed photograph. The picture was of a family: a man, a woman and two kids. Replacing the picture, he turned back to Simmons. "It's about Joey."

MAUREEN WATCHED ALAN step inside the house and close the door. She was glad he hadn't offered to let her come with him. She wasn't the least bit interested in entering that house. Simmons obviously wasn't particular about his living conditions—not the type of man she'd care to meet.

Never very good at sitting still, she got out of the Jeep to stretch her legs. The rest of the yard and outbuildings were in even worse shape than the house. The yard was littered with all sorts of debris, from old broken-down vehicles and spare tires to rusted farm equipment she couldn't name.

It seemed a shame. So much waste in such a beautiful setting. The clearing was a good size, yet the forest surrounded them. She felt as if she were in the middle of a vast wilderness, though she knew the highway was only a few miles away. And the mountains. They sat behind the house, silent and majestic, the perfect backdrop for a not-so-perfect homestead.

Then she saw him. A boy, maybe nine or ten, watching her from the barn door. She smiled, feeling guilty for her unkind thoughts about this place, which must be his home.

"Hi," she said, tentatively taking a few steps toward him. Instead of answering, the boy turned and disappeared into the dark interior of the barn.

Maureen stopped. Reason told her to let him go, but instinct urged her to follow. Shrugging off her disquiet, she crossed the yard to the barn.

As she stepped inside, a rancid odor hit her. She didn't have much experience with animals or farms, but she knew they shouldn't smell like this. Where was the aroma of fresh hay you always read about? Or the scent of leather tack?

"Hello," she called out, hoping the boy would show himself. She moved a little farther inside, fighting the urge to cover her nose and mouth with her hand.

"I'm Maureen," she said. "I'm new in town. What's your name?" She knew she should turn around and walk out, back to the light and fresh air. But something drew her on, deeper into the barn toward the child she'd seen a few minutes ago. She passed rows of empty stalls. It seemed odd that the place should smell like this when it housed no animals.

"Do you live here?" she called again, knowing he heard her even if he didn't respond. She walked toward a dim light at the rear of the building. When she got closer, she saw that the light came from a small open window. If nothing else, she'd get a breath of fresh air.

Moving toward the sunshine, she found him in the last stall. But he wasn't alone. He knelt next to a small deer lying on what was probably the only clean straw in the entire place. The animal was hurt and someone had bandaged its leg.

"Oh my," Maureen said, dropping down next to the boy. "Is it yours?"

For a moment she thought he would run again. Then he visibly braced himself. "No, ma'am."

Maureen bent to get a closer look at the animal, and the boy stiffened next to her. Not wanting to scare him, she pulled away, leaning back on her heels. "Have you had a vet look at him?"

The boy shook his head.

"I won't hurt him," she said. "I don't know much about animals, but I know a little about people medicine." She stopped, giving the boy time. "I could look at him if you like."

She saw the turmoil in his eyes. He was afraid. She thought of the conversation at Rita's dinner table, and a knot of outrage tightened her stomach. This boy and his brother had been deserted by their mother. With an effort she suppressed her anger.

"Would you like me to take a look?" she asked again, willing him to trust her.

Still he hesitated for a moment before nodding.

She reached down and gently removed the makeshift bandage. As she did, the boy steadied the animal. "What's your name?" she asked, surveying the damage done to the animal's leg.

"Tommy."

"Nice name." She laid the bandage aside, wondering if she knew enough to help this creature. Her nursing career hadn't done much to prepare her for doctoring a deer. "It looks like he got his leg caught in something."

"A trap."

She raised her gaze to the boy's. "A trap?"

"Wasn't meant for the deer."

"I see." But she didn't. She didn't know anything about traps, or deer for that matter. Looking back at the animal, she said, "It looks like his leg is broken."

"Yes, ma'am."

She looked at the boy again. He probably knew more about doctoring animals than she did. "You can call me Maureen."

"Yes, ma'am."

Smiling, she turned back to the animal. The boy certainly wasn't short on manners. "You did a good job cleaning it, Tommy, but I think we better set that leg." She glanced around the stall for something she could use. Before she could ask, the boy took off. When he returned, he brought several flat pieces of wood for her to choose from.

"Great," she said. "These will do fine. Now, I think we should go ahead and clean his leg again while it's uncovered. What do you think?"

Tommy scurried away again and returned in a few minutes carrying a stack of clean rags, hot water and an over-the-counter antibiotic.

"Thanks," she said.

Tommy knelt down beside her and once again steadied the animal. She did what she could, trying to think of the deer as a person, cleaning the wound and applying the antiseptic. Then, using the wood and strips of rags, she set the leg. The boy had good instincts—holding the animal steady and soothing it as needed.

"You like animals, Tommy."

"Yes, ma'am."

"You're very good with them."

She finished tying the last rag to secure the makeshift splint and leaned back on her heels to survey her work. "There, that's about all I can do." She glanced at Tommy, who still held the animal's head, stroking it with gentle fingers. "I think he's going to be all right. Just keep the wound clean and covered."

Tommy nodded his response.

The sound of Alan's voice surprised her, and she threw a quick glance toward the barn entrance. "I've got to go," she said.

She started to stand, but the boy stopped her with a hand on her arm. "Don't tell no one, please."

Maureen looked down into his pleading eyes, and something melted inside her. She hated to think what could make this boy so afraid. And why would it matter if she told someone he sheltered an injured animal? Whatever the reason, she knew she wouldn't betray him. "Of course not," she said. "It's our secret."

Rising, she turned and hurried out of the barn, nearly colliding with Alan as she reached the door. "Where have you been?" he asked, obviously irritated.

Shrugging, she turned toward the Jeep. "Oh, I was just exploring."

"Exploring?" Alan reached out and grabbed her arm, stopping her retreat.

"Yes," she answered. She met his gaze, then turned her eyes purposely toward the hand that held her. "Exploring."

He released her suddenly, and she met his gaze again, unconsciously rubbing at the spot where his hand had been. Then she turned away and headed across the yard.

She got into the Jeep and closed the door before realizing Alan hadn't followed. Instead, he'd stopped a few feet away and stood motionless, his back to her, facing the house. Straining to see around him, she let out an involuntary gasp as a bear of a man stepped out of the house—a rifle dangling from one hand.

CHAPTER SIX

AT MAUREEN'S SURPRISED gasp, Alan stiffened. He had to get her out of here. Under normal circumstances Simmons possessed a mean streak a mile wide. After a few beers and the unpleasant words they'd exchanged inside, he was worse than mean. He was unpredictable. Cursing himself for getting them into this situation, Alan shifted his hat to the back of his head before settling his hands on his hips. He should have seen this coming.

"Put the gun away, Bud."

Simmons lifted the rifle to rest across one arm. "This here's private property, Parks."

Alan stood still, knowing he had only two options. He could bully Simmons into getting rid of the gun or he could get into the Jeep and drive off. Backing down was the safest course, but it ate at him. Then, out of the corner of his eye, he saw a slight movement by the barn.

Damn! It was one of the boys.

"Go on, now." Simmons made a sweeping gesture with the hand holding the rifle. "Git."

The decision had been made. With Maureen behind him in the Jeep and one of the boys hiding in the barn, there was only one course of action. Without taking his eyes off the other man, Alan backed up and climbed into the Jeep.

"Remember what I said, Bud."

"Ain't no reason for you to come back here, Parks."

"I hope you're right," Alan said with a nod. "Hope you're right."

Starting the engine, Alan forced himself to move at his own pace, unconcerned, deliberate. He even sat for a few seconds while the engine purred, his gaze never leaving Bud. Then he shifted into gear, backing out slowly before turning and heading for the road.

The few seconds it took to reach the trees stretched like minutes, but he took it slow and casual. Finally the woods closed around them, blocking his view of the ranch in the rearview mirror. Only then did he pick up speed, putting the Simmons place as far behind them as possible.

The meeting had been a disaster. Still, Alan had thought he'd contained it—until Simmons stepped outside. He thought of Maureen and the boy, and his anger at Simmons resurfaced.

The Jeep gained momentum as they left the dirt road behind and skidded onto pavement. For the first time since Bud had walked out of his house, Alan risked a glance at Maureen. She sat with one hand braced on the roll bar, her features set in concentration. It struck him that she hadn't uttered a sound. He was pretty sure she was scared senseless, yet she'd kept her head. He'd discovered another layer to this multifaceted woman. The lady had guts.

She must have sensed him looking at her. Meeting his gaze briefly, she acknowledged his concern with a nod. Then she released her death grip on the roll bar and turned away, visibly trying to relax.

Alan cursed under his breath. How could he have been so stupid? He knew Bud Simmons's reputation. He never should have taken Maureen with him. A deputy or two would have made sense. Not a woman. And what if Katie had come with them?

"Damn!" he said aloud, bringing his fist down hard on the steering wheel.

He caught Maureen's quick glance in his direction, and in a flash he knew the reasons for his carelessness. He'd wanted to get her alone, to back her into a corner and win this little game of cat and mouse they'd been playing. He'd told himself he wanted to know who she was and what she was doing in Waiteville. That had been true. At first.

Lately, however, he'd been more interested in the woman herself, in making her admit the chemistry between them. Hell, he'd wanted to finish what they'd started on Rita's back porch weeks earlier. Like a sex-starved adolescent, he'd been thinking with the wrong part of his anatomy. And he was just lucky—damn lucky—that no one had gotten hurt because of it.

"We need to go back," she said, her voice cutting into his thoughts.

It took a moment before he realized what she was saying. "Are you kidding?" He shot a quick glance her way and saw she was serious. "We can't go back."

"Tommy's back there."

"I know he is," Alan said, another rush of guilt washing over him. He'd worried about the same thing. What about those boys? He'd stirred up their father. Would they pay the penalty? He'd been trying to help, for God's sake, not make matters worse.

"He'll be all right," Alan said aloud.

"You don't know that!"

He looked at her again. She'd turned toward him, one hand braced against her seat while the other gripped the dashboard. Her eyes sparked, and she looked ready to make a grab for the steering wheel. Alan pulled the Jeep off the road and brought it to an abrupt stop.

"Look," he said, turning to face her. "We can't go back. Not now. The gun was for me. A warning gesture. A way of telling me to mind my own business. If we go back, someone *will* get hurt."

"So we just leave Tommy there with that maniac?"

"Bud's not a maniac." Alan pulled off his hat and tossed it on the dashboard. How could he make her understand? After all, he'd wondered the same thing. Only he had the advantage of knowing Bud Simmons and his boys. "You just don't understand how things are around here. We aren't in Chicago."

An angry flush brightened her cheeks. "Don't give me that good-ol'-boy routine. Abuse is abuse, no matter where you're from."

"Bud's drunk and he's angry, but he's not going to hurt Tommy." Alan ran a hand through his hair, suddenly feeling very tired. "He may be a little heavy-handed with the belt occasionally, but there's never been any evidence of abuse."

"How would you know?" Her voice rose, adding a level of hysteria to her words. "They live way out here, miles from town."

"They go to school, Maureen. In a town this size, I and everyone else would know if Bud beat those boys."

She didn't look reassured, and his patience, what was left of it, wore thin. Retrieving his hat, he placed it back on his head. Still, he tried to reassure her one more time. "I wouldn't leave Tommy if I thought he was in jeopardy."

Maureen wanted to believe him. She didn't want to think of Tommy in danger. And, in a way, what Alan said made sense. Hadn't she discovered just how hard it was to keep secrets in a small town? Still, she wasn't sure. She kept remembering how skittish Tommy was. And she was an outsider. Would Alan tell her the truth if Bud really did abuse his boys?

After a few minutes, Alan turned back around and started the Jeep. Before he could put it in gear, Maureen stopped him with a hand on his arm. When he turned a questioning face to her, she met his gaze, begging for the truth. "Are you sure, Alan?"

He smiled softly. "I'm sure."

She hesitated a moment longer, thinking that when this man smiled he could convince a woman of anything. The warmth of his eyes and the gentle slope of his mouth stirred parts of her she considered best left dormant. Pushing her wayward thoughts aside, she nodded and released his arm.

Alan pulled back out onto the road. After a few minutes, he said, "Those boys have been dealing with their father all their lives. More than likely they do a better job of it than I just did."

Detecting a note of self-reproach in his voice, Maureen considered asking what had happened inside Simmons's house. Obviously things had not gone as planned.

When she'd seen Bud Simmons with his rifle, she'd never been so frightened in her life. In the hospital, violence was an all too familiar adversary. But it was always the aftereffects she saw. For the first time in her life, she herself had faced the possibility of violence. It left her weak-kneed and sick to her stomach. She had a right to know what had happened. Didn't she?

Glancing at Alan, she saw his smile was gone, and something told her now wasn't the time to ask. Despite his confident words, he was tense. His body showed the strain, from the straight, rigid lines of his jaw and the hard focus of his eyes, to the way his hands gripped the steering wheel.

She also saw the strength in him, and a slow swell of desire curled inside her. This man drew her. And she didn't understand it. All her life she'd been surrounded by powerful men, and she'd always avoided them.

First there was her father. She'd loved him so much. Yet he'd pushed and pulled at her, trying to mold her into someone she didn't want to be. She'd fought him every step of the way and finally ended up marrying David against his will. Quiet, gentle David, who didn't try to change her.

Then there were the doctors. Always the doctors. Smart, aggressive men who always wanted something from her. She would have nothing to do with any of them. She always went home to David, assuring herself that he was what she needed. Never admitting—even to herself—that she'd married a weak man.

Looking at Alan again, she realized that here was a man whose strength matched her own. And instead of resenting him, she wanted to soothe the lines of tension from his brow and kiss away the hard lines of his mouth.

She fought it. She didn't want this. He would bring her nothing but pain. Turning away, she forced thoughts of him aside.

She considered Tommy instead. Why was he hiding the deer? What must he go through on a day-to-day basis living with a man like Bud Simmons? She knew about growing up without a mother. Her own had left when she divorced her father. But her father, although often overbearing, had never brandished guns at visitors in the front yard. How much worse must Tommy's life be?

He was such a quiet boy, with good instincts and gentle hands. When she'd looked into his eyes, something inside her melted. She wanted to know more about him, about his brother, his mother, and yes, even his father.

The night Millie and Rita had talked about the Simmons boys, she had listened with half an ear, grateful the conversation had turned away from her. And then today, when Alan told her about stopping at the Simmons ranch, she'd been curious. Now she wanted to know more, and she wanted to help. But what could she do? This wasn't her town. And she had Katie to think about.

Within minutes they were back on the highway, heading for Seattle. Maureen absently watched the passing scenery. The sun was a little higher, the air a little warmer, but otherwise it was as if they had never stopped.

As they got closer to Seattle, her thoughts shifted to what lay ahead. The night before she had lain awake trying to determine how she was going to pull this off. For weeks she'd wanted to go to Seattle to discover if the authorities were searching for her and Katie. She was almost there. But so was Alan Parks.

Hunting through back issues of a newspaper took time. Would Alan give her that time? Plus, there was the small matter of finding the library. All she had was a street address in downtown Seattle. How was she going to get Alan to drop her off somewhere in the middle of the city, preferably close to the library, without telling him where she was going?

The problem kept her mind busy until the hills and trees gave way to the evidence of civilization. Suddenly, they were in the middle of the city and she was out of time.

To her surprise, Alan gave her no argument when she told him where she wanted to be dropped off. She'd picked a street number several blocks higher than the library's address, hoping she'd guessed right about a suitable location. Her luck held out. Alan dropped her off in the middle of bustling downtown Seattle, and she walked the few short blocks to the library.

Once her objective was in sight, however, she hesitated, suddenly unsure as to whether she wanted to go inside. The building itself looked more like a college library than the public library she'd expected. Constructed at right angles with a lot of cement and glass, a flat roof and an unrecognizable piece of modern sculpture in the middle of a dry fountain, it would have fitted very nicely onto the University of Miami campus.

But it was not the building itself that held her back. It was what she might find inside.

She could do this, she told herself. She had to do it. Taking a deep breath, she walked inside and was immediately surrounded by the hushed tones common to all libraries. The familiarity comforted her, and she felt the rightness of what she was doing. The feeling fled, though, when she finally found the article she was looking for in the *Miami Herald.*

When she saw it, she thought her heart would stop. Dated four months ago, it was just a small piece, buried on page four. There wasn't even a picture. She read it once, and then again.

Adoptive Parent Sought in Abduction

Miami police issued a warrant today for the arrest of Maura Anderson of North Miami Beach. Anderson was charged in the abduction of her three-year-old adopted daughter, Katie Ann. Anderson was involved in a custody suit with the child's birth mother, Roberta Sanchez. Authorities believe Ms. Anderson has fled the state in an attempt to prevent Ms. Sanchez from regaining custody of the child.

Ms. Anderson was a nurse at . . .

The room dimmed around her.

She saw nothing but the words blurring in front of her eyes. She felt nothing but a tight, choking pain in her chest. She closed her eyes. The words screamed at her. She tried to breathe deeply, but her lungs refused air. In that moment, she didn't know how she could endure this.

Minutes passed, or was it hours, before her reflexes took over, doing what needed to be done. Her eyes opened. Trembling hands rewound the microfiche and removed it from the viewer. She took a deep breath. Her hands put the film back in its container.

Time to stand up.

At first she wasn't sure her legs would hold her, yet somewhere, deep down, she knew her body would not fail. Survival. She would survive this. She stood and somehow managed to return the microfiche container to the reference desk. And then she walked. Back outside. Back to where things were as they had been when she'd walked into the library.

Dropping onto a stone bench, she let the pain engulf her. She sat, she couldn't have said for how long, lost, her mind oblivious to everything but fear.

Eventually her turmoil gave way to numbness, and small things broke through. The low drone of an insect carrying out its business in the bushes behind her. The bench, hard and unyielding beneath her. The midafternoon sun, hot on her bare head. People walking briskly to and from the flat, featureless building that was the library. A small boy, absorbed in his make-believe world, flying a model airplane.

You knew this would happen, she told herself.

She couldn't pretend that she hadn't known the consequences of what she had done. Kidnapping. A federal offense. She dropped her head into her hands and for a moment let the pain overwhelm her again. Behind closed eyelids, she saw her daughter's face, that sweet, cherub face she loved so dearly.

It wasn't fair!

She was Katie's mother! The only mother she'd ever known. Katie needed her. The thought gave her strength.

It wasn't right!

She wouldn't allow them to take Katie away and give her to a stranger—even if that stranger had given her life. Where had that woman been for the past three years?

No, Maureen thought, *I'm not wrong.* She'd done the right thing, the only thing possible. She'd protected her daughter.

With an effort she pulled herself together. For Katie. It was all for Katie. Glancing at her watch, she was surprised to see it was time to go. How long had she been sitting here? She needed to start walking. Alan would be waiting, and somehow she had to face him.

ALAN PROPPED A FOOT on the dashboard of his Jeep, pulled his hat down over his eyes and rested his head back against the seat. He was pleased with himself. Something had finally gone right today.

He had told Rita he'd have a talk with Bud Simmons, but even as he'd made the promise, he had known it wouldn't do any good. Bud needed more than a talking-to—hadn't the way he'd warned them off his property proved that? Bud needed to get off the bottle.

After dropping Maureen off, Alan had headed out of town to an alcohol rehabilitation center he'd read about. He'd mentioned the center to Bud this morning. That, like everything else, had only served to make Bud angry. But Alan had planted the seed, and this afternoon he'd gathered the information to go along with it. Now it was up to Bud.

Alan glanced at his watch and realized it was getting late. Maureen should be along anytime now. He shifted sideways in his seat and adjusted his hat so he could watch the street for her. He spotted her when she was still a block away. She walked quickly, head held high, arms wrapped tightly around her waist.

Something was wrong.

It was in the way she moved and the furtive glances she threw at the people around her. Alan climbed out of the Jeep, all his senses alert. He scanned the crowd but couldn't spot anyone trailing her.

She crossed the street, heading for the Jeep. No one followed. As she got closer, she dropped her arms, but her hands fluttered nervously. They moved to grab her purse strap, shifted to the pockets of her jeans and then back to her purse again.

"What's wrong?" he asked when she was within earshot.

She acknowledged him with a slight lift of one hand but didn't answer. Then she got into the Jeep without looking at him. Perplexed, Alan climbed in next to her.

"Maureen?" he said. Again she didn't answer. He touched her shoulder. "What is it?"

She turned to him then, a little too quickly, her smile a little too bright. His mind registered these things, but it was her eyes he saw. Deeper blue than he remembered, they stared at him: wide, dry and brimming with pain. He suppressed the urge to pull her into his arms.

"What's wrong?" He searched her face for further clues, wondering what or who had brought that haunted look to her eyes.

She shook her head. "Nothing."

"Maureen..." He slid his hand to her face, laying his palm against her cheek. "Let me help?"

To his surprise, she turned her face into his palm and closed her eyes. Time stopped. Suddenly nothing mattered but this woman and his own need to hold her, to comfort her. Shifting sideways, he moved to pull her into his arms.

She stopped him.

Opening her eyes, she turned away, effectively removing his hand from her face. "I'm okay," she said. He could hear the effort the words cost her.

"Tell me."

She shook her head. "No, it's all right." She looked back at him with another forced smile. "It's nothing, really. I had a bit of a shock, but I'm all right now."

He moved to touch her again, but she brushed his hand aside before it made contact. "Maureen," he said. "Whatever it is, I can help."

Leaning her arm against the door, she toyed with the ends of her hair. It struck him again, the way her hair seemed ill-suited to the rest of her—its color, lifeless and flat, like...

"There's nothing to help," she said, pulling him back from his musings. He started to protest, but she stopped him again. Putting two fingers to his lips, she beseeched him with her blue eyes. "Please, Alan," she said. "Let it be."

He sat for a moment, torn. All the questions he had about this woman, all the things he didn't know, flooded his mind. From the very beginning he'd felt—no, he'd known—she held secrets. He'd wanted to know what they were. For weeks he'd told himself he was only doing his job.

Somewhere along the line, his motives had changed. She'd stirred his blood and refused to acknowledge it. He'd watched her straighten her spine and deny—even to herself—the chemistry between them. She'd become a challenge. A game he'd indulged in because of the way she affected him. Maureen Adams made him want. And it had been a long time since any woman had done that.

Now things had shifted again, and he wasn't even sure why. It was no longer a game. Suddenly he didn't care who she was or why she'd stopped in Waiteville. Even the way his body responded every time he was near her meant nothing. It only mattered that she was here, and she needed him. She might not know it yet, but she did.

Patience, he said to himself. *Give her time.* "Okay," he said aloud. "Let's go home."

AS THEY LEFT THE CITY behind, the mountains rose to greet them. Once again, the sun was at their backs, this time casting shades of mauve and violet across the deep green. The quiet beauty of their surroundings calmed Maureen's frayed nerves, soothing the pain deep inside her.

"It's pretty special out here," Alan said, as if reading her thoughts.

"Yes." She'd ridden a Greyhound bus across the country, viewing miles of spectacular scenery. She couldn't remember any of it being more beautiful than these mountains. "It's almost magical," she added, more to herself than Alan.

"My father used to say these mountains held the answer to all of life's questions." Alan spoke absently, as if he, too, were speaking to himself. "If only one knew how to listen."

"Sounds like a very wise man." Maureen felt she understood exactly what Alan's father meant. There was serenity here and an untouched peace that urged one toward openness. She thought how sweet it would feel to be lost here, with nothing but the sight and sounds of the mountains surrounding her. Then she glanced sideways at Alan, embarrassed by her mental wanderings.

He didn't seem to notice. "He was quite the philosopher—or so my mother used to say." He chuckled. "It always seemed like a strange combination to me. Town sheriff and weekend philosopher."

That surprised her. "He was a sheriff, too?"

"Yeah." This time Alan glanced at her and smiled. "I'm sure he would have had something profound to say about that, too. You know, life coming full circle or some such thing. Man makes his living as a small-town sheriff. His only son vehemently declares he'll be anything but. Then son follows in father's footsteps after all."

Maureen had to grin. She understood about parents wanting their children to be reflections of themselves. How many years had she struggled against her father's will. "That sounds familiar."

"You, too?"

"Sure. My father's a lawyer. You know, the rich, sleazy kind." She was a bit surprised that she could joke about it after all the anguish he'd put her through. "He couldn't understand why his daughter didn't want to join his practice."

Alan laughed. "Well, at least one of us succeeded in breaking the mold."

"I broke the mold, all right." Maureen had a brief flash of just how dramatically she'd gone against her father's wishes. What would he say about kidnapping? She pushed the thought aside. She'd done enough thinking for one day.

"What about your mother?" he asked, interrupting her thoughts.

"My mother?"

"Yeah. What did she want you to be?"

Maureen shook her head. She hadn't thought about her mother for a long time. "I never really knew her. She and my father were divorced when I was young. Father got custody."

"That's unusual."

"Father's a bit unusual." She had to smile to herself at the memories of their father-daughter battles. Then the memory of their last encounter wiped all mirth away. "He's used to getting his own way."

Alan threw her a sympathetic look. "But didn't you ever see your mother?"

"Not much. I vaguely remember a couple of times when I was small, but that's about it."

He didn't question her further about her mother, and she was glad. She didn't want to start thinking about her. After all, she'd put that part of her childhood away a long time ago.

Instead, she turned her musing toward Alan and what Rita had told her about his family. Glancing at him, she tried to imagine the kind of child he'd been, how he would have handled his father's death. She could almost picture him as a ten-year-old, his copper eyes stoically refusing to shed a tear, standing rigidly next to a woman dressed in black. A woman who, according to Rita, was unable to stand on her own.

She considered asking Alan about his father, how he died, but she decided against it. The day had held too much sadness, too much emotion already. She needed to think and talk of lighter things, things without the power to cause pain.

"Hungry?" Alan asked abruptly, breaking into her thoughts.

"A little."

"One of my favorite places is only a few miles from here. Want to stop?"

"Shouldn't we be getting back?" she asked.

Alan shot her a quick glance. "What's the hurry? It won't be dark for hours."

"Well, Katie..."

"Don't worry. Rita loves having Katie to herself. She'll probably be upset if we show up too early. Besides, we've got another couple of hours to drive yet, and I'm starving."

Maureen was hungry, too. What could it hurt? Spending a little extra time with Alan wasn't an unpleasant thought. Maybe she could get him to tell her a little more about the Simmons boys and their father. Besides, she rationalized, after the day she'd had, she could use a little diversion.

"Sure, why not?" she finally answered.

"Good. You'll like this place. Nothing fancy, just good food and a great view. I make a point to stop there every time I'm within fifty miles."

CHAPTER SEVEN

CLIFF'S, as the little restaurant was so aptly named, clung to the side of a mountain. Made of split logs, it resembled a long, narrow log cabin of a hundred years ago. Even the small windows and stone steps leading to a wooden porch spoke of another era. Feeling as though she were stepping back in time, Maureen followed Alan through the door.

The minute they stepped inside, the illusion of age vanished. There was nothing old or dilapidated about the inside of Cliff's. Everything gleamed of polished wood. A hardwood floor, tables and chairs of rich rosewood, a carved bar complete with brass trim—all gave the place a warm, homey feel. But the real pièce de résistance, the feature proclaiming itself as twentieth century, was a solid wall of glass windows open to the mountains and overlooking the valley below.

Maureen couldn't hide her delight. "What a fantastic view."

"Want to eat outside?" Alan motioned toward a patio beyond the windows. From inside it looked as if the deck hung suspended above the valley floor.

"Absolutely."

Pleased with her response, Alan led Maureen outside. Cliff's had always been one of his favorite spots. He only wished it was closer to Waiteville. As it was, he ate here every time he drove to Seattle. And sometimes when he found himself needing to clear his head, he ended up here.

They settled at a table next to the railing. Maureen leaned over the edge, just a little, and scanned the valley below.

"What would you do if you were afraid of heights?" she asked, laughter in her voice.

Alan warmed to her mood. "Eat at the bar."

Maureen laughed and settled back in her chair, inspecting the restaurant patio with the same intensity as she had the valley. "Is it always this empty?"

Alan followed her gaze. Only one other couple sat on the patio, while several men occupied stools inside at the bar. Glancing at his watch, he said, "It's early yet. In another hour or so, this place will be jumping."

"Local hot spot?" she teased, picking up her menu.

Alan returned her smile. "Complete with country band."

He'd so seldom seen her like this, her soft blue eyes lighting with amusement and pleasure, the lilting sound of her laughter filling his senses. There had been that first Sunday night at Rita's, before she'd known he was there. She'd come bouncing into the kitchen with Katie on her hip, and he'd felt the first flush of longing in his gut. Occasionally he'd catch glimpses of this side of her at the diner, when she'd let down her guard for a moment or two. But most of the time it was with Katie. It struck him just how badly he wanted to be the cause of her laughter, the reason for the light in her eyes.

Cliff himself showed up to take their order, interrupting Alan's thoughts. "Hey, Alan, good to see you." Slapping Alan on the back, Cliff dropped down into a chair next to them, pad in hand. "What'll it be today?"

Alan smiled. He'd known Cliff for years, yet he knew nothing about him. Likewise, Cliff knew him only as Alan, a guy who stopped in every now and then.

Both Alan and Maureen ordered hamburgers and fries, with all the trimmings. Alan was grateful Cliff didn't linger, or mention that Alan had never before brought someone here. He always came alone, and he wasn't sure how Maureen would take that piece of information.

Watching her across the table, he thought how easily she fitted here. She'd turned back to the view, once again letting her eyes explore their surroundings. Sometimes people were born in the wrong place. He figured she must be one of those people. Born and raised in a big city, she seemed at home in these mountains. He liked the combination, and it gave him a hint of what it might take to keep the spark of laughter dancing in her eyes.

When Cliff delivered their drinks, Maureen turned back to Alan and smiled. This place, these mountains, had worked wonders on her. All the pain and mystery had vanished from her face.

"So," she said when Cliff disappeared again, "what brought you back to Waiteville after college?"

"It's a long story." Alan tore open a couple of sugar packets and dumped them into his tea. "Are you sure you're up for it?"

Maureen grinned, the late afternoon sun casting a pearly glow across her cheeks. "Sure. Why not?"

"Well..." Alan took a sip of tea and winced. Grabbing another couple of packets of sugar, he added it to the drink.

"Fattening," she teased.

Alan grinned and waved his spoon in the general direction of Maureen's diet soda. "Better fat than whatever the chemicals in that stuff will do to you." Stirring his tea again, he took a sip and sighed. "Better. Much better."

"Actually," she said, "I figured you more as the beer-drinking type."

He chuckled. "I am. But I thought you might like to get back to Katie tonight. Beer and driving in these mountains don't mix."

"Conscientious to the end." She smiled, but he couldn't tell whether she was serious or making fun. "You were about to tell me how you ended up back in Waiteville."

"Oh, yeah." Alan leaned back in his chair, casually resting one leg on top of the other. "Actually, I spent most of my youth planning on how I was going to get out of Waiteville."

"You hated it that much?"

"Hate's a pretty strong word." He paused, considering. "I don't think I ever thought of it quite like that. I just wanted out. That's not particularly unusual for kids raised in small towns. You have this idea that there has to be something else out there, something better than what you have."

"And was there?"

He shook his head. "No."

"So where did you go?"

"College first. Western Washington University, up in Bellingham. Luckily, I had good grades and a knack for football. Between the two, I managed to wrangle a partial scholarship. But it only lasted a year."

"You lost the scholarship?"

"No." He took another sip of his tea. "I went to Vietnam."

"Drafted?"

"I enlisted."

"But why?" The look on Maureen's face spoke volumes. Alan instantly knew what side of the war she'd been on. "If you were in college..."

Alan thought of that year, of his anger. He'd felt superior, infinitely more mature than the other students around him. He and Maureen would probably have clashed violently. But he'd been a kid. Different from the others, but no less a kid.

"A small-town boy, raised by a lawman, had no place on a college campus in the sixties. I didn't fit in. I didn't want to fit in." He paused, thinking of the day he'd chucked his scholarship. "One day I said the hell with it and walked into a marine recruitment office."

"The marines?" Maureen grimaced and leaned back in her chair. "Man, you are a glutton for punishment."

Alan laughed. He'd been such a cocky young man. "Hell, I was out to prove a point."

"To whom?"

Alan's smile turned to a wry grin, and he shrugged. "Who knows?"

Cliff showed up with their food, and a lull fell over the conversation. They both seemed content for the moment to dig into the thick burgers and steaming fries. Cliff returned a few minutes later and refilled their drinks. Then he left them alone again.

"So Vietnam was what brought you back to Waiteville?"

Alan could hear the caution in her voice, the hesitation to ask the question. Obviously she, too, knew they'd been on opposite sides of the Vietnam fence.

"Eventually. It taught me that maybe I didn't want all those things the outside world had to offer."

Maureen nodded. Alan wondered if she had ever faced the same doubts, questioning the choices she'd made, realizing she'd been wrong. Something told him she had.

"Anyway, when I got back from 'Nam, I finished school. Then I came back to Waiteville. End of story."

"But no law school."

"Nope. Waiteville needed a sheriff, and I no longer needed to be a lawyer."

"And you're happy?"

Alan hesitated a moment. The answer to that question was not as simple as it might have been a couple of months ago. He'd been happy, or at least he thought he had. Maybe the word that best described how he felt about his life up until now was content. He'd been content—with his job, with his town.

Now there was this woman, this Maureen Adams, with her startling blue eyes and porcelain skin. A woman who made him ache with the gentle sway of her hips and her all-too-feminine bottom. A woman living in a cloud of mystery so thick he could feel it. And suddenly, contentment no longer fit.

"I'm happy," he said finally.

She looked at him, questioning. "You don't sound so sure."

"Why don't you tell me something about yourself?" he suggested, trying to change the subject.

Maureen smiled, gracefully acknowledging his tactic. "I think you and everyone else in town already know my entire life story."

Alan chuckled. "Small towns."

"Yes, small towns." She glanced away for a moment before meeting his gaze again. "I can't quite get used to it. In Chicago no one knows or cares about anyone else."

"You're exaggerating."

"Maybe a bit. Still, it's nothing like here."

Cliff showed up to retrieve their empty plates and offer dessert. The special for the day was homemade strawberry pie, and Alan convinced her to try it. Once Cliff was out of earshot, Alan informed her that at this time of year, the special dessert was always fresh strawberry something.

"So," he said, wanting to bring the conversation back to a personal level, "if you won't tell me about yourself, tell me what you were doing at the Simmons place today."

She shrugged. "I met Tommy."

Alan lifted an eyebrow, encouraging her to go on.

"I was stretching my legs," she said. "He appeared out of nowhere. I went to talk to him."

"Tommy Simmons doesn't just talk to anyone."

"Well, he was a little shy at first." At his dubious grin, she added, "Okay, he was a lot shy."

"So?" Alan knew there was something more here. Something she wasn't telling him.

"We talked."

Alan considered pushing a little harder but changed his mind. Instead he let the subject slide, not wanting to dim the smile in her eyes. But he couldn't help thinking he'd never met a more closemouthed woman.

"What about you and Simmons?" she asked after a few minutes of silence.

He hesitated. Something warned him this was dangerous ground, but he couldn't refuse to answer. "It wasn't what you'd call a successful meeting."

"I take it Bud didn't agree to keep Joey on the straight and narrow?" She smiled, but there was a tenseness about her that denied the lightness of her tone.

"Hardly. He told me to mind my own business."

"And will you?"

"Not if Joey continues to break the law."

"But what if Millie's right?" She leaned forward, her hands clasped together on the table. "What if the boy's supporting his family?"

Alan sighed. "I admit it's not a good situation, but if the boy's driving without a license—"

"But it's such a minor infraction. Under the circumstances, can't you ignore it?"

"Minor infraction." Alan sat forward in his chair. "Do you think if I let Joey get away with this, it will stop with his driving without a license?"

"I don't know, but—"

"What do I allow him to get away with next? Robbing a liquor store? Or stealing old ladies' Social Security checks?"

Anger flashed in her eyes. "Of course not."

"You sound like a typical do-gooder. You want me to let the boy break the law as long as he doesn't bother you."

"That's not what I meant." Maureen held her ground, never flinching under his gaze. "And you know it."

"Do I?" Alan leaned back and crossed his arms. "Do you believe circumstances dictate whether you respect the law? That sometimes it's okay to break the law, if the situation warrants it?"

Maureen didn't answer, and Alan repeated his question. "Do you?"

"Yes," she said at last. "I do."

Silence fell hard between them. There were small sounds: the couple talking on the other side of the porch, the men at the bar cheering over a game on the television and the distant sound of a truck on the highway.

"You're wrong," he said quietly. "No one has the right to decide when a law is right or wrong. As soon as you allow an individual to make that choice, you have chaos."

He saw the stubbornness in her eyes. But there was something else there, too. Something that went beyond a discussion of ideologies. The fight drained out of him and he said nothing more.

Cliff delivered their dessert: big slices of strawberry pie smothered in whipped cream. Alan picked up his fork, but food no longer interested him. He stole a glance at Maureen, who sat staring off toward the mountains, where the sun had dipped just below the ridge.

"Maureen?" he said tentatively.

She turned back to look at him, her eyes cold. "What about Simmons?" she asked, her voice as chilly as her eyes. "Isn't he breaking the law?"

Alan sighed and dropped his fork. "Not technically."

"And technicality is all that counts here. Is that it? He's neglecting his sons. Possibly worse."

"I told you, there's no abuse going on out there."

"And I'm just supposed to take your word for that?"

"This isn't your concern, Maureen. This is my town. I'll handle it."

Again, an uneasy silence fell between them. Alan picked up his fork and took a stab at his pie. Maureen didn't even pretend. She sat there, once again staring out toward the mountains.

"Millie was right," she said, almost absently. Then she turned back to meet his gaze. "You're stubborn, hard-nosed and narrow-minded."

THEY RODE IN SILENCE back to Waiteville.

There was no need for words. Everything had been said back at the restaurant. They were opposites. Like the two poles of a magnet. Neither understood how the other saw things.

Yet despite everything that had passed between them, tranquillity stole into Maureen's heart. The top of the Jeep was open, and an array of stars covered the night sky. The cool evening breeze kissed her face, while soft strains of music wafted through the air. Alan had picked a classical station. She laid her head back on the seat and closed her eyes. The music fitted her mood.

It seemed odd, Alan choosing Mozart.

A man so firmly embedded in his concepts of right and wrong wasn't the type to listen to this kind of music. He should listen to something hard and jarring, she decided, with no rhythm. Smiling, she laughed silently to herself. Who was she to judge or typecast Alan Parks? Still, he was a man full of contradictions. She tried to focus on all the reasons why she should dislike him. Instead her mind drifted, and images of him throughout the day flitted before her closed eyes.

She recalled the way he'd looked this morning, when she had first opened the door. He'd stood on the porch with his hands stuck in the pockets of his sinfully tight jeans, while his eyes raked her from head to toe. Even now, remembering that look, she felt an uncomfortable warmth steal over her.

He'd reminded her of the boys her father used to warn her about. The ones none of the good girls dared speak to, while they all secretly wondered what it would be like. And like the girl she had been, this morning she had wished Alan had worn his sheriff's uniform, even as she drank in the sight of him in skin-tight denim.

Later, at the Simmons place, he'd put on his badge before going in to see Bud. It hadn't helped. Not with Bud. Not with her reaction to him. The scene played out in her mind, and she remembered details she hadn't noticed at the time. There was the smell of dust and the utter stillness of the yard. But mainly there was Alan, standing with his back to her, the tension in his shoulders pulling the fabric of his shirt tight across his broad back. His masculinity had screamed at her, making her forget all the reasons why she should avoid him.

Then, when he'd picked her up in Seattle, his copper eyes had offered comfort. She'd wanted nothing more than to crawl into his lap and cry. For a moment she'd been tempted to unburden herself to him, to let someone else carry her problems for a while. She had needed it desperately, and he'd been willing. The memory warmed her, making her realize that this was the most threatening side of this very dangerous man.

When they pulled up in front of Rita's house, Maureen didn't want to move. Odd that she should feel this way—after all that had happened today. Alan must have felt the same, because he, too, sat silently, without making a move to get out of the Jeep.

After a few moments, Maureen opened her eyes and turned her head to look at him. He sat sideways in the seat, watching her.

"Thanks," she said softly, so as not to disturb the stillness of the night.

"Thanks?"

"For driving me to Seattle. For dinner."

He reached out and stroked her cheek with the back of his fingers. Closing her eyes again, she savored his touch. She knew she should turn away, but she couldn't. Something stronger than common sense kept her still, treasuring the moment.

She sensed his shift toward her. Opening her eyes, she started to speak. He stopped her words by bringing his fingers to her lips. Trembling, she inched backward and met the hard metal of the door at her back.

"Why are you fighting this?" he asked, so softly that she wasn't sure he'd actually spoken the words aloud.

"Fighting this?"

"Yes." His hand left her mouth, sliding across her cheek and into her hair. He paused there for a moment, his fingers toying with the strands around her ear. "Why are you running from me?"

"I'm not."

"But you are." He came closer, his lips within a whisper of her face. He dropped a feather-light kiss on her cheek. "And you want this as much as I do."

"No."

He kissed her again, lighter still, on her temple. "Then why are you trembling?"

"I'm not."

He pulled away, just enough to look deeply into her eyes. She saw the amusement there, the acknowledgment of her lie.

"It could be good between us," he whispered.

"No." But she couldn't put force into her voice or conviction into the word. His closeness overwhelmed her, draining her strength.

"Yes." He found her mouth. Soft, like a summer breeze, he teased her with just the lightest brushing of his mouth against hers.

"Please, Alan." It took all her willpower to get the two words out and all her strength to say the last word. "Don't."

He stopped, a mere breath from her lips.

She edged backward, just enough to put a little distance between them. "It won't work." Once again, there was no certainty in her voice, no potency.

His lips touched hers again, briefly. She moaned. She wanted this. Damn him!

Abruptly, he released her. With catlike grace he moved away from her, leaving a wall of cold darkness between them. She sat for a moment, stunned, unable to make order of the chaos in her mind. He sat staring out the front window, his expression unreadable in the dim light.

She fought the urge to touch him, to beg him to pull her back into his arms. At the same time she wanted to run, to get out of the Jeep and flee for her life.

There was no telling which choice would have won. Before she could act, Alan climbed out of the Jeep and came around and opened her door. She thought maybe he was angry, but she couldn't be sure. There was no reading the expression on his face.

They walked toward the house. When Maureen reached for the doorknob, he stopped her with a hand on her wrist. This time, without asking, he pulled her into his arms until she felt the entire length of his body against hers. And he kissed her. Not the feather-light kiss of a moment ago. But a deep, yearning, searching kiss, which stole the breath from her lungs.

Letting go of her mouth as quickly as he'd taken it, he said, "Tell me this isn't right." His voice was a low growl, daring her to lie again. But before she could speak, he stepped away from her. Opening the front door, he entered the house, leaving her alone on the porch.

THE INSTANT Maureen followed Alan into the house, Katie descended upon her. Filled with the day's activities, Katie was eager to share her adventures with her mother. Maureen lifted the little girl into her arms, but her thoughts and gaze strayed to Alan. He stood watching the two of them, his expression devoid of any evidence of what had just passed between them.

Maureen stumbled through the next hour. Later she would recall most of what was said. But as it was happening, she could think only of Alan. Or, more specifically, she could think of nothing but the taste of his lips and the feel of his body pressed close to hers.

Katie and Rita talked of nothing but the Apple Blossom Festival. Katie bubbled over about the rides and ponies. Rita told them about the different craft booths and who was showing what this year. They made plans for the following weekend, Alan promising Katie he would personally take her on the pony rides. And when he was gone, and Katie was tucked into bed, Maureen felt herself on the edge of a gaping pit.

She lay in bed knowing that Alan would be her undoing. And there was nothing she could do about it. Eventually he would prevail. She would lose this battle she fought with herself. She would give in to her desire, and Alan would win. And then she and Katie would be at his mercy.

SAM COOPER GLANCED at his watch, thinking it was just about time to call Anderson. Taking a sip of coffee, he lighted another cigarette. He had time for one more.

It had been a hell of a few weeks, but he finally had something to report.

At first the woman and kid had left a trail easy enough for even the cops to follow—if they'd bothered. Cooper and his men had traced them to a small town just inside the Georgia state line. A waitress in the café attached to the bus station recognized their pictures right away. Or more specifically, she remembered the kid. Evidently the child had been cranky, and the waitress had had a rough night. She'd been in no mood that morning for a toddler's tantrums.

Unfortunately, the waitress didn't know where they'd gone from there, nor had she seen them again. The only thing she knew for certain was that they hadn't got back on the bus with the other passengers. The kid had still been fussing when the bus pulled away.

Cooper had left the diner feeling optimistic. The town was small, and if Maura and her daughter were still here, someone else was bound to have noticed them. Finding her was going to be easier than he thought.

Then nothing.

For weeks his men combed the area, checking all the routes out of town. They showed pictures at every bus station for a hundred miles. Then they checked all the motels and boarding houses, both locally and in the surrounding towns.

Nothing.

No one remembered seeing them, or if anyone did recognize the photos, they weren't talking. It crossed Cooper's mind that she might have gone to Atlanta. Given the right circumstances and enough cash, that's what he would have done. From there, a person could hop a flight that would take them anywhere in the world. And the authorities probably wouldn't check the passenger lists on all flights out of Atlanta, for a woman missing from Miami.

It would have been a smart move.

But everything he'd been able to find out about Maura Anderson told him she was broke. So he doubted whether there was going to be any quick plane rides out of the country for her and her daughter. And he didn't think Atlanta itself was her destination. It was too close to home.

Not for the first time he wondered why she hadn't gone to her father. From what he knew of her situation, it was a case Jacob Anderson would have devoured. And if not, well, there was always the money.... Then Cooper remembered the cold gray of Anderson's eyes. *Yeah,* Cooper said to himself, *maybe I do understand why she didn't go to Jacob Anderson.*

Still, he had a job to do. And he wasn't considered the best for nothing. Finally, he'd followed a hunch and gotten lucky.

Cooper drained the last of his coffee and crushed his cigarette into the overflowing ashtray. Climbing to his feet, he pulled out his wallet. First, he tossed a couple of bills on the cheap formica table, then paused, considering. Finally, he pulled out a third and folded it in quarters. Walking over to the counter, he smiled at the woman who'd just reopened his case.

"Here you go, May." He tucked the folded hundred-dollar bill into the top pocket of her uniform, letting his fingers linger a few seconds too long. "Thanks."

May beamed her appreciation. "You find that woman, dahlin', and you tell her May sent you."

With an effort, Cooper returned her smile. "I'll do that." He turned to leave, but May's voice stopped him as he got to the door.

"You get back this way," she called. "You look me up, you hear?"

Cooper opened the door and turned, giving her his best smile. "Sure thing," he said with a nod. Then he was outside in the hot, late afternoon sun. He paused, taking a deep breath to clear his head. "Sure thing," he repeated to himself, and headed across the gravel parking lot to the pay phone.

The phone rang three times before Anderson picked it up.

"Yes," came the familiar voice on the other end.

"I picked up her trail." Cooper grinned, pleased with himself.

"Where?" There was a slight change in the cool voice, excitement maybe, and Cooper knew he'd broken through the other man's veneer.

"She was in a place called Dapper, Mississippi."

"How long ago?"

"Three months. She worked as a waitress at a truck stop on the outside of town." He paused a moment to organize his facts. "She shared a room with a woman named May who also has a kid. They had an arrangement. They worked opposite shifts, and so they watched each other's kid." Cooper took a moment to pull out a cigarette and light it.

"And?" Anderson prodded.

Cooper took a deep drag of his cigarette before continuing. "One night your daughter just left town. Without warning. Not a word to anybody. This May woman's really ticked off and was more than willing to spill her guts. Evidently your daughter left May with no one to watch her kid the next day."

"I see." There was silence on the other end for a moment, and Cooper imagined Anderson struggling to maintain his composure. "Where did she go from there?"

"There's only one way out of this town if you don't have a car, and that's the bus."

"And you'll check on it?"

"Already done. It didn't take much to jog the night clerk's memory once I woke him. Seems your daughter left here on a 2:00 a.m. bus heading north."

"Good."

Cooper smiled. "That's why you hired me."

"Call me next week."

"Yeah. Oh, and one more thing." Cooper paused, relishing this last bit of information. "She's going by a different name."

"Yes?"

"Maureen Adams."

CHAPTER EIGHT

THE DAY OF WAITEVILLE'S annual Apple Blossom Festival dawned clear and bright. Having promised Katie that he would escort her and her mother to the festival, Alan rose early. First he checked in at the station to make sure nothing needed his immediate attention. Then he went about getting ready, humming as he contemplated what the day would bring.

It had been a long week. Once again, he'd purposely avoided Maureen, this time to let her stew. He'd made his position pretty clear the night of their trip to Seattle, and he'd given her all week to get used to the idea. She'd had time, more than enough. Today he planned to make something else clear. He wasn't going to takc no for an answer.

He arrived at Rita's right at eight, ready for breakfast. With easy familiarity, he walked around back and let himself in through thc kitchcn. The smell of fresh-brewed coffee and frying bacon made his mouth water. But the sight of Maurccn in a floral print skirt and soft blue blouse aroused a different type of hunger.

He let his gaze rest on her for a moment. He'd never sccn her in anything but jeans. He liked the way the fabric of the skirt floated around her legs, and how the color of her blouse emphasized the blue of her eyes. She looked soft and feminine, and utterly alluring.

Maureen met his gaze and colored visibly. Then defiance sparked in her eyes and she turned away. Alan grinned at her reaction. Yes indeed, this was going to be one fine day.

"'Morning, ladies," he said, forcing himself to head first for Rita, who stood over the stove. Dropping a kiss onto her cheek, he headed next for Millie, who brushed him aside with a wave of her hand.

"Kiss! Kiss!" insisted Katie with outstretched arms. Alan went over to the little girl, rescuing her from the confines of her high chair. Lifting her high above his head, he planted noisy kisses on her bare belly to the accompaniment of her delighted squeals.

"No!" she screeched in between fits of giggles.

Alan brought her back down to eye level. She captured his neck with her chubby arms and smacked him on the mouth.

"Yuck," he said in between her wet kisses. "Girl kisses!"

Katie giggled and continued her assault on his face. Finally, as he settled her on his hip, she said, "Mommy's turn."

Alan turned and caught Maureen's warning glare. Ignoring it, he inched toward her. "What about it, Mommy? Are you up for a morning kiss?"

Maureen flushed prettily. "I think I'll pass, thank you." Sidestepping him, she headed for the refrigerator.

"Aw, come on." Alan put a hurt tone into his voice.

She returned to the table with orange juice, trying to ignore him. But he knew from her bright cheeks that she wasn't quite as oblivious to him as she wanted everyone to think.

"Kiss her! Kiss her!" Katie insisted.

Maureen, obviously having had enough of her daughter's antics, reached out and took the squirming child from Alan. "Come on, Katie, time to eat your breakfast."

"Gee, Mom," Alan said, dropping onto a vacant chair. "You're no fun." Catching her exasperated glare, he grinned. "So, is everyone ready for the festival?" he asked, thinking it best that he change the subject, at least for the moment.

"You mean now that you've got Katie all wound up," Millie stated in her usual no-nonsense manner.

Rita joined them at the table and smiled affectionately at Maureen. "Isn't that what holidays are for?"

Maureen smiled in return, thawing somewhat before Rita's warmth. "I guess so." Then, shrugging in resignation, she turned to Alan. "Do you think you can behave for the rest of breakfast?" The smile in her eyes softened her words.

"I can behave." His gaze locked on hers, emphasizing his words. "For a while, anyway."

He nearly laughed aloud at her startled expression and the color that once again flared in her cheeks. But he didn't look away or temper the meaning of his words. He meant what he'd said. He would behave. For a while.

Breakfast continued to be jovial, with Alan and Katie setting the tone. It was almost ten by the time they set off for the center of town. Millie was manning one of the quilt booths, so she'd left earlier. Katie rode on Alan's shoulders, while Rita and Maureen walked alongside.

When they reached Main Street, Rita waved goodbye and headed for the booth she'd promised to work. Returning Katie to her mother, Alan took Maureen's hand and led them into the growing crowd of people heading toward the town square.

Waiteville's festival was unlike anything Maureen had ever experienced. She'd expected it to be more like an overgrown school bazaar, similar to those her high school used to throw to earn money for band uniforms. Instead, it was a full-fledged fair, without the seaminess that usually accompanied the state fairs she'd been to.

On the north side of the town square, rows of booths sold handmade goods of all varieties—pottery, quilts, furniture, jewelry, macramé, stained glass, artwork—almost anything made by a craftsman was for sale.

"I had no idea there would be so many wonderful things," Maureen said, stopping to admire a display of children's smocked dresses. "These are beautiful," she said to the young woman behind the booth. "What did you use to do the smocking?"

"I do them by hand," the woman answered with a smile.

"By hand?"

"Everything here is handmade," Alan said, moving up next to Maureen. "It's the only rule for setting up a booth."

"I have the perfect dress for your daughter." Nodding toward Katie, the woman retrieved a royal blue dress from a nearby rack. "With those dark eyes and hair, it would look great."

Maureen smiled and shook her head. "You're right, it's really nice, but I can't afford it. Thanks."

They drifted away from the display of children's dresses and continued working their way down the rows of booths.

"Where do all the artists come from?" Maureen asked a few minutes later.

"All over," Alan answered. "A lot of them are from around here. They live in the hills and come down every spring to sell what they've made. Others travel around. They go wherever there's a show."

Maureen and Alan spent a while looking at the various work displayed, until Katie became restless. Then they headed toward the section of the festival devoted to rides and games.

They had stopped at a shooting gallery, where Alan attempted to win Katie a big pink elephant, when Maureen spotted Tommy Simmons. He was with an older boy, walking among the crowd.

"Can you watch Katie for a moment?" she asked Alan, who nodded but continued his attempt at knocking down floating ducks. "I'll be right back." She left Katie sitting next to him and worked her way through the crowd toward Tommy.

"Hi, Tommy," she called.

Tommy stopped and turned. When he saw Maureen, he broke into a grin. "Howdy, ma'am."

"How are you?" Maureen asked, not knowing what else to say. Her mind raced to a dozen other questions she wanted to ask him, but she knew better than to voice any of those. "Are you having a good time?"

"Great," he answered.

Maureen smiled warmly and turned to the other boy. "I'm Maureen Adams. I don't think we've met."

"This is my brother, Joey," Tommy said, the pride evident in his voice.

Maureen did her best to hide her surprise. Joey looked nothing like his younger brother. Where Tommy was small and fair, Joey was big and dark. He looked every bit of eighteen, though she knew he wasn't yet sixteen. There were other differences, as well. Differences not so easily defined.

"How are you doing, Joe?"

Maureen turned abruptly at the sound of Alan's voice behind her. He held Katie, who gripped a stuffed pink elephant. Without thinking, she took Katie from him, and Alan dropped his hands to his hips, facing the boys.

"I'm okay, Sheriff," Joey answered, placing a hand on his brother's shoulder.

"You behaving yourself?"

Maureen saw the anger flare in Joey's eyes. "Alan," she began, unable to stop herself from intervening in this boy's defense. But when Joey's angry gaze turned on her, she refrained from saying another word.

Joey shifted his attention back to Alan. "Widow Cellar brought me and Tom into town. She's working over at the quilting booth, if you want to ask her."

"It's the truth, Sheriff," added Tommy. "Honest."

Maureen shifted her gaze back to Alan. He looked as if he were considering challenging their answers. She grew irritated at his treatment of these boys.

Then Alan nodded. "Okay, boys. I'll take your word for it. Just don't let me find out you're lying."

"We ain't lying," Joey said flatly. "Come on, Tom, let's get out of here."

Tommy shot Maureen an apologetic grin but followed his brother's lead. She watched the boys disappear into the crowd and then turned on Alan. "What was that all about?"

"Stay out of it, Maureen."

"Stay out of it!" The absolute arrogance of the man stunned her. "I was trying to talk to Tommy. You're the one who came barreling up here with your macho sheriff attitude challenging Joey."

She saw the anger creep into his eyes. "I was doing my job."

"And that job includes threatening young boys?"

"Mommy!" Katie interrupted, squirming in her mother's arms. Maureen looked at her daughter and saw the concern on her face. "Don't be mad."

"I'm not mad," she tried to reassure her, but Katie knew better.

"It's okay." The child patted her mother's cheek in imitation of an adult comforting a small child. Maureen felt the anger seep out of her, and she smiled softly at her daughter.

"Okay, sweetheart," she said. "You win. I won't be mad any more." She turned back to Alan, who still stood with both hands braced on his hips. Her anger stirred again, but then she caught sight of the stuffed animal in Katie's arms, and she pushed her annoyance aside. She wasn't going to spoil the day. Besides, how could she stay mad at a man who won a bright pink elephant for her daughter? "All right, cowboy, what's next?"

Alan seemed to battle his own temper for a moment. Then he smiled that slow, cocky grin of his and dropped an arm around her shoulder. "I think it's time to put the princess here on a real pony."

They spent the rest of the morning and early afternoon entertaining Katie. First there were pony rides and cotton candy. Katie got her face painted like a clown, and Maureen had her fortune told. All three of them took a ride on the merry-go-round, and Katie went for another pony ride.

At lunchtime they stopped at the concession stands set up along the river, and Rita joined them. They laughed and talked while Katie fed bread crumbs to the birds. After a while Alan left to relieve one of his deputies so the other man could enjoy some of the day.

Maureen spread a blanket under a tree, and she and Rita sat talking while Katie napped. They weren't far from the playground, and as Maureen watched the older children playing, she thought of Tommy and his deer.

"Rita," she said, "tell me something about the Simmons boys."

Rita shifted on the hard picnic table bench to look at her. "What do you want to know, dear?"

Maureen hesitated. What *did* she want to know? "I'm not sure," she said with a shrug. "Last week when we went to Seattle, Alan stopped at the Simmons ranch. While he was inside talking to Bud, I met Tommy. He seemed . . ."

"Shy?" Rita answered for her.

"More than shy."

Rita sighed. "I'm afraid I can't tell you much. I don't really know the boys very well myself. Their mother left when they were young. And Bud . . . well, I guess you've heard enough about Bud."

Maureen nodded, wanting to ask more about Simmons and the way he treated his sons, but she was unsure if even Rita would tell her the truth. She considered telling her about Tommy's deer and how he kept it a secret, then decided against that, too. She'd promised him she wouldn't tell anyone. Instead she thought of Alan and how stubbornly he refused to cut Joey any slack. "Why is Alan so hard on Joey?"

"He's not any harder on Joey than anyone else. It's just that he believes so strongly in the law."

"But he's so adamant about it. Surely the things Joey's doing are minor."

Rita smiled sadly. "Has Alan told you how his father died?"

Maureen shook her head. "What does that have to do with how he treats Joey?"

"Everything." Rita paused, as if considering what to say next. "It was an accident. A stupid accident."

"Aren't they all?"

Rita glanced at her and nodded. "Probably. But this accident was particularly unnecessary." She paused again and took a deep breath. "Jud Morris was drunk and beating his wife, Celia. It wasn't the first time. One of the neighbors had called in and complained. Usually a deputy would have handled it, but that night Mel, Alan's father, decided to go over there. He was determined to get Celia to press charges. Instead, he died."

Maureen could see that the memory hurt. The pain in Rita's eyes was sharp, bitter.

"It seems Jud's sixteen-year-old son had had enough of his father beating up his mother. The bullet went wild, hitting Mel just as he forced his way into the house."

Maureen groaned, feeling the senselessness of such a death, knowing how it must have affected Alan.

Rita nodded. "Alan has never been able to get past the fact that Jud's son was taking things into his own hands."

"But surely he doesn't blame that boy."

"That boy killed Alan's father." Rita looked at her hard. "It should never have happened."

"Yes, but..." Maureen let her voice trail off, her understanding of Alan's pain conflicting with empathy for the boy who'd tried to help his mother. And there was Joey Simmons, supporting his family any way he could. Were they wrong? And if she believed that they were wrong, what about herself and what she'd done to protect Katie?

No, she decided, she'd done the right thing.

She could feel for Alan's loss. Maybe even understand a little better why he saw things the way he did. But she'd done what she had to. Just like those two teenage boys.

Still, the tragedy of both situations bothered her. Couldn't something be done before Joey and Tommy's predicament turned into something more serious? Shouldn't someone be trying to prevent a repeat of the disaster that had taken the life of Alan's father? If someone took the time to intervene with Bud Simmons and his boys, maybe tragedy would be avoided. With that in mind, she decided to go out and see Tommy again. She'd check on his deer. Maybe if she could get closer to him, she could help.

WHEN KATIE WOKE from her nap, they spent the rest of the afternoon strolling amid the booths, repeating the child's favorite activities.

As the daylight dimmed, they found a spot beneath a gigantic oak tree within sight of the bandstand. Maureen spread the blanket again and dropped their accumulation of purchases and prizes on one corner. Rita lowered herself with a sigh, resting against the bark of the old tree. Katie immediately crawled into her lap, and Rita slid loving arms around the child. Maureen sat cross-legged next to them, a sense of peace and wistfulness stealing over her.

All around them, the townsfolk began settling. Some carried baskets of food, others sleepy children. For a while the evening grew quieter, with only the sounds of friends and families talking in hushed tones or laughing softly among themselves. Even the children, those still awake, seemed subdued.

The air cooled. In the woods across the field, the first fireflies of the evening flickered. Birds chattered overhead, saying farewell to the daylight before quieting for the night.

Maureen stretched her legs, tucking her skirt around her knees. Leaning back on her elbows, she felt the warmth of the soil and the springy grass beneath the blanket. The sun dipped lower, and the streetlights along Main Street blinked on. She fought the urge to close her eyes, not wanting to miss one second of this evening.

"Are you hungry, dear?" asked Rita quietly.

Maureen lifted her gaze to Rita, who rested her head against the tree, her eyes closed. Katie, too, hovered close to sleep, her head nestled against Rita's chest. Only the slight movement of her baby fingers against Rita's arms indicated she still held on to wakefulness.

"I couldn't eat another thing," she answered.

Rita sighed. "Me, neither."

Silence slid easily between them, the evening sounds turning softly into those of night.

"What about Katie?" Rita asked a few minutes later, still not opening her eyes. "Should we feed her?"

Maureen saw that the tiny fingers had stilled. "She's sound asleep. You could probably lay her down, if you want."

"In a minute."

Maureen smiled, understanding the sweet sensation of holding a sleeping child against your breast. Rita would hold Katie for some time yet.

She let her attention drift back to her surroundings, back to the bandstand, where preparations for the evening's entertainment had begun. The scene seemed somewhat unreal—not unlike the rest of the day. Six men, dressed in white slacks, red candy-striped shirts, navy blue bow ties and white straw hats, set up sound equipment. She even recognized most of them. There was Abe Bollow, who owned and ran the grocery at the end of Main Street. Doc Readon, Waiteville's sole claim to the medical profession. Jake Balwin, one of Alan's deputies. And Percy, who ate breakfast, lunch and dinner at the diner, and spent the rest of the day reading newspapers outside the grocery.

Never had she imagined that places such as Waiteville still existed. These people, this town, the day's events, none of it should be real. She found herself wishing she was truly part of it all, that she belonged here.

Then she felt Alan next to her. It was as if the air suddenly turned warmer around her. Lifting her eyes, she followed the long line of him until she met his gaze. Smiling, she shifted slightly, giving him room to sit next to her. He dropped a small bundle onto her lap and sat down beside her.

"What is it?" she asked, picking up the package wrapped in plain brown paper.

"A peace offering."

"Hah!" Maureen stole a sideways glance at him while removing the cord that held the package together. "A bribe, you mean."

Alan shrugged and smiled. "Just open it."

Within minutes Maureen had it unwrapped. She gasped as she pulled out the blue hand-smocked dress she'd admired and wanted for Katie. "Oh, Alan."

"It will look pretty on her."

"But..." Maureen felt unreality close about her once more. She didn't understand this man. "Why?" she asked, searching his face for some clue.

Alan shrugged again and looked away. "I thought Katie would like it."

Maureen kept her eyes on him, willing him to turn back and look at her. When he did, he reached over and touched her cheek. "You were right. I was a little hard on Joey today."

Her heart melted. She thought of what Rita had told her about Alan's father this afternoon, and she suddenly felt she understood the forces that drove him. At least a little. She wanted to tell him, but the words wouldn't come. There was still this major obstacle between them, their way of looking at right or wrong. Alan saw things as black or white, she in shades of gray. Maybe in another time and place they could ignore it, but under the circumstances, that was impossible.

"Thanks," she said. And then because she needed to say something else, she added, "Katie will love it." She turned away, letting the hushed sounds of the park surround them.

"The band's about ready to start," he said, his voice as quiet as those around him.

"I had no idea towns like this still existed," she said, conveying the sense of unreality she'd felt all day.

"There aren't many places like Waiteville left in the world."

"It's like being in another time."

"Sometimes it seems a bit unreal. But not to them." Alan gestured toward the others. "This is all they know. This is their reality."

"It's not a bad reality."

"No, it's not." He paused for a moment, as if weighing his words. "That's why I'm still here."

She turned to look at him and he smiled, a soft, gentle smile. A smile that tore at her heart and sent a surge of longing through her.

Who was this man? she wondered. What was he? Not even David had affected her the way Alan did. He was a bundle of contradictions, and she felt both drawn to and threatened by him at the same time. Stronger and more arrogant than any man she'd ever known, he possessed all the traits she usually detested in a man. Yet he loved children and traditions and his hometown. He brought her gifts for her daughter. And he made her want him in a way she'd never wanted a man before.

The band started slowly, pulling her thoughts back to the moment. They played old, soft music that must have brought back memories to some. A waltz, a love song... then, as the crowd on the grass stirred to life, the music grew livelier.

"Come on," Alan said, taking her hand. "Let's dance."

Maureen automatically shook her head. "No, I don't—"

"You don't dance?" He was on his feet now, drawing her up next to him.

"Well, yes, but..."

"Then come on." He didn't give her another chance to protest but started walking, still holding on to her hand.

Maureen threw Rita and Katie one quick glance before Alan hustled her toward the bandstand.

Then she was in his arms, and all other thought ceased. He pulled her close, and she felt the long, lean lines of his body pressed against hers. For a moment they stood still, and Maureen felt the threads of her restraint slip. Then Alan's feet began to move with the music, and she followed.

She was a wonderful dancer, Alan thought. Light and airy, her movements seemed to come to her as naturally as breathing. She followed him faultlessly, not missing a step or nuance in movement. Then there was the feel of her, the underlying strength beneath the sheer femininity. She fitted him perfectly.

He sought her eyes and felt the rest of the world drift away. He could see her struggle at first, like a small animal caught in a trap. She fought him. No. She fought herself. But his patience was gone, and he had no intentions of letting her escape. She was his, and it was time she realized it.

He knew the instant she gave up the fight, the moment she recognized the futility of denying how right this was, how perfect they would be together. At once everything grew easier. And harder. They danced, first fast, then slow, until there was nothing but the two of them.

When he could no longer stand the feel of her without having something more, he guided her off the dance floor. Without a word, he steered her into the woods and toward the river. She followed him willingly, silently.

Once under the canopy of trees, it took all his willpower to keep from pulling her into the bushes and down onto the forest floor. But he kept going until they came to the river. Then he picked his way among the rocks until he found the path leading to a spot he knew.

A few minutes later they stood on an outcrop of rock above the river, a wall of ragged stone at their back. Below them the water sparkled in the moonlight as it wound its way toward the Pacific.

"It's lovely," she said, without taking her eyes off the scene below. "You always find the most beautiful places."

Alan studied her face, thinking the beauty of the silvery river below was nothing compared to her skin. He touched her cheek. She didn't look at him, but he saw the slight flutter of her eyelashes.

"You're beautiful," he said, lifting her hair so he could brush a kiss along the smooth surface of her neck.

Maureen trembled at the feel of his lips, knowing she should stop him, yet wanting him to continue. He slipped his hands around her waist and pulled her close, pressing her head to the side as he continued his sensual exploration of her throat and neck. For the briefest of seconds, she considered stepping out of his arms. Then the thought fled as his fingers grazed the underside of her breast. With a moan, she gripped his arm, loving the feel of his strong muscles beneath her fingers.

"I want you," he whispered.

She didn't answer, couldn't, but turned into his embrace, slipping her arms to his shoulders while he worked his magic along the edges of her collarbone. He held her tight against his hips, his hands spread wide around her waist. And everywhere he touched, with his hands, with his mouth, with the hardness of his body, the heat nearly burned her.

She craved more.

Slowly, he worked his way toward her lips, and the world spun crazily about her as she waited to feel his passion sear her mouth. Instead, he stopped, a mere breath away from what she'd been awaiting. She opened her eyes and met the coppery warmth of his gaze. He smiled and filled her with intense longing. She couldn't wait any longer to taste his lips on hers. Weaving her fingers into his hair, she pulled him down until she could take what she required.

His mouth covered hers, hard and demanding, spreading its fire downward until she ached for more than moonlit kisses and strong arms about her. The extent of her desire frightened her, and she pulled away, not enough so he would release her, but enough to give herself a moment. A moment to think. A moment to breathe.

Maureen lowered her head to his shoulder, and Alan loosened his grip on her waist. He tried to calm himself while his heart pounded in his chest. He'd desired her for weeks now, watching her fluid movements at Jill's. Then he'd kissed her last week, and he'd wanted her desperately, longed to feel her lips beneath his again. But nothing had prepared him for her passion, or the way it sent a sharp claw of need ripping through his gut.

He pulled away slightly, and with one hand, he lifted her face gently toward his. Looking into the blue depths of her eyes, he saw desire reflecting his own.

"Maureen?" He brushed his thumb against her mouth. Her eyes drifted closed and her lips parted, drawing his thumb gently inside. He watched, fascinated, unable to move as she gently tasted the appendage.

After what seemed an endless eternity of exotic torment, she turned her face into his palm and kissed it softly. Alan slid his hands to her shoulders and circled her neck with his hands. She opened her eyes and answered his unspoken question. "Yes."

Stepping back, he took her hand and led her into the shadows of the cliff. She came eagerly, as if she, too, could wait no longer. Her impatience destroyed the last of his restraint, and he claimed her lips with a fierce possessiveness. He invaded her mouth, and in turn, she filled his senses. Her warm, spicy smell permeated the air he breathed, while the sweet taste of her made him ache for more. She moaned, deep in her throat. Or did he?

He pulled her closer, his hands splayed across her back, until he felt the frantic groping of her hands on his neck, in his hair, begging for more. He leaned back against the stone wall and drew her into the angle formed by his widespread legs. His hands cupped her bottom, pulling her even closer, showing her the extent of his hunger.

Maureen needed no urging and she rubbed herself against him, the ache between her thighs growing torturous. He aroused something within her she hadn't known existed. A fire. A yearning. It coiled inside her, burning hotter with each caress, each stroke of his tongue. She needed him. Here. Now. On this moon-drenched cliff. Denying it had become impossible. Stopping it unthinkable.

He slid his hands upward to claim yet another part of her. He found her breasts beneath the thin fabric of her blouse, fabric that was suddenly too thick, too cloying. As if reading her mind, he yanked the offending garment from the waistband of her skirt. The touch of his hands against her bare skin sent shivers down her spine. He worked his way back to her breasts, leaving a trail of heat in his wake. She moaned at his caress, her already taut nipples turning hard and aching.

Maureen thought she'd reached the limits of her endurance. She thought he could take her no higher. Yet when he touched her breasts, she knew she'd been wrong. Nothing had ever felt more right, more natural than the feel of this man's hands on her. Though she'd fought it, she had known from the very beginning that this moment, this physical contact, was inevitable. She'd felt herself drawn to him, spiraling out of control. But she had never expected this rightness, this feeling of belonging.

The feel of Maureen's soft skin was unlike anything Alan had ever experienced. Silky, smooth, rather like fine satin than the skin of a grown woman. And her breasts, full and hard, growing heavier and more taut with each touch of his fingers.

He pulled away to look into her eyes as he stroked her, but she kept them closed, her lips parted in invitation. He nipped at her mouth, and her eyes opened, bright with desire. They held passion, deep and demanding. She wanted him as much as he wanted her.

Her hands pulled at the buttons of his shirt until they were skin against skin. He growled again as her mouth came back to his, and his hands returned to her bottom, grabbing and tugging at her skirt until her soft, rounded flesh was covered only with the thinnest nylon. His hands slipped inside her panties, and he realized he planned to take her right there.

"Maureen," he said, releasing her mouth but not yet able to relinquish his other hold on her. He would stop now if he must, if she asked it of him. But nothing he'd ever done would be more difficult. "Here?"

She didn't answer verbally but drew his head back down to hers while melding herself more firmly against him. It was all the answer Alan needed, and it destroyed what little control he had left. Turning her so her back pressed up against the wall, he lifted her until she straddled his waist. She held him tight with her arms and legs while he struggled with his own clothes. Then he was free, and, ripping the thin nylon, he buried himself deep inside her.

CHAPTER NINE

THEY WALKED in uncomfortable silence back to the square. Maureen kept her arms wrapped tight about her waist, afraid to let him touch her again. It had all happened so fast. She hardly knew what to think, what to feel.

She stole a glance at Alan and saw he felt it, too—the rashness of what they'd done. Turning away, she momentarily closed her eyes and stumbled over a root. Alan grabbed her arm to steady her, but she pulled away as if burned by his touch.

He didn't push it but stopped her with another touch when they reached the edge of the woods. "Maureen, are you all right?"

She saw the uncertainty in his eyes, the concern. He was willing to take this all on himself, to accept the blame as his alone.

"I'm okay," she said. "This wasn't your fault."

He hesitated a moment longer, and she thought he was going to say something else. Then he nodded, and they moved on.

They found Rita sitting where they'd left her, surrounded by a group of ladies, most of whom Maureen didn't know. Katie lay on her stomach next to Rita, sound asleep. The older woman sat with one hand idly caressing the child's back.

Four sets of questioning eyes turned toward them as they approached the group. Maureen suppressed the urge to straighten her hair and check that all her clothes were in place. The unreality of the day was nothing compared with what had just happened. What she'd allowed to happen. There was no doubt that speculation about the two of them had already begun.

"Katie's had a big day," she said, trying to keep her sudden attack of nerves out of her voice. "I need to take her home and put her to bed." As she moved to gather her daughter, Alan intervened.

"Here, let me." He squatted next to the sleeping child and lifted her gently. Katie stirred slightly before settling comfortably in his arms.

Maureen's face heated with embarrassment at the gesture. Not that she didn't appreciate his thoughtfulness. It was just that she could almost hear the gears clicking in the minds of Rita and her friends. Speculation be damned. She knew tongues would be wagging all over Waiteville tomorrow. She and Alan would be declared an "item."

"Thanks," she finally said to him, because there was nothing else she could say. She started to gather the rest of her belongings, then stopped, realizing no one had said a word. They all still watched her.

"I think I'll stay for a while," Rita said, breaking the silence. "I'll bring the blanket."

"Will you be okay here by yourself?" Maureen asked, not knowing whether she should stay with Rita instead of running home. Would staying look less obvious?

"Of course," Rita said. "Go on. Get that baby to bed."

Relieved, Maureen nodded, and they left the little group sitting on the blanket under the tree.

Neither spoke as they made their way through town and up the hill to Rita's house. Maureen opened the door and Alan stepped inside, heading straight upstairs with Katie still nestled in his arms. She followed, expecting him to hand her daughter back to her before reaching the bedroom. But he didn't. He went on into their room and carefully put Katie on the bed.

Katie half woke when he laid her down, a sweet cherub smile creeping across her face. A swell of emotion caught in Maureen's throat as he leaned over and kissed her sleepy daughter.

"'Night, princess," he said ever so softly. Katie's arms slipped around his neck and squeezed before she rolled over and fell back to sleep.

Shoving her warring emotions aside, Maureen moved up beside him to undress Katie. He stepped out of the way, but she could feel his presence close behind her, unnerving her. Her hands trembled and her vision blurred, but she finally managed to get her daughter out of her clothes and into pajamas. When she pulled the covers up around Katie's chin and turned to leave, she nearly collided with him.

"Oh," she said. "I'm sorry."

Alan reached out and brushed a stray strand of hair away from her forehead. "Are you?"

"Yes. I mean, no." His closeness threatened her. Her chaotic thoughts dimmed with the remembered feel of him.

"I'm not," he whispered, lowering his head to brush his lips across hers.

Maureen took a step backward and glanced quickly at Katie before looking at him again. "Not here, Alan."

He smiled and dropped his hand to her cheek. Then he slid an arm around her shoulders and led her out of the room. She went with him but shifted out from underneath his arm once they were outside the bedroom.

"Go on down," she said. "I want to clean up a little."

He hesitated, his gaze sweeping her face before asking again, "Are you sure you're all right?"

"Fine." But she wasn't. She needed a few minutes to herself, a few minutes to come to grips with the evening's events. Then it struck her that maybe he, too, needed time alone. "Maybe you should go," she felt compelled to say, although she wasn't at all sure what she wanted him to do. Leave? Or stay?

Alan's smile softened, and he dropped a gentle kiss on her forehead. "I'll be downstairs. Waiting." Turning, he left her rooted to the spot, all her turbulent emotions ready to engulf her.

What had she done?

She closed her eyes and tried thinking rationally about the evening's events. Instead, all she could do was remember the feel of him. His mouth on hers. His hands caressing her, holding her, lifting her so she could wrap her legs about his waist... The room swayed and she opened her eyes quickly. Steadying herself against the wall, she pushed the memories aside. It took a moment for her to regain her equilibrium and, with it, her ability to view the evening with more objectivity.

It didn't take her long to clean up, to remove the evidence of her lapse by the river. A part of her performed the task swiftly, mechanically, as if it were an everyday occurrence. Another part of her watched in amazement, wondering what David would think. David, who'd been her husband and the only lover she'd ever known. David, whom she'd held off until their wedding night. David, who always said she was too reserved in their lovemaking, too conservative. What would he say now?

A twinge of guilt tightened around her heart. But she was honest with herself. Her regrets weren't due to *what* had happened at the river but rather that it had happened with Alan Parks. Why had she never experienced such abandon with her husband? She couldn't help but wonder if things would have turned out differently if she had. But they hadn't. And now she was here, unable to ignore the way this stranger, this very dangerous stranger, aroused her.

Once she had finished cleaning up, she started toward the stairs, but hesitated before going down. She should just stay upstairs, she told herself. She could end this here and now by going into her room. She would crawl into bed next to Katie and ignore Alan and all the emotions he stirred within her.

But she couldn't.

Even as the idea surfaced, her feet moved, seemingly of their own volition, down the stairs. She knew she couldn't forget him. Not tonight. Alan drew her like a moth to a flame. And just as surely, she would end up burned. He would find out who she was and what she'd done, and then it would be over. She would have lost. He would turn her in, and she'd lose them both, Katie and Alan.

She had just reached the hall when Rita stepped into the house. "Is Katie asleep?" she asked, slipping out of her sweater.

"Yes," Maureen answered, surprised that her voice sounded so normal. Alan joined them, momentarily drawing her attention away from Rita. To her surprise, he looked more handsome than ever, his copper eyes riveted on her with an intensity that left her breathless. With an effort, she dragged her thoughts back to Rita. "I didn't expect you back so soon."

Rita smiled and patted her on the cheek. "These old bones aren't what they used to be." Then, turning and smiling broadly at Alan, she added, "I've had enough for one day. But you two go on. I'll listen for Katie. Go back down to the festival. The fireworks will start soon, and the dancing will go on till midnight."

"Oh no, I..."

"We owe you, Rita." Alan leaned over and kissed his aunt on the cheek while grabbing Maureen's hand.

"Really, Alan, I can't."

"Sure you can," Rita insisted, nearly shoving them out the door. "Now, go on."

Rita closed the front door behind them, and they stood silently for a moment on the porch. Maureen sighed, feeling the walls of inevitability close around her. Looking at Alan, she saw him watching her with the same intensity she'd seen in the house. Then, without speaking, he led her down the steps. They walked to the end of the street, where he stopped, pulling her into the shadows of nearby trees.

"Come home with me, Maureen."

She searched his face. It had all happened so fast. At the river. Now. Yet she'd seen it coming, known maybe from the first moment he'd turned his soul-searching eyes on her that this would happen. That they would be lovers. That they would end up in bed. Or by the river.

"It shouldn't have happened the first time like that," he said, and Maureen wondered at how easily he read her thoughts. "I never meant—"

"It's okay." She touched his lips with her fingers. She couldn't let him take this all on himself. "It happened. And it wasn't one-sided."

He smiled, and she knew he was remembering the wanton way she'd thrown herself at him. She felt the color rise in her cheeks, but she didn't turn away. It was too late for regrets.

"Come with me, then," he said. "Let me make love to you the way it should have been."

She hesitated only a moment before putting her hand back in his. They would have this night, she told herself. Because they would never have anything else.

"Yes," she said. "I'll come home with you."

THE WALK TO ALAN'S HOUSE was short. But then everything and everyone in Waiteville was too close together, Maureen reminded herself. There were no secrets here, no privacy. A short while ago she'd been worried about the town's speculations. No doubt someone would see them together now, and there would be few questions left in anyone's mind. Still, she wished it had taken longer to get there.

As they approached a large house on the street above Rita's, she came to an abrupt halt. "It's not what I expected," she said.

She stood for a moment, taking in the details of the house. Large and rambling, it had obviously been designed for a family, not a bachelor. The huge yard was meant for children, scrambling across the grass in summer, building snowmen in winter. The wide veranda, complete with white wicker furniture, spoke of long summer evenings where a family might sit together and watch the sunset.

Maureen wished that he lived in a small, crowded apartment complex. Somehow it would make being with him easier, less tempting.

"My grandfather built it," Alan said. "I've thought of moving into a smaller place..." He shrugged, letting his voice trail off. Releasing her hand, he slid his arm around her shoulders and led her up the walk. "Come on."

He opened the front door and they stepped inside. Alan flipped on a small table lamp, and a large, graceful foyer sprang into sight. High ceilings, hardwood floors and a long, curving staircase highlighted the entryway. But it was the little things that caught Maureen's eye: the well-worn braided rug, the vase of fresh flowers on a table, the smell of wood polish.

"Very nice."

"I only use the downstairs." Alan shoved his hands into his pockets, and for the first time since meeting him, Maureen thought he looked a bit uncomfortable. Maybe he knew how incongruous it seemed that he should live in a house like this.

"The living room is this way," he said, and motioned toward twin oak doors on one side of the foyer. Maureen followed him into the other room.

Like the outside of the house, the living room was large and comfortable. A massive fireplace dominated one wall, while a cozy seating arrangement invited one to curl up before a blazing fire. There was no fire tonight, but Maureen could imagine the warmth of the room on a cold winter night, and how sweet it would be to make love slowly in rhythm with the dancing flames.

"How about a glass of wine?" Alan asked.

A flush of heat rose to her cheeks as she shifted her gaze to him. "Sure," she said, turning away quickly so he wouldn't see the wayward direction of her thoughts. This house, his house, tugged at her, making her want things she couldn't have. Things that could never be.

While Alan got the wine, she drifted around the room. A bay window faced the street, and she thought it would be a good place to sit on rainy days. She shoved the thought aside and moved to one of the bookcases flanking the fireplace. It contained an odd assortment of books, hardcover and paperbacks, from classics to current bestsellers.

She'd never thought of Alan as a reader, but some of the more recent books must have been his. It reminded her of how little she knew about him. She ran her fingers along the shelf, still wondering what she was doing here.

"Checking for dust?"

Maureen pulled her hand from the shelf and turned at the sound of his voice. "I was just looking at your books." She crossed the room to take one of the glasses he held in his hands.

"Do you approve?" He smiled down at her and took a sip of his wine.

"Sure." Shrugging, she moved away from him, away from the heat of his smile. "I'm just a little surprised."

Alan laughed. "Surprised that I *can* read, or that I *do* read?"

Maureen grinned and shook her head. "At *what* you read. Or more to the point, at the variety of things you read."

He moved up beside her. "I'm full of surprises."

"Yes." She met his gaze for a moment, thinking how easy it would be to lose herself in him. "You are."

"You're uncomfortable. Why?"

Again his perception startled her. "Well," she began, deciding to be as open and straightforward as he, "this evening has been somewhat unusual for me."

"Me, too."

Maureen turned and stepped away from him again. "I wasn't looking for a relationship. And what happened earlier..." She shrugged, refusing to meet his gaze, afraid that if she did, he would see too much. "Anyway, it wasn't supposed to happen."

"But you came here with me." He'd followed her across the room and stood behind her, so close she could feel the heat of his body against her back. She closed her eyes, letting his warmth penetrate her senses.

"Yes. I did." She turned back to face him. "And maybe that's the scariest thing of all."

Taking the glass from her hand, he set it on a nearby table. Maureen followed his movements with her eyes, unable to meet his gaze when he turned back to her. She felt so strange being here. It made no sense after what had happened at the river, but an odd shyness crept over her.

Alan framed her head with his hands and tilted her face to his. "Don't be afraid," he whispered.

But she was. So much more afraid than she'd been of the arrogant cowboy who had taken her by the river. He bent to kiss her, and she trembled when his lips touched hers. The floor shifted with his touch, rendering coherent thought impossible. Their frantic lovemaking by the river hadn't changed that. Why now? she silently questioned. Why did this man affect her like this?

"I'd never hurt you," he said against her lips. "You know that, don't you?"

"No." She shook her head slightly. He started to protest, but she prevented it by deepening the kiss. When she could speak again, she added, "Please, Alan, no promises."

He pulled back a little, searching her face. Maureen's heart went out to him. She could see the confusion in his eyes. How could he know that he would hurt her—badly. That it was inevitable. He started to say something else, another reassurance, she supposed, but she stopped him again.

"No more words," she pleaded. Rising on her toes, she slipped her arms around his neck and hid her face against his chest. "Just make love to me. Like you promised."

Alan held her, fearful that at any moment she would change her mind. Their frantic lovemaking by the river had only whetted his appetite. He wanted her now more than ever, with a force threatening to overpower him. But he didn't want to hurt her, and she seemed so sure that he would.

"Alan," she whispered against his chest, a question in her voice. Her fingers moved restlessly to the hair touching his collar and she shifted against him, reminding him of the sweetness of the body he held.

Bending, he lifted her in his arms. "No more words," he agreed, pressing his lips to the top of her head. He carried her into the bedroom and laid her gently on his bed. He would just have to prove to her that she was wrong about him.

Sitting beside her, he took a moment to admire the sight of her there, her small form nearly overpowered by his massive bed, her pale skin translucent in the dim light. He planned to go slowly. He wanted to savor every touch, relish every whisper, cherish every moment.

She started to say something, but he pressed a finger to her lips. "No more words. Remember?"

She closed her eyes as his hand slowly drifted, tracing the line of her jaw and then her neck, until he came to the top of her blouse. She held her breath as he paused there, teasing her with the gentlest of touches.

"Do you always go braless?" he asked.

Maureen opened her eyes and smiled. "Sometimes."

"I like it."

"Come here." Lifting her arms to his shoulders, she pulled him down until his lips touched hers. After a moment he shifted to lie next to her. They lay there length to length, both fully clothed, as he explored the taste of her.

Maureen treasured the feel of him, his lips on hers, his hands on her body. So strong. So sure. They moved over her with a possessiveness that made her yearn to belong to him. He slipped her blouse over her head, and his hands found her breasts. Strong, callused hands against the soft fabric of her skin. She wanted to feel those hands elsewhere.

She moved to unfasten the buttons of his shirt, but he grabbed her wrist. Shifting his weight, he slid a strong leg between hers, while pinning her groping hand against the mattress.

"Patience," he whispered as he rubbed a muscled thigh against the ache between her legs. He kissed her, brief, nipping touches of his teeth and lips that made her squirm to capture his mouth. A low chuckle emanated from deep in his throat, and he gave her what she wanted—a hard, searing kiss that only managed to intensify the ache where his thigh lay.

"Better?" he asked when he abandoned her mouth.

"No."

"Slowly." He lowered his head to her breast. "We're going to go slowly."

She lost the last shreds of composure as his mouth teased her breast. The room, the world, swirled around her in a dizzy array of sensation and yearning. Her back arched and her legs clamped around the hard thigh that held them apart, while she strained to free the hand he held prisoner. She wanted to touch him, to have him touch her.

She was driving him mad, Alan realized. Nothing had prepared him for this. He felt the desire pulsate through her body, turning his own passion into a hot, raging need. He tasted her fevered skin, while her legs strained against his thigh. Her unbridled moans of pleasure and protest begged him for more. No other woman had ever wanted him this way. And he'd never needed anyone like he needed her.

He freed her wrist to pull at her skirt, and her hands flew to the buttons of his shirt. They both groped, pulling the printed fabric over her slender hips, popping buttons in frantic haste. Shirt and skirt were tossed carelessly aside. He pinned her again, and this time his bulging sex, still restricted by denim, pressed firmly between her thighs with all his weight.

"Please," she moaned, her eyes closed, her hands fumbling at the waistband of his jeans.

He pressed harder, loving the way she wanted him. "Say it again," he breathed against her lips.

Maureen wanted to feel him—all of him—skin against skin. Yet he teased her. It was obvious how badly he needed her—which was no less than she needed him.

"Please," she repeated as her lips met his, her hands slipping around his waist, her legs wrapping around his, pulling him tighter against her.

He answered her with his mouth and the harsh fabric of his jeans rubbing against her aching femininity. He brought her higher, until need and desire wrapped around her like a blinding light, bringing her a release that was both sudden and shattering.

When the room slipped back into focus, she realized he still lay atop her, his own unsatisfied need evident against her. She opened her eyes to find him watching her, hunger and restraint warring in eyes gone dark with hunger. Uncoiling her legs, she reached down to unfasten the snap of his jeans. He didn't stop her this time but held her gaze as she slowly lowered the zipper.

Then she held him in her hands, hot, hard and throbbing. Just the feel of him resurrected her own desire. Closing her eyes, she pulled him gently toward her. With a low growl, he rolled away from her.

"Wait," he said, his voice deep and gravelly. "I can't put you at risk again." Reaching over to the nightstand, he pulled open the top drawer and grabbed a small foil packet from inside. Then he stripped away his jeans in one easy motion and returned to her. She lifted her hips to meet him, wanting him again, wondering if she would ever stop.

IT TOOK A WHILE for the world to stop spinning, but even then Maureen kept reality at bay. She'd promised herself this night, and she wanted all of it. She would lie here with Alan and pretend that this was just the beginning.

Snuggling closer against him, she let herself think how right it felt to be here. His warm, masculine body would be her haven against the world. When things got rough, he would be there with his unique strength to fend for her and her daughter. She would no longer have to be the strong one. And what a father he would be to Katie. Strong, loving, but firm. The perfect father. The perfect husband.

The idea hit her hard, and she yanked herself back to the real world. Fantasizing wasn't her style. There was no future for her and Alan. Lying here dreaming about it was pointless at best. The entire day had been laced with fantasy, but she couldn't allow herself to pretend any longer. In the end, she would only suffer more for it.

Yet everything she'd learned about Alan—from his feelings for Rita to his way with Katie—revealed a man who wanted a family. Pulling away from him, she raised herself on one elbow. "How come you don't have a wife?"

Alan turned and smiled, amusement dancing in his eyes. "Are you applying for the job?"

"No." The word came out quickly, before his teasing tone of voice registered. Then she returned his smile, realizing that she must have sounded forward. "Sorry. I didn't mean to pry."

"Sure you did." Sliding his arm around her shoulders, he pulled her head back down to rest on his chest. "But I don't mind. And the truth of the matter is that I've just never met the right woman."

Though still curious, she hesitated to say anything more. She was reluctant to break the wall of silence she'd built around herself. Since the night she'd left Miami, she had tried to keep her distance from others—not learning too much about them, not giving away too much of herself. Her curiosity won out.

"That's a pretty unoriginal answer," she said.

She felt his low chuckle against her cheek. "But a true one."

Maureen sighed and settled closer to him. Thoughts of keeping her distance dimmed, while contentment clashed with her need to maintain a grip on reality. "There must have been someone."

"Not since I came back to Waiteville."

"How come?"

Alan adjusted his arm and rested a hand on her head, stroking her hair. "I'm not sure. Maybe as you suggested that first night, I've known all the women in this town my entire life. Who knows?" He shrugged and dropped a quick kiss on the top of her head. "Maybe I just developed a liking for city girls."

Maureen laughed lightly. "But not enough to go back to the city yourself."

"That's right."

Silence fell softly between them. His fingers worked magic in her hair, gently caressing her scalp, making her wish he'd never stop. It felt good to be here with him.

"What about before you went away to school?" Maureen asked, breaking the silence. "Was there someone special then?"

"Are you sure you're not applying for the job?"

Maureen pulled away and started to deny it once again, but stopped when she saw the smile on his face. He was teasing her. And again, she had taken him too seriously. "You could just tell me if I'm getting too nosy, you know."

"I was born and raised in a small town. I'm used to nosy." Grinning, he ran a lazy gaze down the length of her, reminding her of the route his hands had wandered earlier. "Other things I'm not so used to."

A flush of heat branded her cheeks, and Maureen quickly covered herself with an afghan that lay across the bed. Alan laughed and reached out to her, brushing his knuckles against her breast, inches above where she held the blanket.

"You can hide under that blanket if you want, but I've got a great memory." Then, as if he hadn't just sidetracked the conversation with his suggestive eyes and talk of hiding under blankets, he added, "Besides, you're not asking anything that everyone else in town doesn't already know."

A wave of disappointment washed over Maureen that he'd returned to their previous topic. With a simple look and the touch of his fingers, he made her want to forget talking altogether. Trying to hide her errant emotions, she settled back down on his shoulder.

"Jill and I dated all through high school," Alan continued, seemingly unaware of the turmoil he'd created. "Everyone figured we'd end up together. I guess I pretty much figured that way, too."

"So what happened?"

"By the time I got back, things weren't the same. For either of us. We went out a time or two, but it just wasn't right."

She thought of the easy camaraderie between him and Jill and wondered if she could ever feel that comfortable with him. She doubted it. Even if all the other problems somehow went away, if by some miracle there was no longer anything to keep them apart, she could never be at ease with him. She would never be able to look at him and not feel this stirring, this burning need to have him.

Alan lifted a hand to stroke her hair. "Maureen, I want you to know that something special happened between us tonight."

She stiffened in his arms, knowing he spoke the truth, but also knowing her secrets would destroy whatever he felt for her.

Tonight had changed nothing.

She was the same woman, guilty of the same crimes she'd been guilty of yesterday. And he was the same man. They were different, and only she realized how explosive those differences were. She never doubted for a moment that he would condemn her for the things she had done.

Alan shifted to look at her, searching her face for the words she hadn't spoken. He'd felt her withdrawal, and a thread of fear tightened in his gut. He wanted to know what her eyes said. When he did, it surprised him. Sadness. Did she think he'd toss her aside now that he had gotten her into his bed?

"Maureen," he said aloud, dropping his hand to stroke her cheek. "Tonight was the beginning. Not the end."

She closed her eyes, but not before he saw the faint shimmer of tears. The fear in his gut sharpened, but his need to comfort stirred stronger, and he pulled her closer. Whatever she was afraid of, whatever ghosts haunted her, he would drive them away. "It's okay."

She shook her head, denying his words while tears dampened his chest. But Alan wasn't ready to give up. "I was beginning to believe I'd never feel this way about someone," he said, more to himself than her. "We can make this work."

For a few minutes, he thought he'd convinced her. She lay still in his arms, and he persuaded himself that she had once again relaxed. Then she moved away, and he knew he'd been fooling himself.

She rolled over to the other side of the bed, dragging the afghan to cover herself as she sat up, her back turned toward him. When she spoke, her voice was thick and shaky.

"You're wrong, Alan. We can't make this work."

He wanted to go to her, to climb out of bed and make her face him. But his experience with this woman told him to stay put. With an effort, he shoved aside the fear eating at his insides and the pain threatening to render his voice unrecognizable.

"Maybe not." He took a deep breath and raised his hands to rest under his head. "But we won't know until we try."

She turned to look at him, and he nearly lost his carefully constructed composure. Her eyes were red-rimmed and haunted. "It's too soon," she said.

"Liar." The word escaped before he could stop it, and anger flared in her eyes. He liked it better than the pain.

"I told you I wasn't interested in a relationship. And I meant it. Tonight has changed nothing."

"The hell it hasn't." He had her back lying fully on the bed, pinned beneath him, before realizing he'd even moved. He stared down into eyes alive with fury and defiance.

"Let me go," she demanded, struggling to free herself.

But he held his own anger barely in check, and he wasn't about to release her until he got the truth out of her. "How can you lie like that?"

"I'm not—"

"Tell me you don't feel anything when I do this." Ripe with frustration and need, he attempted to take her mouth. She fought him, turning her head away, but he wedged his hand between them and grabbed her chin so that she faced him again. Forcing her lips open beneath his, he claimed her mouth and tongue. Only when he felt the resistance drain out of her and her hands move to pull him closer did he release her.

"Now say it," he ordered. "Tell me there's nothing here."

Closing her eyes, she shook her head.

"Damn it, Maureen. Open your eyes and tell me there's nothing between us, and I'll let you go."

It took a moment, but she opened her eyes. The tears almost undid him. He almost begged her forgiveness. He almost told her he loved her. Then he saw her regain her composure, steeling herself, and he knew before she spoke what she would say.

"There's nothing between us." Her voice was cold and calm. Only her eyes told him the effort her lie had cost her.

The anger drained from him, and suddenly he felt very tired. Releasing her, he rolled away to lie once again with his hands behind his head.

"Go, then," he said, refusing to look at her.

He closed his eyes and forced himself to remain still as she dressed. Though he longed to pull her back into his arms, he wouldn't allow himself to go to her. He wouldn't speak to her, though words leapt to his lips. Words that might change her mind. He wouldn't even look at her, because if he did, all his other resolutions would disappear.

Instead he listened as she dressed, imagining, as he did, each item of clothing he'd so recently removed sliding back over her slender figure. The image stirred his desire, and he almost opened his eyes to watch her. He stopped himself and turned to less tempting thoughts—like why he planned on letting her walk out the door.

If he'd learned anything about this woman, it was that feigned indifference was the only way with her. He'd been pursuing her for one reason or the other since the day they'd met. And with every step he took toward her, she took two steps in the other direction. It was only when he left her alone, when he purposely ignored her, that he seemed to make any headway.

With most women, he wouldn't even have bothered. He wasn't into games, and he didn't care much for women who played them. With Maureen, however, he sensed this was no game. She was running scared, and the more he chased her, the faster and farther she ran.

Now the stakes were higher. She could lie all she wanted, but they both knew the truth. There was something between them. Something strong. Something inevitable. And she was terrified. He had no doubt that if he pushed too hard she'd be on the next bus out of town.

"I'm leaving." Her soft voice shattered the stillness, and once again he almost lost his resolve. Somehow he managed a yawn, followed by words that nearly killed him to speak.

"Can you find your way back to Rita's?"

He heard her sharp intake of breath and the hesitation before she answered. "Sure. No problem." The door slammed behind her.

Alan released the tight clamp he'd held on his eyes and turned to look at the closed bedroom door. It was only seconds before he heard the front door slam, as well. Then he was up, pulling on jeans and a shirt, struggling to slip his feet into boots so he could follow her. Although he was going to let her think he didn't care enough to see her home, he was making damn sure she got there safely.

As for her insistence that there was nothing between them, he didn't give it another thought. He knew better. And he didn't give a damn about her fears. He wasn't about to give up on the best thing he'd ever found.

CHAPTER TEN

MAUREEN TOLD HERSELF it was for the best when Alan begged off Sunday dinner at Rita's. After all, the day before had been a strain on both of them. They needed a little time to compose themselves before seeing each other again.

Of course, Katie missed him. She was crabby and difficult to handle all evening. She kept asking for Uncle Alan, while insisting she couldn't go to bed without a horsey ride. Rita said Katie was just overtired from the day before, but Maureen knew it was more than that. Katie had become attached to him—just as Maureen feared she would. And telling the child that Alan had to work because he'd been with them the previous day made no sense to a three-year-old. Katie wanted Uncle Alan, and that was that.

As for the emptiness *she* felt every time she looked at his vacant chair, Maureen figured it was nothing more than she deserved. She had gone to him with her eyes open. She'd known from the beginning that her attraction to him was dangerous. Yet she'd ignored her own common sense. If it hurt a little now, she'd just have to deal with it.

Monday and Tuesday came and went with no sign of him at the diner. She knew it was better this way. Better that they not see each other, especially after the way they'd parted. If she closed her eyes, she could still see the anger in his eyes as he pinned her to the mattress. Better that they both have time to get over that night. Better that *she* have time to forget the way he made her feel, the way she wanted him.

Still, every time the door opened, she faltered, longing and fear tying knots in her stomach. And when it was someone else, she'd return to work knowing in her heart that she was lying to herself. She doubted any amount of time would heal the pain she felt with his absence.

And of course the whole town had an opinion about their relationship. It seemed everyone had seen them dancing or heard about it or knew he'd spent the day with her and Katie. This didn't surprise her. Waiteville was a small town and there was no such thing as privacy. The thing that did amaze her was that everyone seemed to approve.

"You and Alan sure looked good together out on that dance floor Saturday night," Jill said first thing Monday morning.

"He's a good dancer," she answered, hoping Jill wouldn't start in on her.

"I wasn't talking about your dancing."

"We're just friends."

Jill let out a short laugh. "Yeah, I know how *friendly* Alan Parks can be."

Maureen turned toward the other woman, unsure what kind of expression she would find on Jill's face. There was nothing but amusement. Then Jill caught Maureen's look and immediately laughed. "I was just kidding. Alan and I are old friends. We dated ages ago. In high school. Really. He's all yours."

Maureen opened her mouth to protest, then shut it abruptly. The worst thing she could do was start denying things. So she let it go, and so did Jill. For the moment.

But that conversation was only the first of many.

"Hey, Maureen," called Percy later that same morning. "Hear ya got your hooks into the sheriff." The old man cackled as if he'd just told the best joke of the year, and several other regulars joined in.

"Shut up and eat your breakfast," Jill stated, plopping a bowl of oatmeal and a plate of toast in front of him. "And stop bothering my help."

For once Maureen was thankful for Jill's interference. At this point, she would accept all the help she could get. With her nerves stretched taut, she didn't know if she was going to explode in anger or burst into tears. It seemed she would just conquer the urge to give in to one emotion, when the other would set in.

And Tuesday was no better.

One of the women who'd been sitting with Rita Saturday evening came into the diner and hugged Maureen as if she were a long-lost child. Maureen didn't even know the woman's name. That didn't seem to faze the older woman.

"I'm so glad the sheriff's gone and found himself a nice girl," she said. "He's been alone too long. It's not healthy, you know."

By this time, Maureen knew better than to answer. Her own emotions were too volatile. Besides, no one listened to her anyway. They'd all made up their own minds about what was going on. She hoped all the furor would soon die down. Especially when no one saw her and Alan together again.

Wednesday came, and it was the worst day yet. She wished she'd never gotten out of bed, because seeing Alan was even harder than not seeing him.

She had finally resigned herself to his purposeful avoidance of her. Now, when she closed her eyes, she no longer remembered his anger when she'd lied to him Saturday night. Instead, she pictured him stretched out nonchalantly on the bed, his hands behind his head, his eyes shut. He'd fallen asleep while she'd dressed, for God's sake. And he hadn't even bothered to walk her home.

So much for his little speech about there being something special between them. Her first impression of him had been right. He was a cocky, egotistical cowboy, and she was better off without him.

It was time for her to leave Waiteville. Past time. Things were closing in around her fast. The threat of Alan finding out who she was and what she'd done hung over her like a guillotine.

Yet she knew she couldn't leave. Not yet.

The money she made at the diner barely paid their rent and living expenses. No matter how careful she was about spending, there was never very much left to put away. It would be months before she had enough saved to move to Seattle.

Then Alan waltzed into the diner, smiling and greeting everyone the way he usually did. "'Morning, ladies." He claimed his favorite stool and tossed his hat on the counter. "Great day out."

For Maureen, the room slipped out of focus, but he obviously didn't notice. "Abe, how's the leg?" he asked. The conversation between him and Abe was an old one and quickly put aside.

"Hey, gorgeous." He stopped Jill with his usual lady-killer smile. "How about a couple of eggs, over easy, ham and lots of coffee."

His gaze lighted on Maureen, and she wished the floor would open and swallow her. For a moment she thought she saw a flare of warmth in his eyes, but just as quickly, she realized her mistake. He gave her the same vacuous smile he bestowed on Jill, and his eyes held nothing but amusement.

"How's Katie doing?" he asked as Jill poured his coffee. "Did she enjoy the festival?"

Nodding, Maureen barely got the single word past the sudden obstruction in her throat. "Yes."

"And you?" Was there more to his question, more in his eyes than common courtesy?

"Yes, we both enjoyed it," she answered.

"Good." He smiled again, but his smile was empty. He may as well have been talking to Abe or Percy. She opened her mouth to say something more, although she had no idea what, but he'd already shifted his attention elsewhere.

"By the way, Percy," he said to the diner's most frequent customer, "I was at Widow Cellar's place yesterday. She wants you to come out and fix her fence."

Jill delivered his breakfast, and he acknowledged it with lady-killer smile number two. "Thanks, Jill. How about some more coffee."

He didn't glance Maureen's way again, so, turning aside, she tried to go back to work. But his presence pulled at her, and she could hardly keep her mind on the other customers. Instead, she was acutely aware of Alan's every word and gesture.

Yet nothing he said or did was different from any other time he'd come into the diner. He treated her the same as he did everybody else. She stole glances at him, looking for signs, searching his face, his eyes, waiting, hoping to see some memory of the night they'd spent together.

But there was nothing.

He smiled. He talked. He teased. And then he left.

She hardly remembered the rest of the morning. She got through it somehow. And when the worst of the lunch rush was over, Jill cornered her in the kitchen and told her in no uncertain terms to go home. Evidently she wasn't handling things as well as she'd thought.

ALAN LEANED CASUALLY against his cruiser and watched Maureen leave the diner. Glancing at his watch, he smiled. It was only a little past one—an hour earlier than usual. So he'd succeeded in rattling her enough that she'd taken off early. Pleased with himself, he resettled his hat lower on his head and pushed away from the vehicle.

Things were proceeding as planned.

Without another glance at her retreating figure, he headed down the street toward the square. He knew her routine. She'd go back to Rita's and change. Then she'd pick up Katie and bring her down to the park—where he'd be waiting.

He'd planned to stay away from her for a week, but the last three days had been pure hell. Each morning he set a routine for himself that kept him out of town and away from the diner. He'd checked in with every rancher and farmer within fifty miles, talking to people he hadn't seen in a year.

On Sunday his resolve had remained strong. The memory of the previous night's passion lingered like a smoldering ember, while Maureen's stubbornness twisted in his gut. He'd had no trouble calling Rita and telling her he'd have to skip dinner.

On Monday his memories had shifted. He remembered sensations, things that warmed his blood, like the feel of satiny skin beneath his fingers and the taste of honey-sweet lips. He checked his watch hourly, each time making mental calculations on how long it would take to get back to town—just in case he wanted to stop by the diner for a quick lunch. Somehow he'd managed to stay away.

On Tuesday he'd known he couldn't stay away much longer. He kept himself out of town during the day by deciding to stop by Rita's that evening. She was always eager to feed him, and both she and Katie would act as a buffer. That's when he'd gotten the idea of running into Maureen and Katie at the playground the next day, and he'd been able to keep himself away for another night.

Then he'd walked into the diner this morning and almost lost his resolve. She'd looked so fragile, with her pale skin and soft blue eyes. He'd wanted nothing more than to go to her and pull her into his arms. But he'd kept his distance, somehow managing to follow through with his charade.

Arriving at the park, he skirted the playground and headed down the path leading in the other direction. No need for Maureen to see him waiting. After they arrived, he'd wander over as if he were just passing by. He knew that wouldn't fool her, but that was okay. It was the element of surprise he was after.

Thirty minutes later, it was Katie who spotted him as he approached the playground. She was on the swings, while Maureen sat on a nearby bench with her back to him.

"Uncle Alan!" She was off the swing and in his arms before Maureen had a chance to stand up and turn around.

"How's my princess?" To his surprise he realized that he'd missed her almost as much as he'd missed her mother.

"Where were you?" Katie asked.

Laughing, he walked over to Maureen and sat down on the bench she'd just deserted. "Sorry, sweetheart. I had to work Sunday."

"But you promised."

Smiling, he tapped the little girl lightly on the nose with his finger. "So I did. I guess I'll just have to make it up to you next Sunday."

"You shouldn't make promises you can't keep." Maureen's words brought his head up abruptly, and his gaze locked with hers. In her eyes, he saw a reflection of his own sleepless nights. If he'd had any doubts about her sharing the hell he'd lived through these last three days, they dissolved in that moment. Her eyes held pain and longing similar to the pain he'd seen in them on the day they'd driven to Seattle. Only this time he knew he'd caused it.

Again he resisted the urge to wrap her in his arms and tell her everything would be all right. He knew she wouldn't allow it, nor would she believe it. Instead, he settled Katie on his lap while wondering what to say to her mother.

"You look tired." He motioned toward the bench where he and Katie sat. "Come on. Sit down."

She stiffened at his invitation, and he had to smile. She was as skittish as a new colt. He wondered what she thought he'd do in the middle of the park, in broad daylight, with Katie sitting between them.

"Don't worry." He tried without success to keep the teasing out of his voice. "Katie's here to chaperon."

Irritation sparked in those great blue eyes of hers, and he knew his words had hit home. "I hardly think a chaperone is necessary."

His smile broadened. "Don't you?"

A hot flush of color rose to her cheeks. He thought how beautiful she was when aggravated. He liked the fire in her eyes almost as much as the way they danced with laughter or became bright with passion.

"No," she said, her voice laced with sarcasm. "I think I can restrain myself." As if to prove her point, she joined them on the bench. "If *you* can."

Alan laughed aloud. She was so damn stubborn. It drove him crazy. At the same time, it was one of the things he liked best about her.

"Well," he said, thinking he might just break through that stubborn streak of hers, "I'm just not sure about that, sweet thing." He smiled as his eyes raked over the most intimate parts of her. "You see, you're just about the hottest—I mean the best—thing to come into Waiteville in a long time."

"Why, you—"

"Truth hurt?"

Her anger nearly scorched him, but he reveled in it. He wanted to throw her off guard, to see her respond, make her scream, curse him, anything. Maybe then he could get the truth out of her. She looked ready to slap him. Then, just as quickly, she reined in her anger.

Alan shook his head and shifted his attention back to the little girl on his lap. "So, did you miss me?"

"Uh-huh." Katie nodded and gave him a hug that tied knots in his heart.

"How about your mom?" He threw a sideways glance at Maureen. "Did she miss me, too?"

Maureen met his gaze without flinching. "I meant what I said about not making promises to Katie."

"I know you did." He paused, holding her with his eyes, willing her to understand his words. "And *I* meant everything I said." Without waiting for a reply, he turned back to Katie. "Come on, princess. I'll push." Lowering the little girl to the ground, he followed her over to the swings. "How high?"

"Way high."

Maureen watched them go, desire and anger warring within her. The man had no scruples. First he threw their passion in her face, and then he used her daughter to get to her. He stood behind Katie's swing, pushing her just high enough to keep her satisfied.

Katie laughed and called to her mother while urging Alan to push higher. Maureen smiled and waved at her daughter, though both gestures were forced.

She still felt the urge to slap him—almost as strongly as she wanted to feel his lips on hers again. Shaking both feelings, she forced her thoughts down less dangerous paths. Like how she was going to deal with him. If only Katie hadn't taken to him, she might have been able to ignore her own feelings. But Katie adored him, and it tore at her heart.

Glancing at the two of them at the swings, Maureen saw how he watched her. Even at a distance, the hunger in his eyes reached her.

I want you.

She heard the words as if he'd spoken them, and the most feminine parts of her stirred in response. For the briefest of moments she gave herself over to its warmth. Then Katie giggled and Maureen pulled her gaze away, forcing herself to deny her body's response to his silent plea.

Silence hung around them for long minutes. Maureen didn't dare look at him but pretended instead to concentrate on something at the other end of the park.

"Okay, princess." His voice, ripe with frustration, sliced through the air. "That's it for today. I need to get back to work."

Katie started to protest but stopped when he pulled her off the swing to give her a hug.

"I'll see you on Sunday," he said. Then, setting her back on the ground, he nodded to Maureen.

She met his gaze again briefly. His eyes had turned hard and brittle, his anger stabbing her like a knife in her heart. She started to reach out to him but stopped herself. Instead, she gathered Katie into her arms and held her tight, as if the child could protect her from her own desires.

"See you around," he said, and started to leave.

Suddenly she couldn't let him go. Not like this. "Alan."

Her voice stopped him. As he faced her, she let herself be drawn by his eyes again, and for a few moments she forgot all the reasons she couldn't have him. His eyes brought back memories of their time together, and all the unchecked emotions of that night swirled about her. Their wild abandon by the river. The sweet seductive lure of him as he asked her to go home with him. Her own driving desire to have one night with him. His anger when she'd lied. She longed to go to him and curl into his arms. He would protect her and Katie. Surely when emotions ran so strong, nothing could stand in their way.

"Yes?" His one word broke the spell, bringing her back to the real world.

Closing her eyes for a moment, she took a deep breath. She couldn't go to him. If he knew who she was, what she'd done, what would he think? Now that he had become fond of Katie, perhaps he would understand. Possibly everything would be all right if she just told the truth. But she couldn't take the chance. He might not understand, he might despise her, and she didn't know if she could live with that.

"I'm sorry," she said, thinking she had never spoken truer words. Looking deep into his eyes, she willed him to understand, to know that she regretted having to turn away from him more than anything in her life. But he just stood there, without a word, and she knew he expected her to say more. And she owed it to him.

"The way I've been acting, and what I said Saturday night..." She hesitated, pulling her gaze from his long enough to set Katie on the ground. "You were right. I lied."

"I know."

"Yes, I imagine you do." She raised her eyes back to his, knowing she needed to face this head-on. She owed it to both of them. He started to move toward her but stopped when she took a step back.

"What are you afraid of?" he asked.

"I'm not afraid." She glanced away, and then with an effort met his gaze once again. "No, that's not true. I am afraid. This isn't what I want. It's just not right for us now. Not for Katie or me."

"But?"

"I want you to leave us alone. Please."

Alan sighed. Removing his hat, he shoved a hand through his hair and half turned to stare off into the distance. Maureen held her breath, unsure what she would do if he pushed any harder. If he took another step toward her, or touched her, would she be able to resist?

"Sorry," he finally said. "I can't do it. Not this time." Looking back at her, he resettled his hat on his head. "You see, this isn't exactly what I wanted, either. But it happened. And I have no intention of leaving you alone."

A flood of emotions rushed through her, and she sat down to try to pull herself together. She couldn't speak, because she wasn't sure whether it was fear or relief coiling relentlessly within her stomach. Either way, she just stared at him.

"In fact I plan to spend a lot of time with you and that little girl of yours." He grinned that cocky, little-boy grin of his, and her heart melted. "So you may as well get used to the idea."

He tipped his hat and waved to Katie, who had made her way back to the swings. "See you, princess." Then he was gone, walking away casually, not realizing he had just handed Maureen a jail sentence.

She watched him go and understood that it was her heart, and not Alan, that would betray her. She knew now that it was relief that she felt. And Alan had known it, too. If she'd truly wanted him to walk out of her life, he would have gone.

Fate had played a cruel trick on her. She wanted more than friendship from Alan. She felt more than friendship for him. And it was those feelings that had betrayed her.

It had just been a matter of time.

AS SPRING DRIFTED into summer, the weather turned warmer, and Alan remained true to his word. He spent all his free time with Katie and Maureen. There were no more passion-filled moments like the night of the Apple Blossom Festival, but neither were there any empty days like the three that had followed.

He gave them the grand tour of the surrounding countryside. They drove east, out of the Cascade Mountains and into eastern Washington, where they explored apple orchards. A little farther north and back into the foothills, they swam in the cool blue waters of Lake Chelan. And they hiked. With Katie mounted on Alan's shoulders, it became their favorite activity. He showed them the splendor of the high mountains of the North Cascades Highway, where they picnicked within sight of the majestic Liberty Bell Mountain.

He ate lunch at the diner and dinner at Rita's, where he turned dull, weekday nights into warmth-filled evenings. He spent time at the playground, pushing Katie on the swings while entertaining Maureen with humorous stories about small-town life. He made her laugh, he made her yearn, and he made her want him.

Fighting her desire became a losing battle. It was her own heart she warred against. She couldn't help it if she enjoyed every moment she spent in his company, or if she lay awake at night remembering the way it had felt to be in his arms. He was male and exciting, and the very air around him reverberated with life.

Occasionally, she reminded herself that she and Katie would soon be leaving Waiteville, but those moments came less and less frequently. More often, she wondered when he would touch her again. Not the friendly, warm touches he constantly bestowed on them, but the hot, passionate caresses they'd shared the night of the Apple Blossom Festival.

At the same time, she became closer to Tommy Simmons. A couple of weeks after the festival, she ran into him at his school. She and Katie had gone out walking, enjoying the late spring afternoon. Without planning to, they ended up at Waiteville's Middle School just as it let out for the day.

Swarms of preteens milled about the school yard, talking in groups or waiting to board buses. She hadn't realized that there were so many children in the surrounding mountains who attended school in Waiteville.

She approached the school slowly, wondering if Tommy was old enough to be in middle school. Her mind had been so occupied with Alan, it had been days since she'd thought about the shy little boy and his wounded animal. In fact, she'd almost forgotten her resolve to go out and check on him and his deer. When she saw him, she felt a renewed determination to get closer to him.

"Hi, Tommy," she called.

Surprise registered on Tommy's face as he caught sight of her. Glancing anxiously over his shoulder, he moved to intercept her. "Miss Adams. What are you doing here?"

"I was just passing by." She shrugged and smiled, trying to put him at ease. "So this is your school."

"Yeah." He followed the direction of her gaze toward the one-story, featureless building. "Not much, is it?"

"Oh, I don't know. It looks nice to me."

Tommy shoved his hands into his pockets. "I guess it's okay." Then, nodding toward Katie, he asked, "Is that your little girl?"

"Yes. This is Katie."

"Uh . . . hi, Katie."

Katie smiled sweetly, shyly resting her head against her mother's shoulder.

"She's a little bashful," Maureen said. "So, how are you doing?"

"Fine." He smiled but threw another quick glance over his shoulder.

She realized that he might be embarrassed to be caught talking to an adult—especially a woman and child—in front of his friends. She decided to make their conversation quick. "I'm sorry we didn't get a chance to talk at the festival."

"That's okay."

"How's your friend?" She didn't want to ask outright about the injured deer since he'd sworn her to secrecy.

"My friend?" He looked puzzled at first, then smiled. "He ain't walking yet, but I think he's better."

"Would you like me to come out and check on him again?"

Tommy's face lit up. "Could you?"

"Sure."

"That would be great." Suddenly his smile faded. "But, I don't know . . . my daddy don't take kindly to strangers."

"Maybe I could come when your father's not home." She felt guilty even suggesting it, but something about this boy pulled at her and she wanted to help him. If she had to do it without his father's knowledge, then so be it.

"Okay." Tommy nodded and smiled again. "Can you come on Sunday? He ain't never home on Sunday."

"Hey, Simmons," a boy called from across the yard. "Come on. The bus is gonna leave without you."

Tommy glanced over his shoulder and then turned back to Maureen. "I gotta go."

"Go on," she said. "I don't want to cause you to miss your bus. I'll see you Sunday."

Tommy grinned and nodded, then took off in the direction of the waiting school buses.

Maureen watched him go and realized she hadn't felt this good in days. She'd let herself get too tied up over Alan. He'd made her forget her priorities. Sure, she was attracted to him, maybe even cared for him, but that was no excuse to lose sight of what was important. Katie was important. And this boy, Tommy Simmons, was important. And she couldn't do anything to jeopardize either of them.

Turning away from the school, she headed home. She needed to borrow Rita's car on Sunday. She planned on keeping her promise to Tommy.

Convincing Rita, however, turned out to be more difficult than she had expected.

"Please, Rita, I have no other way to get out there." It was later that same day. Katie was asleep, and Maureen and Rita sat in the kitchen drinking coffee.

Rita shook her head. "You know I don't mind you borrowing the car. And I'd do anything for you and Katie..."

"But?"

"I don't think going out to the Simmons place is a good idea."

"Why?"

"Bud doesn't take kindly to strangers. And he can be . . . difficult."

Maureen leaned forward in her chair. "But I'd be going to see Tommy, not his father."

"I don't think that would matter to Bud. In fact, that would probably make matters worse."

"But he won't even know I'm there."

Picking up her empty cup, Rita rose from the table and moved to the counter with the coffeepot. "How can you be sure?"

"He had no idea I was there the day Alan and I went to Seattle. At least not until Alan got him all riled up."

"Finding you out there won't exactly make him happy." Rita refilled her cup and returned to the table.

"He won't know I'm there, I promise. Besides, Tommy said he's never home on Sunday."

"I don't know." Rita shook her head again. "I think you're asking for trouble. What did Alan say about this?"

Maureen hesitated for a moment. "I didn't tell him." She met Rita's gaze and added, "We both know he wouldn't approve."

The other woman looked away, her face clouded with indecision. "Those boys need someone," Maureen added. "Please, let me borrow your car."

Eventually Maureen succeeded in enlisting Rita's help. Rita agreed to let Maureen borrow her car and also offered to watch Katie for the afternoon. The following Sunday, Maureen was off to see Tommy Simmons and his deer.

CHAPTER ELEVEN

IT WAS A RISK borrowing Rita's car to go see Tommy.

Technically, Maureen still possessed a legal Florida driver's license, so she was within her rights. But if she was stopped for any reason, she'd be in trouble. She couldn't show anyone her license because she couldn't allow them to see her real name. So she'd be arrested for driving illegally.

It was a chance she had to take.

Following Rita's directions, she recognized landmarks from the day she had driven this way with Alan. She remembered seeing the small church sitting on the side of a hill, boarded up, needing paint and nearly hidden by the surrounding woods. It looked desolate and alone, doomed to lose its struggle to remain standing. In a flash she thought of her own situation. Although she was determined to retain custody of Katie, circumstances seemed to conspire against her. She too might lose her battle for survival, just like the little white church on the hill.

Shaking away the depressing thoughts, she turned her attention back to the surrounding countryside. Spring had become summer since she'd last been this way. The mountains, which had just started to awaken a month ago, were now alive with their summer growth. Everywhere she looked she saw new life, whether it was the broad green leaves of deciduous trees sprinkled among the evergreens, a patch of wildflowers caught in a stretch of sunlight or a baby rabbit darting among rocks at the edge of a stream.

These mountains, once again, soothed her soul.

Her thoughts drifted back to the day she and Alan had driven to Seattle. So much had changed since that day, yet so much had remained the same.

To those around them, it appeared as though Alan and she were developing a relationship. They spent a lot of time together. They had even shared a night of passion. On the surface, they'd come to know each other well.

Yet Maureen knew they'd never been further apart.

She was on her way to visit Tommy Simmons and she had purposely hidden the fact from Alan. She knew he wouldn't understand or approve. Just as she feared he would never understand about Katie. When it came to important things, they knew very little about each other.

Nothing had really changed.

A half hour later, she pulled slowly into the Simmons yard and parked under a copse of trees near the barn. The ranch was as she remembered, a rundown shambles of a place set against the stark beauty of the Cascades. She wondered how it would look, how it might have looked at one time, the yard clear of debris, the house and barn repaired and painted. It would be a peaceful place to live. Somewhere you wouldn't mind calling home.

Once again she shook her melancholy thoughts and made a more practical survey of the yard. Bud's truck was nowhere in sight. That meant Tommy had been right and Bud was off somewhere.

Or maybe Joey had the truck.

She didn't want to think about that possibility. Memories of a big man wielding a rifle rippled through her thoughts. She didn't want to encounter Bud Simmons. It occurred to her that maybe she shouldn't have come. Maybe she should have listened to Rita and minded her own business. But everything was quiet, and no one—not even Tommy—was in sight.

Getting out of the car, she closed the door soundlessly. If Bud *was* in the house, he might not even know she was here. She glanced around again and started slowly across the yard.

"Tommy? Are you here?" She kept her voice low, not wanting to call out and possibly attract any unwanted attention. When she reached the open barn door, she stopped, taking a minute to peer into the dim interior.

"Tommy?" she called a little louder.

Suddenly, someone stepped out of the shadows directly in her path. Maureen's hand flew to her mouth to stifle a gasp as she stumbled backward. Then she realized who it was and she shook her head. "You startled me."

"Sorry." Tommy dropped his hands into his pockets and grinned sheepishly. "I didn't mean to."

Maureen stood there another minute, giving her heartbeat a chance to return to its normal rate. "It's okay," she said. "I guess I'll live." Then, after another momentary pause, she added, "Is anyone else here?"

"Nah. Pa and Joey are..." He let his voice trail off and shrugged. "They're out. Won't be back till dark."

Maureen nodded and glanced around, feeling suddenly awkward, wondering what she was doing here.

She'd purposely come out when this boy's father was away. What was she trying to accomplish?

"I wasn't sure you were coming."

Tommy's words brought her back to the moment. She met his gaze and saw the uncertainty there. "I told you I would come," she said, responding to the unspoken plea in his eyes.

With a shrug, he started to turn away. Maureen stopped him with a hand on his shoulder. "I keep my promises, Tommy."

He studied her for a moment, as if trying to decide whether to believe her. Then he smiled. The dim light of the barn didn't have a chance against the brilliance of that smile. Maureen's heart tightened within her chest, and her doubts about being here dissolved. Somehow this shy boy had crept into her heart and taken hold.

Slipping out from under her hand, Tommy moved deeper into the barn. "Come on. Pesky's waiting."

"Pesky?" Maureen followed, steeling herself for the smell of the unkept barn. To her surprise, the air was clear.

"I named the deer Pesky 'cause he can't seem to stay still."

"Very appropriate." Maureen glanced around and noticed the other differences in the barn. "Looks like someone's been doing some barn cleaning."

"Yeah. I thought Pesky might want a clean place to live." He stopped at the last stall. "Here he is. What do you think?"

Maureen was surprised at the changes in the animal. He stood in the middle of the stall—formerly two stalls—gazing at her with big brown eyes.

"He started walking yesterday," Tommy said.

Maureen's gaze wandered to where the wooden railing between this stall and the next had been removed.

"He needed more room," Tommy said, as if reading her thoughts. "I just took down some of the boards."

"By yourself?"

Tommy nodded and slipped his hands back into his pockets. "It wasn't any big deal." Opening the stall door, he moved inside to the deer. Pulling a handful of small granules from his pocket, he held out his hand to the animal. Pesky immediately took the boy's offering. "If you're quiet, he'll let you touch him. Come on in slow and close the door behind you."

Maureen did as he directed, approaching the deer with caution while the boy crooned soothing words. "He's so soft," she said, running her hands down the animal's sleek sides. "How you doing, Pesky?" She met Tommy's gaze and smiled. "What are you feeding him?"

The deer nuzzled the boy's pocket looking for more treats. Laughing, Tommy drew a few thinly sliced apples from his other pocket. "Here you go. I should have named you Greedy." Then, glancing at Maureen, he grinned. "Most of the time I just give him sweet feed—you know, the stuff they feed horses. But he likes apples better."

Maureen took the opportunity to squat down and take a look at Pesky's leg. Tommy had removed the bandage and makeshift splint. It looked as though the animal's leg were healing nicely. "How's he walking?" she asked.

"He doesn't look too steady yet. But he seems to get around the stall all right."

"Let's see."

Tommy got the deer to follow him by holding out another handful of sliced apples. Maureen watched as the animal limped behind him.

"Well, it doesn't look like he's going to win any races real soon," she said.

"I can't let him go..."

"You're right. Not yet, anyway." Maureen didn't know much about deer, but she could guess what would happen to any animal in the wild that couldn't run. "Give him some more time. He'll heal. But sooner or later, Tommy..."

The boy nodded and continued stroking the animal. "Yeah, I know. I'll have to set him free."

"Yes. You will." Maureen watched Tommy and his deer for a moment in silence and then sat on an overturned bucket in the corner of the stall. "Does your father or Joey know about Pesky?"

A flicker of apprehension crossed Tommy's face, and she wished she hadn't asked the question. "Don't know about Joey," he answered. "He hasn't said anything."

She thought about letting the subject drop, but she wanted to know more about what was going on out here. "What about your father?"

He shook his head. "Pa don't know."

"I see."

"Pa don't like animals much," Tommy offered.

"But surely he wouldn't object to your helping a wounded deer."

He shrugged, and the gesture told her more than words ever could. Bud Simmons would definitely not care for his youngest son harboring a stray deer. She couldn't for the life of her understand why, but it was one more thing about Bud Simmons that made her want to shake the man.

"So how have you been able to keep Pesky a secret?"

Tommy finally met her gaze. "Pa never comes out here."

"And Joey?"

"If he's seen him, he ain't said nothing."

This time, she let the subject alone. Tommy obviously was uncomfortable talking about it, and she'd pushed far enough for one day. Still, the whole situation bothered her. It didn't make sense—unless Bud was a lot harder on his boys than anyone was admitting. Yet both Rita and Alan had been adamant that there was no sign of abuse. She just didn't understand it all.

"So why'd you come?" Tommy asked, breaking the silence.

Maureen looked at him, surprised at the question. "I told you I would."

"But why?"

Maureen met his gaze. In some ways this boy was old beyond his years. He felt too deeply, and he saw things most ten-year-olds would never notice. He reminded her of someone, and suddenly she realized why she had risked so much to come see him again.

"I guess," she said, picking up a piece of straw from the floor, "it's because you remind me of someone else I know."

Tommy looked curious. "Who?"

"Me." Maureen shrugged and smiled. "Actually, you and I are a lot alike. I didn't know my mother, either."

"Really?" Tommy left the deer and came over to sit next to her on the floor. "Did your ma run off, too?"

"Sort of." Maureen twirled the bit of straw between her fingers. "She and my father got divorced when I was seven. My father got custody."

Tommy didn't say anything for a moment, and Maureen wondered what his young mind was making of her revelation. When he spoke again, she saw the effort the question took him. "Did you ever see her again?"

Maureen shrugged. "Once or twice."

"Then what happened?"

"I'm not sure. I think she didn't like being around my father. They fought a lot."

Tommy nodded knowingly. "Yeah. That's what Joey says about our ma. He says Pa was always yelling and she was always crying..."

Maureen felt a momentary twinge of empathy for the woman she'd never met. She could understand how Bud could strike fear in his wife. "That's too bad," she said aloud.

"I don't remember her."

"I'm sorry."

"Joey tells me about her, though." There was a wistfulness in his eyes that tore at Maureen's heart. "He says she was real pretty."

"I'm sure she was." Maureen reached over and brushed a stray lock of blond hair from his forehead. She wished there was some way to comfort this boy. "I'm sure she loved both you and Joey very much."

"Then why did she leave us behind?"

Maureen shook her head. She didn't have an answer for him. Not really. How could she know what his mother had been through, what had made her leave without her children? She'd asked the question a million times herself about her own mother. Why hadn't she at least come back to see her own daughter?

"I don't really know, Tommy. Sometimes adults do things..." Maureen hesitated, searching for the words to ease this boy's pain, words she'd never found herself. "I just don't know."

Silence fell between them. They both sat, lost in their own thoughts. Then he asked, "What about your pa?"

"He was a bit of a tyrant."

"Yeah. Mine, too." Tommy shook his head. "Man, if we don't toe the line, there's hel—heck to pay."

"Mine, too." Maureen paused, weighing her next words carefully. "He never hit me or yelled, though. He'd just fix me with this icy stare that meant he was *really* disappointed in me."

"You're lucky. Pa can bring down the roof when he's mad enough, and his belt smarts on the backside..." Tommy blushed and fell silent. Then, after a few moments, he stood and made his way back over to his deer. "Will you come out again?" he asked. "To check on Pesky?"

"Sure," she answered, rising from the floor, feeling as if she'd been dismissed. "I promise." Tommy glanced back over his shoulder and met her gaze. "I don't break my promises," she added. "I'll be here again next week." Then she turned and let herself out of the stall.

Maureen drove back to town feeling more confused than ever.

The boy didn't talk as though his father beat him. Not that she was an authority on child abuse, but while working in the emergency room of an inner-city hospital, she'd seen her fair share of battered women and children. Nothing Tommy said made her think he fitted that category. As Alan had indicated, Bud seemed to be a little heavy-handed with the belt, but that was all. It was only when she'd asked about the deer that Tommy had become apprehensive.

Something was going on with Tommy. But as the weeks went by and she saw more of him, it didn't seem as important as it once did. It was Tommy she went out to see. Tommy who was growing to trust her. Tommy who had become her friend. And whatever secrets he held were his own.

SUMMER PROGRESSED, and Maureen learned that not even Waiteville was spared a tourist season. She thought it a bit ironic. She'd traveled almost four thousand miles from Miami, the tourist mecca of the world, just to be besieged by a summer crowd cruising the Cascade Mountains. The fact that it was summer, rather than the Florida winter season, didn't make dealing with hordes of outsiders any easier. It just made it hotter.

For one thing, the town changed with the onslaught of the sightseers. Strangers walked the streets day and night. The town's one motel, which Maureen had always thought of as more of a landmark than a business, suddenly thrived. Townsfolk transformed their homes into bed-and-breakfast inns, while a regular flow of travelers rented Rita's two extra rooms. At the diner, the usual easygoing pace became hectic, and Jill hired several local teenagers to help with the summer rush. Maureen made more money during July than she'd made in the three months she had been in Waiteville.

The money made her start thinking about Seattle again, although for the most part she'd convinced herself that the urgency was gone.

She and Alan were getting along well. She told herself that they were friends. She felt more comfortable with him than she would have thought possible, probably because he had stopped probing. He took her and Katie places, showed them things, but he kept his distance.

It was the best of arrangements, even though at times she thought she'd scream from wanting to feel his arms about her. Then she would push the thoughts aside, chastising herself for being a fool. She knew it was safer that she and Alan not become any more involved. As it was, she had the best of him. He was there for both her and Katie, with his dancing eyes and easy manner, without the complications a more serious relationship would entail.

Without his being intent on uncovering her past.

Still, at the oddest moments an inner voice whispered to her that it couldn't last—sooner or later she and Katie would have to flee. She was a criminal, wanted for kidnapping. Eventually Alan would find out. And even if he didn't turn her in, he would never understand. He'd never forgive her for what she had done.

Sometimes, usually in the dead of night when she couldn't sleep for wanting him, the voice got louder, telling her that her time was running out. Those nights were the worst. She would lie awake for hours, the windows open, listening to, but not hearing the night sounds of the town. She would imagine the worst during those lonely times. They were like waking nightmares. And they always ended the same, with Alan finding out what she'd done...and hating her for it.

It had been one of those rough nights, and the diner was particularly busy. Maureen had a dull headache, the kind that hovers at the edge of your awareness, sapping your strength. She counted the minutes until she could go home and take a long, cool shower. Then it seemed the very ground collapsed beneath her, and once again her world fell apart.

CHAPTER TWELVE

THE FRONT DOOR of the diner slammed open, and a hush fell over the room. Turning in that direction, Maureen saw a huge bear of a man framed in the doorway. The light was behind him, so she couldn't quite make out his features, but something about him looked familiar. Then he took a couple of steps into the room, and she recognized him immediately.

"Well, if it isn't Bud Simmons," Jill said, stepping in front of the big man. "What brings you to town?"

Bud ignored her greeting while his eyes scanned the room. "I'm looking for that woman."

"Now, what woman might that be?" asked Jill.

His gaze landed on Maureen. "Never mind. I see her." Brushing past Jill, he moved across the room.

Maureen imagined she could feel the floor quake as he lumbered toward her. He was big and scruffy, like an aging grizzly. For a moment she felt pity. Then he stopped in front of her, smelling of stale beer and cigarette smoke, and her sympathy vanished.

"You the woman's been hanging around my boy?"

Setting down the plates she'd been carrying, Maureen wiped her hands on her apron. "I take it you're Mr. Simmons, Tommy's father." She extended her hand toward him, but he ignored it.

"You bet your ass I am, lady." He dropped his two hamlike fists to his waist and leaned closer, his foul breath nearly gagging her. "And I don't like people messing with my boys."

For a moment, Maureen stood stunned. She didn't quite know what to make of this man storming in here, accusing her of "messing" with his boys—whatever that meant.

"I'm afraid I don't know what you're talking about," she said, folding her arms across her chest.

"Like hell you don't."

Maureen glanced around and realized they had caught the attention of everyone in the diner. Then, looking back at Bud, she shook her head. "No, I don't. If you'd like to explain—"

"I'll explain it, all right. You've been sneaking around my place, filling my Tom's head full of nonsense."

With an effort, Maureen stood her ground. This overgrown bully might scare his two half-grown boys, but she'd be damned if she would let him frighten her. She had stood up to men twice as smart and three times as intimidating. "I've been out there a few times, if that's what you mean."

"Messing with my Tom's head—"

"Bud," Jill interrupted, stepping up beside him. "I think you better leave."

Shifting his angry gaze to Jill, he took a step in her direction. "I ain't done."

"That's okay, Jill," Maureen said, placing a hand on her friend's arm. "I can handle this." Turning back to Bud, she added, "I don't really see what the problem is, Mr. Simmons. I've talked to Tommy a few times. That's all."

"You ain't got no right to interfere with the way I'm raising my boys."

"Interfering! Why, that's ridiculous. We're just friends."

"Yeah. Well . . ." He took another step toward her, and Maureen squelched the urge to step back. "He don't need friends like you."

"I think that's enough, Bud." There was no mistaking the threat in Alan's voice. Maureen had been so involved with Bud that she hadn't noticed Alan enter the diner and move up behind the bigger man.

Bud half turned. "This ain't none of your affair, Parks."

"You're disturbing the peace. That makes it my affair."

Bud turned on him, but Alan didn't budge. He looked deceptively casual, arms crossed, legs spread wide. A sick fear churned in Maureen's stomach. Bud towered over Alan by a good six inches and outweighed him by at least a hundred pounds.

"Look," she said, trying to dispel the sudden tension between the two men. "Mr. Simmons, I'm sorry. I didn't mean—"

"You have nothing to apologize for, Maureen." Alan's words were directed at her, but his eyes never left the other man. "Bud here is just a little overprotective of his boys. Isn't that right, Bud?"

Bud glanced around at the hushed group of people watching his every move. Then his gaze fell on the two deputies who had followed Alan into the diner.

"Yeah," he finally growled. Looking back at Maureen, he added, "But I better not catch you hanging around my place again. You hear?"

"You're not threatening the lady, are you, Bud?" Like his stance, Alan's voice remained deceptively calm.

Veering back to face him, Bud gave Alan a slow, sarcastic smile. "Wouldn't dream of threatening, Sheriff. Just stating facts." Brushing past Alan, he stomped out of the diner.

Everyone in the room gave a collective sigh.

Maureen closed her eyes and took a deep, calming breath. She couldn't account for how frightened she'd been. Not of Bud. It had never crossed her mind that he would actually harm her. She'd been afraid for Alan. Alan, with his sheriff's badge and macho attitude, hardly seemed a match for Bud's towering strength. If Bud had hurt him because of her, because of what she'd done...

Then, opening her eyes, she met Alan's gaze across the room. The spark of anger she saw there stunned her, and she instinctively took a step backward.

"Are you all right?" he asked, his voice a study in rigid control.

She nodded, even thought the hard look in his eyes promised this wasn't over. "Yes," she said aloud. "I'm fine."

Alan stood staring at Maureen for a moment longer. How could she be so naive, so reckless? He had the strongest urge to cross the room and shake her. And if he didn't get out of here right now, he might just give in to the temptation. Pivoting on his heels, he headed for the door.

"Alan," she said, stopping him before he reached the door. "Thank you."

He couldn't face her, not without losing the tight rein he held on his temper. Instead, he acknowledged her words with a nod and quickly left the diner.

He wasn't a moody man, nor was he prone to losing his temper. Yet twice in as many months, Maureen had managed to rouse his anger. The first time had been the night of the Apple Blossom Festival, when she'd lied about the feelings growing between them. And now. It looked as if she'd been lying again. Evidently she'd never stopped. One lie after another—the woman had a real talent for it.

True, she'd never said anything one way or the other about going out to the Simmons ranch. But he'd heard enough of Bud's ravings to realize she had been making regular excursions out to see Tommy—and she'd never even told him about it. She knew he wouldn't have allowed it, so she just hadn't mentioned her trips to the Simmons place.

A lie of omission was still a lie.

Funny, he thought he'd broken through to her over the last few weeks. He'd enjoyed every minute he'd spent in her and Katie's company, and she'd finally begun to relax with him. Now this. Frustration, sharp and bitter, ripped through him. It seemed Maureen still danced to her own tune, and he'd been following her lead.

Yet, he'd ignored all the warning signs.

Maybe that's what really bothered him, infuriated him. He'd been sucked in. He'd allowed himself to become attached to her when he knew—had known from day one—that she was hiding something. He'd let it go by, disregarded his instincts and had been taken in.

Taking a deep breath to calm himself, he glanced around. His deputies had preceded him out of the diner and followed Bud, who was just pulling away from the curb on the other side of the street. Seeing Alan, he paused for a moment and then gunned his truck, leaving tread marks on the road. Alan shook his head but let it go. Right now, Bud wasn't what bothered him.

"Thought for a minute there we were going to have ourselves some fun," Jake said, walking up behind him.

"Yeah." Alan nodded absently, his mind still on the woman he'd left inside. "Rolling around Jill's with Bud Simmons would have been a hell of a good time."

Jake laughed. "So, what was that all about?"

Alan shot a quick glance at his deputy. "I don't know. But I intend to find out."

"You want me to follow Bud?"

Alan nodded again. "But give him a few minutes. I don't want him getting all riled about us harassing him."

The deputy nodded and started toward his cruiser. Alan stopped him before he got more than a couple of feet. "Jake," he said. There was something else that had just struck him, something that had been eating at him since the day he first met Maureen, and he'd suddenly realized what was wrong. "Why do you think women dye their hair?"

The deputy stopped and turned, a bewildered look on his face. "You asking me, Sheriff?" At Alan's nod, Jake added, "Hell, I don't know."

"Humor me." Alan shoved his hat to the back of his head and closed the distance between him and his deputy. "What's the reason most women change the color of their hair?"

"Well . . ." Jake hesitated, then grinned. "I guess if they want to be a blonde."

Alan nodded. "Yeah. There's that. But what other reason would they have?"

"Well, don't mention I told you, but my mom colors her gray hair. Like on those commercials. She says the gray makes her look older."

Alan smiled. Jake's mother *would* be angry if she knew her son had just revealed her secret—even though it was really no secret at all.

"But what about young women?" he persisted. "Those who *aren't* trying to be blondes. Why do they do it?"

"Beats me." Jake shrugged. "Maybe they just don't like their real color."

"Yeah. Maybe." Alan shifted and stared off into the distance. *Or maybe if she's running from something.* After a few minutes, he said, "Thanks, Jake. You go on and make sure Bud doesn't decide to head back into town."

Jake looked ready to ask another question but nodded instead. "Sure, Sheriff."

"I'll be at the station if you need me."

Alan made his way over to his office. Inside, he tossed his hat aside and lowered himself into the chair behind his desk. Propping his feet on an open drawer, he leaned back and tried to decide what to do.

Maureen Adams. He wondered if that was even her name. *Don't be an idiot!* Of course it wasn't her real name. So he might as well forget about calling Chicago and trying to locate some lawyer named Adams who just might be her father. Hell, maybe that was a lie, too. No, he thought, that little piece of information had been an unintentional slip of truth. He'd have bet his badge on it. And the dead husband? Unless she was a hell of an actress, that was true, as well.

So what else was she lying about? Her hair color. Hadn't he spotted that on day one? Hadn't he noticed a lot of things that first day, things he'd sort of pushed aside because he didn't want to look too hard? Like the fact that she didn't move like any down-and-out drifter he'd ever seen.

"Damn!" he said, dropping his feet to the floor.

Glancing at his phone, he thought of his friend Mac Credal at the Seattle Police Department. One call would be all it would take. "Hey, Mac, it's me, Alan Parks. You know that favor you owe me..." A description of Maureen and Katie would go out on the wire within the hour, and he'd bet he'd know all he needed to know by the end of the day.

Then what?

Shoving a hand through his hair, he leaned back in his chair again. He couldn't do it. Not yet. Not without giving her a chance to explain. After all, it might not be the law she was running from. Maybe an ex-husband or an abusive boyfriend. Yeah. That could be it. Just because the lady was running didn't mean she was running from the law.

Then why the hell hasn't she come clean with you, Parks?

The question leapt at him from nowhere. He tried ridding himself of it, yanking it from his back and tossing it aside. But it dug its claws in deeper and held on, eating at him, so that by the time he arrived at Rita's after dinner, he felt as surly as a wolf nursing an injured paw.

MAUREEN KNEW Alan was upset, and sooner or later he'd come demanding an explanation. She'd kept her visits to Tommy a secret because she knew Alan wouldn't approve. In fact, she was sure he would have tried to stop her.

Her headache grew worse as the day wore on, and the crowd at the diner refused to let up. She'd never been happier to see two o'clock come around, when she could finally leave for the day. As she left the diner, she almost expected Alan to be waiting for her. Thankfully, she made it back to Rita's without seeing him.

All she wanted was a few aspirins—three or four at least—a cool shower and a nap. But there was Katie to think about. So she settled for the painkillers and headed to the playground with her daughter.

As they passed Alan's office, she noticed him standing at the window. She expected him to follow them. He had a way of cornering her when Katie was around, so she figured this time wouldn't be any different. But he didn't show, and instead of making her feel better, his absence made her feel worse.

Later, she told Rita about the incident. The older woman patted her hand and told her not to worry. Alan angered quickly—that was like him—but his anger was also quick to cool. Maureen would, of course, have to stop going out to see the boy.

For the first time all day, Maureen thought of Tommy's situation and immediately felt a rush of guilt. How had Bud found out about her visits? Had he found out about the deer? Tommy's reasons for keeping the deer secret still remained a mystery to her, but she knew for certain that the boy's father was a big part of it. If Bud had been angry enough to come into town and threaten her, what had he done to his son? No matter what happened with Alan, she needed to make sure that Bud hadn't taken his anger out on Tommy.

She and Rita were just finishing the after-dinner cleanup when someone knocked on the back door. Maureen nearly dropped the plate she'd been drying.

Tossing her a reassuring smile, Rita opened the door. "Why, Alan," she said, stepping back to let him enter. "We expccted you for dinner."

"Sorry." Removing his hat, he stepped into the kitchen.

"Is something the matter?" Rita asked, her voice laced with innocence.

He shifted his gaze to Maureen. If anything, his mood had deteriorated. "Rita," he said, "do you mind watching Katie for a few minutes? I need to talk to her mother."

Rita glanced quickly at Maureen. "Of course." When Rita looked back at Alan, Maureen wondered if she, too, saw the simmering anger behind his eyes. "Katie and I will be in the living room." Then, turning to Maureen, she added, "If you need me." She leveled a warning look at her nephew and left the room.

Neither of them spoke at first. Maureen finished drying the plate she'd been holding and set it on the stack of clean dishes. She took her time putting them into the cupboard and then folding the dish towel on the rack.

"Are you through?" Alan asked, irritation and impatience evident in his voice.

"Yes." Not daring to meet his eyes, she nodded and glanced around the kitchen. "I think so."

"Good." Alan moved toward the door and held it open. "Let's go out back then."

Maureen took a deep breath and walked out onto the back porch. It was still light, but the day had settled and the sights and sounds of evening filled her senses. Too bad she wasn't going to be able to enjoy them.

Alan closed the door behind them and moved to stand by the rail with his back to her. Bracing herself, Maureen decided to take the offensive. "Is this an official visit, Sheriff?"

He spun around, and she wished she'd held her tongue. His eyes sparked and his voice dripped with annoyance. "We could make it official. If that's what you want."

Maureen looked up at him for a moment, then shook her head in resignation. There was no point making this any harder than necessary. "No."

He took a step toward her. "Then how about telling me just what the hell you think you were doing out at the Simmons place?"

"What a silly question." Maureen threw up her hands in exasperation and moved away from him. "You sound just like Bud."

"I'm not Bud." He followed her across the porch, coming close enough to pin her against the railing. "And I deserve an answer. What were you doing out there?"

"Okay. Okay." Alan's closeness accomplished what Bud's size had failed to do. She felt small and defenseless, and unwilling to defy this man any further. "I wasn't doing anything. I simply befriended a young boy."

"Bud Simmons's boy."

"That's right." She lifted her chin in a silent gesture of defiance. "I wasn't aware that was against the law."

"Damn it, Maureen." Dropping his hands to his hips, Alan stepped away from her. "You know the situation out there."

"No, I don't. Or at least I didn't." She crossed her arms and moved farther away from him. "All I knew was what you told me—which didn't agree with what I'd seen."

"You thought Bud was abusing his boys."

"Yes!" She shot him another defiant look. "Tommy was so painfully shy and so afraid of...something."

"But I told you—"

"I know what you told me," she snapped. Then, almost apologetically, she added, "I needed to see for myself."

Alan shook his head and turned away. "So, do you believe me now?"

She looked away guiltily. "Yes. Although I still don't know why he's so afraid."

Shifting to lean against one of the roof supports, Alan half sat on the railing, leaving one foot firmly anchored on the floor. "So is that why you kept going out there?" The hard edge of anger had disappeared from his voice, but she sensed it was still there, just below the surface, ready to emerge again at a moment's notice. "Because you couldn't figure out what Tommy was afraid of?"

"Yes." She met his gaze. "And there was something else he needed my help with."

Alan raised a questioning eyebrow.

"There was this deer." Even now she felt guilty revealing Tommy's secret. But she figured Bud had already found out about the animal, and it might smooth things with Alan if she told him the whole story.

"A deer?" Pulling off his hat, he ran a hand through his hair.

She moved up to lean against the railing next to him. "The day we went to Seattle, I found Tommy in the barn. He was nursing a wounded deer."

Alan frowned. "Why didn't you tell me about this?"

"Tommy asked me not to."

Alan didn't say anything for a few moments but just stared out at the woods bordering Rita's backyard. Then he turned to her and asked, "How was the animal hurt?"

"His leg. It was broken and pretty badly chewed up—"

"No. I mean how was it hurt? What caused it?"

"Tommy said it was a trap."

Surprise registered on his face. "A trap?"

"I didn't see it, but that's what he said." She shrugged. "Why? What difference does it make?"

Alan shook his head. "That's why Bud was so riled up. He's using traps for big game."

"I don't get it."

"It's not trapping season. And even if it were, trapping big game like deer is illegal."

"But Tommy said the trap wasn't meant for the deer."

"Maybe not, but if the trap was big enough to break that animal's leg, my guess is that Bud isn't after small game. He's probably using old illegal traps, as well." Slipping off his perch, he turned to rest both hands on the wood railing. "Damn!"

Maureen didn't know what to say. Bud's ravings in town today suddenly made much more sense. He'd been afraid she knew about his illegal hunting activities. If only he knew the mistake he'd made. She didn't know the first thing about hunting of any kind. If he'd only kept his cool, Alan wouldn't be standing here considering what to do about it.

Suddenly she was more afraid than ever for Tommy. Over the last several weeks she'd come to the conclusion that Bud didn't beat his boys. But he was a violent, unpredictable man. And if he'd found out about her and the deer...

"Alan." She moved up beside him and placed a hand on his arm. "I have to go out there again."

"Forget it." His eyes darkened, warning her that his anger stirred close to the surface. "You were trying to help Tommy, but it's over now. Things have taken on a whole new flavor here. You can't go out there again."

"But I have to." She tightened her hold on his arm, begging him to understand. *I have to make sure Tommy's safe.*

"Maureen..." The muscles under her hand bunched, his voice threatened, but she chose to ignore both warnings.

"Once more. I promised him. And I won't break that promise." She turned and started to walk away.

Before she knew what was happening, Alan grabbed her and spun her around. Taking hold of her upper arms, he pulled her against his chest, trapping her hands between them. "No! I won't let you."

She should have been furious. There was nothing gentle about him—not the look in his dark eyes nor the hands gripping her arms. She should have resented his tone of voice, hated his attitude. Not even her father dared treat her like this. She should have slapped his face, or at least demand that he unhand her. She didn't do either. Instead, she held her breath, wondering if he could hear the pounding of her heart.

She felt the shift within him as his temper gave way to something else. His eyes warmed, hunger replacing anger. His hands gentled, stroking, working their way to her waist, where they pulled her even closer.

It felt like coming home. As if she'd been away and finally arrived back where she belonged. For two months she had pretended not to want this, trying to forget how good it felt to be in his arms. Now she knew it had all been for nothing. She would never be able to forget. She loved him.

Slipping her arms around his neck, she lifted her face to his. He accepted her offer, lightly grazing her lips with his own. It was like touching a match to dry kindling. The bridled flame between them ignited, and the gentle touching of lips became a blaze of longing and desire.

Alan had dreamed about this far too long to resist. Soft, demanding lips met his. Low, urgent moans echoed her desire for him. He reveled in the feel of her slender body curved next to his and imagined her soft skin, fevered with wanting, beneath the fabric of her shirt. Without thinking, he yanked her blouse from the waistband of her jeans, wanting to feel . . .

Suddenly he stopped himself. Ending the kiss, he pulled back enough to see her face. He couldn't quite bring himself to let her out of his arms. "This isn't a good idea, Maureen."

"No. Not now." Her words agreed, but her eyes and lips said otherwise. They enticed him, inviting him to continue. He was tempted. It would be so easy to drown himself in her, to take what she offered until he lifted her in his arms and carried her into the woods to satisfy them both.

"Not here," he said aloud. Smiling, he took one more taste of her honey-sweet lips, one soft, gentle sip, then reluctantly released them.

She smiled and rested her head against his chest. Removing his hands from the smooth skin of her back, he lifted one to cradle her head against him.

"This doesn't change anything," he said after long minutes of sweet silence. "I can't let you go out there." He kept his voice soft. "It's too dangerous."

Sighing, she nestled closer against him. "That's why I have to go. I'm concerned about Tommy."

"I'll go and check on the boy."

She raised her head to look into his eyes. "He won't talk to you. I'm his friend. He trusts me. And I promised."

"Do you have any idea how serious this is?" Annoyance crept back into his voice. The woman had no idea what she had walked into out there. "Bud's not just letting his son drive without a license, he's illegally trapping big game. That's a criminal as well as a civil offense. And you know about it. What's to keep him from shooting you for trespassing?"

"He won't be there," she insisted. "I go on Sundays, and he's never there. I don't know how he even found out, unless he found the deer and Tommy told him. That's why I have to talk to Tommy—just to make sure he's okay."

Alan released her and turned away, shaking his head. He couldn't believe how obstinate she was being about this. She planned on going out to Simmons's place again. And it seemed nothing he could say would change that. Turning back to her, he searched her face, looking for some way to break through her stubbornness. He saw none. There was only one way to make sure she was safe.

"Okay," he said. "I'll take you."

His offer seemed to throw her off, and for a moment she didn't know what to say. Then she shook her head. "That would only make things worse. Bud will think you're coming out to arrest him or something."

"I thought Bud wasn't going to be there."

"Well, I can't guarantee it, and if he is—"

"I'll be there to make sure he doesn't shoot you."

He'd stumped her, and he could see she wasn't happy about it. In fact, she looked pretty irritated. But that was just too bad. "Okay," he said, considering the discussion closed. "I'll pick you up Sunday morning. Around nine."

She looked ready to argue again, but then resignation set in and she nodded. "Okay. But you have to stay away from Bud."

"Don't worry about me." Lowering his mouth to hers, he kissed her lightly. "Then we need to talk about us." Releasing her, he turned to walk away but changed his mind. "One more question."

Maureen stopped with her hand on the doorknob. "What?" She smiled, and he almost lost his resolve. Then he forced himself to remember the one thing he'd promised himself he would ask.

"Why do you color your hair?"

Shock registered in her eyes. Her hand flew first to her chest, then fluttered to her hair. "My hair?"

"Yeah." Alan nodded, holding his breath.

She glanced sideways and dropped her hand, wrapping her arms about her waist. "How did you know?"

"A wild guess."

She still didn't look at him. Instead, her gaze skipped over inanimate objects: the porch, the sky, the trees behind his back. "Premature gray runs in my family," she answered after a moment's hesitation.

"Premature gray?" A queasiness began in the pit of his stomach, making him wish he hadn't asked the question. Maybe it was better not to know.

"Yes." She met his gaze for a moment then looked away again. "I mean, who wants to be gray at thirty-five?"

MAUREEN SHUT THE DOOR behind her and collapsed against its solid frame. Her hand drifted to her hair again. He knew she colored it. What else did he know? He'd had a strange expression on his face just now that frightened her beyond reason. He had looked disappointed.

Closing her eyes, she took a deep breath, trying to calm herself. She felt as nervous as she had when she'd first come to town three months ago. She'd been a woman running scared, jumping at shadows, shying from every badge she saw. Except now she had cause to be frightened. If Alan suspected her of something and checked up on her...

No. She pushed the thought aside. He wouldn't do that. He wouldn't investigate her behind her back. After all, they'd become friends—and there was this other, stronger emotion between them.

On the porch, when he'd taken her into his arms, she had finally understood that she loved him. She wasn't sure when it had started. Maybe it was the day of the festival, or the afternoon they had sat and watched the sunset at Cliff's. Possibly she'd fallen a little in love with him the first time she'd watched him bounce Katie around Rita's living room. When didn't really matter. She loved him. It was as simple as that.

And she knew he felt something for her, too. The thought warmed her. Whether he was in love with her, she couldn't say, but he cared. She'd felt it in his arms, seen it in his eyes. He wouldn't, couldn't go behind her back.

But what if he did?

Fear chilled her. She knew this man and his view of right and wrong. He would never understand about Katie. If he found that Maureen was wanted for kidnapping, she wasn't sure he would even bother to let her explain before arresting her. The way he felt about Katie, she doubted it. He'd turn Maureen in first and ask why later—if he ever bothered to ask why at all.

It was time to go. No more stalling. She and Katie would leave tomorrow on the first bus...

"Maureen dear, are you all right?" Rita's voice snapped her back to the present. "Alan didn't upset you, did he?"

"No." Her answer was automatic. Funny how she'd learned to lie without giving it a second thought. "I'm fine." She pushed away from the door and crossed the room to the older woman. "He was angry, but it's okay now."

"What happened?"

"Just what you predicted." Maureen smiled and thought how much she would miss Rita. She had become more than a friend—she was more like the mother Maureen had always wished for. Rita would never have left her alone to deal with her domineering father. "He got all angry and gruff and told me not to go out there again."

Rita laughed lightly. "And..."

"He's going to take me out to the Simmons place this Sunday." At Rita's surprised expression, Maureen added, "Just to make sure Tommy's okay."

It was a couple hours later, after explaining everything to Rita, before Maureen had time to think again. She lay in bed next to Katie and tried to put her thoughts in order.

She and Katie couldn't leave tomorrow.

Katie was invited to a birthday party on Sunday. It was her first. Josh, the little boy whose mother watched her while Maureen worked, was turning five. Katie had talked of nothing else for days. How could she explain to the child that she would miss the party because they were leaving? It was going to be hard on her anyway, but it might be a little easier after the party.

Besides, she couldn't leave Tommy without saying goodbye. Sometime while talking with Rita, she'd realized that in order to leave tomorrow, she would have to break her promise to the boy. At first she'd pushed the thought aside. She had to think of Katie. Tommy would be fine. Maybe Alan would go out and see the boy on his own now that she'd alerted him to the possible danger. But the thought nagged at her, and she knew she had to go out to the Simmons place one more time.

It was Friday. She would just have to take her chances that Alan hadn't quite gotten to the point of checking up on her. But first thing Monday morning, she and Katie would be on their way to Seattle.

CHAPTER THIRTEEN

THE SHARP RING of the telephone brought Jacob Anderson awake with a start, his heart pounding. A quick glance at the clock on the nightstand told him it was the middle of the night. Grabbing the offending instrument, he didn't try to hide his displeasure at being so rudely awakened.

"What is it?"

"I found her," said Cooper's disembodied voice.

Jacob bolted upright as a surge of hope streaked through him. "Where?"

"Washington State. Northeast of Seattle. A placc called Waiteville."

Jacob took a moment to calm himself. Then, reaching over to the nightstand, he switched on the lamp and grabbed a pen and paper. "Never heard of it." In neat block letters he wrote the name of the town.

Cooper chuckled softly. "I don't think many people have."

"Is she okay?"

"Fine. She's been here awhile. Working in a local diner and living in a boardinghouse."

"And the girl?"

"Good. They're here to stay." Cooper paused before going on. "It even looks as though your daughter has something going with the local sheriff."

"Something going?"

Cooper let out another short laugh. "Yeah. According to the local gossip mill, the two of them are a real item."

"Does he know about her?" Having Maura involved with a local lawman complicated matters.

"I don't think so. From everything I can gather about the guy, he's a straight arrow."

Jacob wondered what the hell Maura was thinking of to allow such a thing to happen. If the man knew who she was, then he was as guilty as she. And if he didn't...well, she was skating on thin ice. But that was only part of the problem, Jacob realized. Because now that he'd found her, he wasn't sure what he should do about it.

"What now?" Cooper asked, as if reading Jacob's mind across the miles.

"Let me think." Jacob sat lost in his own thoughts for a moment.

His first impulse was to catch the next flight to Seattle. But he had no idea how Maura would react to finding him on her doorstep. And what would he say to her? "Hello, dear, remember me? I'm the reason you're in this mess. The person who turned his back on you. Your father. But now I've come to help. Now that your husband's dead, now that they're trying to take your baby away from you, I'm here." He wouldn't blame her if she slammed the door in his face.

He would have swallowed his pride anyway and taken the chance, if not for another possible problem. By going to Seattle and then on to Waiteville, he could be leading the authorities straight to her. And although he knew he could help her if she turned herself in, it had to be voluntary on her part.

"Anderson?" Cooper's voice once again pierced Jacob's thoughts, but he still didn't answer immediately. Making decisions usually came so easily for him. But not this time. It was an odd and unsettling experience.

"Watch her," he said at last. He needed time. "Give me a number where you can be reached, and I'll get back to you." He wrote down the number Cooper gave him and hung up the phone.

With a sigh, Jacob leaned back against the headboard of his bed. Thank God, Cooper had found her. Closing his eyes, he once again considered his options. None of them seemed a clear choice. He couldn't go to her. And if Cooper approached her, she might run again.

The dilemma pulled at him.

Somehow he had to let her know he could help. He needed to convince her to give herself up and put herself in his hands. He knew time was running out. If Cooper found her, the authorities might be right behind. Or her boyfriend, the sheriff, might turn her in if he discovered her identity.

No, Maura had to be convinced to trust him, Jacob realized.

With a derisive laugh, he shook his head. That wasn't likely. And who could blame her? At least there was the note, he remembered. He'd thought far enough ahead to send something in case Cooper found her.

Jacob couldn't remember the last time in his life when he was so unsure of his next move.

ALAN STOOD in the shadows next to Bollow's grocery and watched the stranger. The man approached the phone booth across the street and then stopped, looking around, evidently searching the darkness. For a brief moment his gaze seemed to light on the spot where Alan hid, and he thought he'd been spotted. Then the other man stepped into the booth, leaving the door open behind him.

Alan took a deep breath, willing himself to stay put. He wanted to stop that call. He didn't know why, but something told him the call was important. And it had to do with Maureen.

But the man hadn't done anything wrong. Not yet. And as odd as it seemed for him to be making a telephone call in the middle of the night from a phone booth on Main Street, there was no law against it. So Alan settled back into the shadows and waited, wishing he could hear what was being said.

There was no telling how long the stranger had been in town. And that made Alan nervous. At any other time of the year he would have spotted this man immediately. As it was, with the town overflowing with summer tourists, Alan couldn't say for sure how long the stranger had been hanging around asking questions.

But Alan knew him now, and there was no doubt in his mind that the man was watching Maureen. Strangely enough, Alan would have preferred to think that the stranger had picked Maureen at random—just a woman alone—as a likely victim. But he had a feeling that wasn't the case.

He glanced around, trying to find a way to get closer to the phone booth. Unfortunately, he was on the wrong side of the street. Across the way was the park, where dozens of ancient trees cast their deep shadows in the night. But on this side, street lamps lighted the closed storefronts, and the only cover was provided by the building he hovered near.

He'd first become aware of the man this afternoon, during Bud's little scene in the diner. The stranger had been sitting alone in one of Jill's corner booths, sipping coffee. Like everyone else in the room, he'd been all eyes. But there had been something else as well...a tension, a readiness about the man that made Alan's skin crawl. If he and Bud had come to blows, Alan had no doubt that the stranger would have been ready.

But ready for what?

The stranger in the phone booth turned his back to the door and Alan saw his chance. Still he didn't move. The distance to the park was too great. Besides, he doubted that he would be able to get close enough to hear what was being said anyway. Cursing silently, he resigned himself to staying put.

Once Alan had left the diner this afternoon, he had forgotten about the stranger. He had been too preoccupied with Maureen. He wanted to confront her immediately, but he was so angry that he dared not go near her. But as usual, he was aware of her activities. He knew when she left the diner for the day and he had stepped to the windows in his office to watch her and Katie make their way to the park.

That's when he had noticed the stranger again.

The man sat on a park bench near the playground, a newspaper open in front of him. Only he wasn't reading. His eyes remained locked on Maureen and Katie, following their every move.

But even that wouldn't have been enough to make Alan skirt around after midnight, scrutinizing this guy's every move. It was the last time Alan had seen him that was responsible for this particular vigil.

Alan had been distracted when he left Rita's earlier this evening. He had confronted Maureen about her involvement with Tommy Simmons and been disturbed by what he'd found out. Then he'd asked her about her hair, and he knew she was still lying to him.

But he'd noticed the stranger right away.

Once again, the other man was all innocence. He stood across the street from Rita's, talking to one of her neighbors. From what Alan could gather from the conversation, the man was asking for directions.

Alan couldn't put his finger on it—call it gut instinct if you will—but something about the man's presence didn't seem right. He was alone, for one thing. If he was a tourist, where was his family? Waiteville wasn't exactly on the businessman's circuit. He was dressed like a vacationer...only he wasn't. Then there was the little matter of his watching Maureen.

Shaking the distracting thoughts, Alan brought his attention back to the present. Across the street, the stranger hung up the phone and stepped outside. He stood and fished a pack of cigarettes from his breast pocket. For a second, a brief flicker from a match illuminated the man's features, and then he was swallowed by the darkness once again. He crossed the street, coming straight toward Alan. When he reached the sidewalk, however, he turned, heading toward the outskirts of town.

Alan never considered letting him go. It was time to see what this man was up to. He let the other man pass before stepping out of the shadows behind him. "Pretty late to be roaming the streets."

The stranger stopped, his back suddenly rigid. He turned slowly, hiding any surprise he might feel to find the town's sheriff facing him in the middle of the night. "'Evening, Sheriff."

Alan got his first close look at the other man and knew his instincts had been right. This was no tourist. He towered over Alan by a good three to four inches, but it was the hard lines of his face and his well-disciplined stance that spoke the loudest.

"Mind telling me what you're doing out here this time of night?" Alan asked.

The man took a long drag of his cigarette before answering. "Have I broken the law?"

"Not that I know of." Alan shook his head and crossed his arms. "Just seems mighty peculiar, your wandering around this late."

The other man smiled and flipped his cigarette into the street. "I couldn't sleep."

"And what about the person you called?" Alan nodded toward the phone booth. "Couldn't they sleep, either?"

To his surprise, the other man chuckled softly. "Not anymore."

When Alan didn't respond, the stranger's smile faded. Silence enveloped the two as they stood their ground, each sizing up the other.

"How about some ID?" Alan said finally, knowing he was on shaky legal ground here but not really caring. This man was up to something, and it had to do with Maureen.

"Sure thing." The man reached into his back pocket to retrieve his wallet. Pulling out a driver's license, he offered it to Alan. "Name's Cooper. Sam Cooper."

Alan took the plastic-laminated card and quickly memorized the details. He knew the man's credentials would appear in order. But what would he find if he ran the name through his contacts in Seattle? Out loud he asked, "What are you doing in Waiteville?"

Cooper shrugged. "Just passing through, Sheriff."

"I think not."

Alan saw a spark of anger in Cooper's eyes. "Well maybe I don't care what you think."

"Maybe you should start. You've been hanging around, asking a lot of questions. I don't like that."

"You don't say."

"What's your interest in Maureen Adams?"

Cooper shook his head. "Don't know the woman."

"You sure? Maybe you'd like to come over to my office. That might refresh your memory some."

"Don't threaten me, Sheriff." Cooper met his gaze. "I'm not one of your local boys."

Once again the two men locked gazes while the air around them sparked with tension. This time it was Cooper who spoke first. "I'm not here to cause any trouble, Sheriff. And I'm sure not looking to lock horns with you."

Alan studied the man for a moment longer before returning his license. Cooper still made him uneasy, but there was truth in his words, in his eyes. Besides, the man had done nothing illegal—yet.

"I think it's about time you moved on, then," Alan said.

Cooper returned his wallet to his back pocket and smiled. "I was planning on leaving first thing in the morning."

IT WAS ALMOST DAWN before Cooper got around to calling Anderson again. This time he didn't bother going to a phone booth but called from his tiny motel room at the edge of town.

Anderson was awake and picked up the phone on the first ring. "Yes."

"I'm coming in," Cooper said, rubbing his eyes. Damn, he was tired. It had been a rough couple of months. And he sure didn't need that little confrontation with Parks. "The sheriff's spotted me."

He could almost hear Anderson's disapproval. Cooper no longer cared. He'd done his job. He'd found the girl and her kid. Now he was looking forward to a little time off.

"Do you have somebody else who can keep an eye on her?" Anderson asked. "Someone you trust?"

"Yeah. Couple of guys. They look like college kids. I'll put them in scruffy jeans and boots and they'll fit right in around here."

Anderson paused a moment. "What about the envelope I sent you?"

"Got it a couple of days ago."

"Good. Make sure she gets it before you leave."

"Okay. I'll hand deliver it." Cooper leaned his head against the wall, eyes closed, and stifled a yawn. Maybe he could catch a couple hours' sleep before heading back to Seattle. "I'll be by in a day or two to pick up the rest of my money."

"No."

Cooper opened his eyes. "What?"

"We're not done yet. Fly to Miami and check in at the Airport Hilton. I'll meet you there."

Anderson hung up, leaving Cooper holding a dead line. Cursing under his breath, he considered calling

Anderson back and telling him to go to hell. Instead, he dropped the receiver into its cradle and lay back on the bed.

"Damn!" he said aloud.

ON SATURDAY, Friday's headache had intensified, and so had the crowds at Jill's. The combination left Maureen short-tempered and irritable. One man repeatedly snapped his fingers at her, calling her everything from nurse to waitress, and then grumbled about slow service. Maureen's temper snapped and she suggested he and his partner try the burger place in the next town down the road.

The couple stormed out, complaining loudly to Jill as they went through the door. Jill shrugged and shot Maureen a reassuring grin.

Maureen wanted the day to end.

She told herself that now she had made the decision to leave Waiteville, she was ready to go. Anxious, even, to put this town and everyone in it behind her.

At two o'clock she gathered her things from the back storeroom. She said goodbye to the cook, waved to one of the kids helping out for the summer and headed for the kitchen door. The moment she stepped back inside the dining room, however, she couldn't go any further.

Jill sat at the counter laughing and talking with one of their regular customers. It suddenly struck Maureen that after today she would never set foot in the diner again—never see Jill again, either. On Monday, instead of showing up for work, Maureen would be on a bus heading west.

She walked over to the counter.

Jill broke off her conversation and smiled. "Don't worry about the jerk who was in here earlier, Maureen. We'll survive without his kind."

"Thanks." Maureen nodded and forced a smile, saddened at the thought of betraying this woman. Jill had been good to her. A friend. And Monday morning she'd be short one pair of hands. It was no big deal, Maureen told herself. Jill would hardly notice it. She'd call any one of a dozen locals to help her get through the morning. Still, Maureen wished she could tell her. She wished she could say goodbye.

"Are you okay?" Jill asked.

Maureen snapped back to the moment, realizing that she'd been standing there staring, lost in her own thoughts. "Yeah. It's just a headache."

"Well, you go on home. Skip the park today. Get Rita to watch Katie and lay down for a while."

"I think I'll do that."

"Good. Now go." Jill shooed her toward the door with a wave of her hands. "And have a nice day off."

Maureen nodded, feeling the sudden urge to cry. "Sure." There was nothing else to say. Nothing else she *could* say. She left quickly before she did or said anything she would regret.

She'd take Jill's advice. She picked up Katie and headed home, finding Rita in the kitchen.

"Rita, would you mind watching Katie for a little while?" Maureen hated to ask, but her head was pounding and she needed some time alone. "I'm not feeling very well, and I'd like to lie down." Except for her excursions to see Tommy, Maureen had made it a point not to impose on the older woman by asking her to watch Katie too often. Not that Rita ever seemed to mind. Maureen just hated being a burden. But then, she told herself, after tomorrow, she and Katie would be out of Rita's hair for good.

"Of course." Rita took Katie's hand and squatted down until she was eye-level with the child. "We'll make cookies for Josh's birthday party tomorrow. How does that sound, Katie?"

Katie grinned. "Can I paint the faces?"

"You bet." Rita gave the child a hug and then stood. "Go on, dear," she said, waving Maureen out of the room. "Go lie down."

Maureen smiled her thanks and headed for the stairs. She was halfway up when Rita came bustling into the hall after her. "Just a minute, Maureen. Something came for you today."

Rita moved to the table where she kept the incoming mail and picked up a large manila envelope. "A man came by this morning and left this for you."

"A man?" Maureen met Rita at the bottom of the steps and reluctantly took the envelope.

"Yes. He said he was a friend of yours from Chicago. He was really disappointed he missed you."

"Chicago." Maureen's hands trembled. "Did he give you his name?"

"Let's see." Rita wrinkled her brow. "Something starting with the letter *J*. John or Jason..." She shook her head. "I knew I should have written it down."

"Jacob?"

"That's it. Jacob."

Maureen's legs nearly gave way beneath her, and she grabbed the railing for support.

"Are you okay?" Rita, evidently alarmed, reached for Maureen.

"Fine," Maureen said, pulling herself together with an effort. Could her father be here? "I guess I just feel worse than I thought."

"Let me help you upstairs."

"No. That's not necessary." Maureen started to move away. "Just watch Katie for me."

"Are you sure? Maybe I should call Doc Readon."

"I just need some rest." Maureen took a few more steps, the envelope clutched in her hand, then stopped. It couldn't be him. "Did the man tell you his last name?"

Rita shook his head. "No. Just his first name. And then he left the envelope."

"What did he look like?"

"He was a big man. Blond. Good-looking."

"Young?"

"He is a friend of yours, isn't he?"

"Was he young?" Maureen repeated.

Rita shrugged. "Mid-thirties."

Maureen let out her breath and forced a smile. "Yes, I know him," she lied. "Thanks." It couldn't be Jacob.

Somehow she managed to climb the remaining stairs, though her legs threatened to give out beneath her. In her room she collapsed on the bed.

She didn't want to open the envelope.

She told herself that she wasn't interested in knowing who had sent it. So she just sat staring at it, the blood pounding behind her eyes. She knew no tall blond man from Chicago. No one named Jacob. Except . . .

As if her hands belonged to someone else, she watched them tear open the flap. Inside was another envelope, cream-colored and legal-size, which she drew out with trembling fingers. She saw the insignia in the upper left-hand corner and the bold hand-printed name across the front. For a moment she froze, unable to move. Then the letters swam in front of her eyes and she fought back the sudden nausea.

He'd found her.

Her father. She would recognize his handwriting anywhere. She dropped the envelope as if it had the power to burn and fell back on the bed, covering her face with her hands.

How long had she waited, hoped to hear from him after he'd shut her out? How many nights, while David still lived, had she lain awake wondering how her own father could turn his back on her? She'd needed him then. And it would have been so easy for him to help her. Instead he'd refused. He wouldn't take her calls, and her letters had come back unopened.

She squeezed her eyes shut, but the tears came anyway.

Now this envelope. A lone message delivered by a stranger. What would she find inside? Accusations? Smugness? A reprimand? And then would he offer his help?

Now that it was too late.

She rolled over on her side, burying her face in her hands, and surrendered to tears. She cried for her father, who had sent a note after years of silence. She cried for Katie, who knew nothing of the legal system threatening to give her to strangers. She cried for David, whom she'd lost. And she cried for herself, because on top of everything else, she'd fallen hopelessly in love with a man who could destroy her.

When she opened her eyes sometime later, long shadows filled the room. She must have fallen asleep.

Her head felt somewhat better, though her eyes were gritty from crying.

Sitting up slowly, she saw the envelope on the floor where she'd dropped it. Once again the name Maura, written in bold letters across the front, seemed to beckon from some other time and place. Leaning over, she picked it up. Nothing had really changed. She still didn't want to open it, but now she knew she had no choice. She needed to know what her father wanted from her. What he expected.

And there was only one way to find out.

She carefully slit open the seal. Inside was a piece of her father's stationery. The sight no longer had the power to surprise her. Sometime in the last few hours she had come to accept the fact that he knew where she was. Now she felt only curiosity and fear. How had he found her? And who else knew about her?

The note itself was a disappointment. There was none of the frigid prose she expected. No condemnation or accusations. No threats. Only three short sentences, written in Jacob's unique bold script.

"Maura. Contact me. I can help."

CHAPTER FOURTEEN

ALAN PARKED the Jeep under the shadow of trees at the edge of the Simmons yard. Shutting off the engine, he turned toward Maureen. Neither of them had spoken on the way here, and an uncomfortable stillness lay between them. Alan wished he could reach out and pull her into his arms. Maybe then they could talk, really talk. Maybe then she would stop lying to him.

Maureen started to get out but stopped when he said, "I ran into someone Friday night whom you might know." He hadn't meant to bring up his encounter with Sam Cooper, though it had been on his mind.

Maureen visibly stiffened, then turned to meet his gaze. "Oh?"

"Yeah. Tall blond man." When she didn't respond he added, "Said his name was Sam Cooper. *Do* you know him?"

Maureen hesitated, and Alan saw the indecision in her eyes. "Sure," she said. "I know him."

"Where from?"

"Chicago. He's a friend." She lifted her shoulders in a gesture of nonchalance. "He stopped by Rita's to see me, but I was working."

"Funny." Alan shifted his hat to shield his eyes. "I wonder why he said he didn't know you."

Maureen flinched but recovered quickly. "You must have misunderstood."

Alan held her gaze for a moment longer and then shrugged. "Sure. I must have misunderstood." He didn't believe her. Not for a moment. But he didn't know what to do about it.

"Are you sure you won't change your mind?" he asked, nodding toward the barn. No matter what else was going on, he still didn't like her being out here. "We could just leave."

"No." She shook her head. "I'm not changing my mind. Besides, you're forgetting I've been out here before—without an escort."

"I'm not forgetting a thing." Alan pulled off his hat and tossed it on the dashboard. "In particular, I'm not forgetting Bud Simmons."

"Bud's not here. And besides, you're the one who told me he wasn't dangerous."

Exasperated, Alan ran a hand through his hair. "I said he didn't abuse his boys. Make no mistake, the man is dangerous. I would think you'd understand that after his little display at Jill's the other day."

"I'm just here to see Tommy—"

"Which Bud particularly warned you against doing."

Irritation spread across her features. "Am I going to have to listen to you lecture me all over again?"

Sighing, Alan shook his head. "Would it do any good?"

"No." Maureen got out of the Jeep and reached in the back to retrieve the bag she'd brought along. "Besides, if anyone gets Bud Simmons riled, it'll be you."

He just looked at her and shook his head. The woman was deluding herself. If Bud caught her out here again, there would be hell to pay.

"Remember," she said, "you promised to stay put. And if Bud does show, don't go stirring up things with him."

"I'm not going anywhere." Alan propped one foot on the dashboard as if to emphasize the fact that he would wait. "Now, go on. Get this over with."

He watched her walk toward the barn, wondering what he was going to do. She had him so tied up in knots he couldn't think straight anymore. He hadn't forgotten about her hair, nor did he believe her explanation. Not about the hair. And not about Cooper. That's why he'd stayed away from her yesterday. He couldn't decide what to do about her. He knew she was lying. He couldn't say how, but deep down he knew. Yet he also knew his feelings for her ran deep, and he wanted to think there was a logical explanation for her secrets.

She was halfway across the yard when he heard the shot, followed by an ear-splitting howl. Coming from the barn, the sounds echoed through the yard, shattering the mountain stillness. He sprang from the Jeep before the din died and raced toward the barn.

"Stay here," he shouted at Maureen, who'd dropped the bag to head toward the barn.

Alan stopped at the door, back against the wall, gun in hand. Maureen fell in next to him. "I thought I told you to stay put."

She didn't answer but stood rigidly where she was. He threw her another exasperated look before edging around the door, trying to see into the dim interior of the barn. What he saw tore at his insides.

"Help us!" It was Joey, on the ground cradling his brother's head in his lap. "Tommy's shot."

Alan dashed to the boy's side.

Blood. There was blood everywhere—on the ground, on Joey's hands, but mostly on Tommy's leg. Ripping the boy's jeans away from the source, Alan checked for the seriousness of the wound. Blood spurted in an all-too-familiar pattern, a pattern he'd seen far too often in Vietnam. Yanking off his shirt, he pressed the fabric hard against the flow.

"What happened?" he asked Joey.

"He grabbed my rifle...and fell..." Joey could hardly get the words out.

"Where's your pa?"

Joey shook his head, tears streaming down his face. "Don't know."

"It's going to be okay, Joe," Alan said, trying to reassure him. Then he leaned over the injured boy. "Tommy, can you hear me?" Tommy's eyelids fluttered open for a brief moment, and Alan thought the boy recognized him. Then they closed again.

"Damn," Alan muttered. Grabbing Joey's hand, he guided it toward the shirt he held against Tommy's leg. "Here, Joe, hold this firmly in place. I need to stop that bleeding." Unbuckling his belt, he yanked it off.

"No! Wait!" Maureen had followed him into the barn and crouched down on the other side of the injured boy. "Hold his leg, Alan. I need to get his boot off."

"What are you talking about? His artery's been severed. He's going to bleed to death if I don't stop it."

"It may be only nicked," she said, while her fingers probed the area around the bullet wound. "I need to see if there's still circulation in his foot." She met his gaze, and the calmness in her eyes startled him. "I know what I'm doing," she added, never taking her eyes from him. "If you want to save this boy's life *and* his leg, I need to get his boot off."

He believed her. Later he couldn't say why, but something in her eyes, something in the steadiness of her voice and the way her hands moved so confidently on the boy, convinced him.

"Keep the pressure on, Joey." Leaning down, he held Tommy's leg while Maureen worked the boot off. Then he held his breath while she pressed her fingers against the pulse point of the boy's ankle. Alan prayed she knew what she was doing.

"There's still circulation," she finally said. "Most likely the artery's only nicked. Alan, take over for Joey and put pressure on that wound. Joey, go call for help. Then bring me blankets, clean sheets and rags—tear up sheets if you have to—and water."

"I can't call!" Joey's voice was near hysteria. "The phone's out. Pa ain't paid—"

Maureen turned to him and grabbed both his hands. "Calm down, Joe."

Joey nodded, but his eyes were wild, scared.

"I'll go," Alan said. "The boy's—"

"I need you here." Maureen's voice remained calm but firm. "Joe's going to be fine, aren't you, Joe. And you want to help Tommy, don't you?"

Taking a deep breath, Joey closed his eyes. When he opened them, he looked calmer, steadier.

"Okay," Maureen said. "What are you going to get for me?"

"Uh... blankets, clean sheets, rags..."

"Clean rags."

"Yeah, clean rags. And water."

"Good, now go on. Hurry!" Maureen gave Joey a slight push, and the boy raced out of the barn.

While they waited for Joey to return, Maureen worked over his brother. She loosened Tommy's shirt, then rechecked his leg and the pulse in his foot.

As he watched her, a sharp realization sliced through Alan. She was too calm, too confident. Her movements too smooth, too efficient. She'd done this before, and it wasn't something she'd learned in a six-week first-aid class. She knew what she was doing, and she was good at it.

"We need to get him to a hospital," she said, breaking into his thoughts. "He's going into shock."

Alan shifted his attention back to Tommy. The boy shivered despite the ninety-degree heat of the barn. And his face had a gray, clammy look to it.

"Where's Joey?" he growled. He didn't like being this helpless. "He's taking too long."

"He'll be here." Maureen brushed the hair from Tommy's forehead. "Can you hear me, Tommy?" He didn't respond.

"I should have gone." Alan shot a furtive glance at the barn entrance. "Maybe—"

"How far's the nearest hospital?" Maureen asked, once again pulling his attention away from Joey.

"Wenatchee. It's a good hour and a half drive."

Maureen shook her head. "It's too far. We can't risk it. What about a phone?"

"Jean Cellar's place. Twenty minutes."

"Can we get him airlifted out of here?"

He nodded. "The forest service has rescue helicopters. It'll take them about thirty minutes to get here, though. Another thirty to get him to the hospital in

Wenatchee." He hesitated before asking the next question. "Is he going to make it?"

Maureen met his gaze. Despite her calm, he could see the worry, the fear. "I don't know."

"What about the bleeding?"

"The pulse in his foot is still fairly strong, and the swelling isn't too bad." She paused, taking a deep breath. "I think we've got the bleeding under control."

"I'll go as soon as Joey gets back."

She shook her head. "No. I need you here. Let Joey go."

"Joey can't drive, he's—"

"Alan, Joey's no good to me. He's too upset. Get him out of here. Send him for help."

Before Alan could answer, Joey returned carrying blankets and sheets. "Will these do?" he asked. At Maureen's nod, he added, "Okay, I'll be right back with the water." Then he raced off again.

Alan felt Maureen's gaze on him, but he refused to look at her. He held Tommy's leg, keeping the pressure constant, and thought about Joey.

"You've got to let him take your Jeep," she said, as if reading his thoughts.

She was right, and he knew it. He could do more good if he stayed here with her and Tommy. Still he hesitated—more for fear of Joey's being unable to get help rather than the fact he shouldn't be driving. Maureen wouldn't believe that, however, so he kept his mouth shut.

When Joey returned with two jugs of water, Alan threw a glance at Maureen and then turned to the boy. "Are you okay, Joe?"

"Yeah." Joey dropped down next to Maureen. "How's Tommy?"

"We need to get help." Alan held Tommy's leg steady while Maureen unfolded a blanket and prepared to shift it under Tommy. "Take my Jeep and go to Widow Cellar's—"

"What if she ain't home?"

Alan paused, then took a deep breath. "Break in if you have to."

"Alan," Maureen interrupted, "let me hold his leg. You lift him up and Joey shove this blanket underneath him."

Tommy groaned when Alan lifted him, but in a matter of seconds he was back on the ground.

Alan turned his attention back to Joey. "Call the station. Jake's working the switchboard. Tell him we need a helicopter and Doc Readon. Got it?"

Joey nodded, his eyes bright and scared but steady.

"Anything else?" Alan asked Maureen.

"Make sure they understand he's lost a lot of blood."

Alan nodded. "Go on, Joe. My keys are in the Jeep."

Joe shot one more worried glance at his brother and then tore out of the barn.

They waited for help.

Alan watched silently as Maureen tended the boy. She kept a constant watch on his pulse, checking every few minutes to make sure blood still flowed to his foot. Then she would check his leg, explaining to Alan that she was looking for excessive swelling, a sure sign that the bleeding had started again or was internal. Occasionally, Tommy's eyelids fluttered open, and she whispered soothing words while trying to get him to take a few sips of water.

Alan couldn't ignore the facts. Maureen knew something about medicine. The knowledge was like a clamp, squeezing his heart till he thought it would burst. Lies. Everything about her was a lie. She lived them. And he had believed them.

Once more he'd let this woman get to him, and here was the proof. The day Bud came into town he had known she was lying—about a lot of things. Lies that indicated she was running from someone or something. He'd planned on demanding the truth that night.

Then he'd pulled her into his arms, and it no longer seemed important. He'd forgotten everything but how much he needed her, how much he wanted her. The only question he had forced himself to ask was about her hair, something she could easily explain away. A lie he could easily ignore. And then he'd met Sam Cooper. Alan couldn't shut his eyes anymore.

When the Jeep finally pulled up outside, he went out to meet it. Jean Cellar had been home and she'd called for help, then driven back with Joey.

Help arrived a few minutes later. Once again Maureen took charge, giving directions to the paramedics as they loaded Tommy into the helicopter. There wasn't room for anyone to go with the boy, so Alan drove Joey and Maureen to the hospital. Jean Cellar agreed to stay behind. She'd try to get hold of Bud and let Jake know that Alan was going on to the hospital in Wenatchee.

MAUREEN HATED WAITING. She'd never been a patient woman. But her impatience was nothing compared to how much she detested not knowing what was happening inside that operating room. She would have much preferred to be in there, assisting Doc Readon. Instead, she sat on a hard plastic chair in the waiting room, trying not to pace. She now understood what it was like to be on the other side of things. Never again would she take lightly a friend or loved one's request for information.

At one point Alan suggested she go home and get some rest. She'd looked up, surprised to see him still there, and was shocked by the coldness in his eyes.

It hit her then. He knew.

Everything she had said and done since the moment she'd heard the shot had betrayed her. And he had seen. Her worst nightmare unfolded before her, and she had the strongest urge to take him up on his offer. Only she wouldn't stop when she reached Waiteville. She'd just keep on going.

She turned down his suggestion. Right now Joey needed her and she would stay with him. Later, she would deal with Alan. And if she was lucky, she and Katie would still make that bus tomorrow morning.

After Joey's initial rush of hysteria, he had shut down all emotions, following her orders without question. Now he sat like a dead man himself, stiff as a board, waiting to hear if his brother would survive. Still, when Maureen reached over and took his hand, he didn't try to pull away.

"Do you want to talk?" she asked him after the three of them had sat there in silence for what seemed like hours.

Joey shook his head.

"It might help. Maybe if you told us what happened..."

He shot a distrustful look at Alan. "And have him arrest me? No thanks."

"Joe." She squeezed his hand, bringing his attention back to her. "Did you shoot your brother?"

Pain registered in his eyes. "No way! It was an accident."

"Well then I don't think you have anything to worry about." She looked back at Alan. "Does he?"

"Look, Joe..." Alan crossed the room to sit on the chair next to him. "I know you didn't shoot Tommy. And I'd like to be here for you as a friend. Honest."

Joey looked at him for a moment, then shook his head again. Maureen sighed and decided to let him be. The boy would explain when he was ready.

They'd been there three hours when Bud Simmons arrived. As always, his size filled the room, but this time he looked more like a lost soul than a grizzly bear. He pulled Joey into his arms for a rough hug, holding him for several minutes. It wasn't until he released the boy that his expression turned angry.

"What happened?" he growled at his oldest son.

Joey yanked away from him. "It wasn't my fault."

"What happened?"

"He tried to pull my rifle away from me and he tripped. Somehow it went off..."

"Tripped! You were supposed to be watching him. You're the eldest."

"Yeah, well where were you? He tried to stop me. And you weren't anywhere around." He threw a quick glance at Alan, then turned back to face his father. "If you hadn't chased that deer of his off, none of this would have happened."

"What are you talking about, boy?"

"He was afraid I'd kill it."

Silence fell hard and accusing. Bud and his son faced each other, so much alike, yet separated by more than years.

"Bud..." Alan stepped up and laid a hand on Bud's arm. "It wasn't Joe's fault."

Angry eyes turned on Alan, and Maureen held her breath. Then she saw something else in Bud's eyes. Fear. The man was afraid.

"It's okay," Alan added. "It was an accident. And Tommy's going to be all right."

It took a moment, but the last of Bud's anger drained from his face until nothing was left but the fear. Closing his eyes, he nodded. Then he turned and dropped his massive frame onto one of the chairs. Joey returned to his own seat, and the four of them waited.

When Doc Readon finally entered the waiting room, he looked exhausted. But he nodded and smiled at Joey and Bud as they sprang to their feet.

"That boy's one hell of a fighter," Doc said. "Lost a lot of blood. But he's going to make it."

Joey sank back down into his chair. Bud crossed the room to claim the doctor's hand, tears streaming down his face. "Thank you, Doc, thank you."

"Don't thank me," Doc said, nodding toward Maureen. "That young lady over there is who you should thank. Not only did she save his life, she saved his leg, as well."

Maureen's cheeks reddened as everyone turned to look at her. "Nice work, Ms. Adams," Doc added. "If you ever want to go back into medicine, you let me know."

Maureen's gaze shifted to Alan. At the doctor's words he had gone rigid. Turning quickly to Doc

Readon, she attempted a smile. "Thank you, Doctor, I will."

"Can we see him?" asked Bud.

"He's still unconscious, but you can go in for a few minutes."

They started to leave the room, then Bud stopped and turned toward Maureen. Taking a few hesitant steps, he stopped in front of her. "I guess I owe you—"

"It's not necessary."

"An apology." He lowered his head, and she could see he fought to contain his tears. "Thank you for saving my boy's life."

He raised his eyes to hers, and she smiled. She knew then that no matter what waited ahead for her and Katie, she wouldn't have done things differently. "You're welcome."

Bud followed Doc Readon and Joey out of the waiting room. When they were gone, the room seemed empty and eerily quiet.

"Well," she said, wrapping her arms around herself to fight off the sudden chill. "We should probably get back to Rita's."

Alan stood and looked at her. She could see the internal battle raging across his features. "Yes," he said. "There are a few things we need to talk about."

Maureen took a deep breath and met his gaze. It was time to face up to what she'd done. "Yes. I guess there are."

CHAPTER FIFTEEN

RITA'S HOUSE was empty.

Maureen glanced at the clock standing against the wall, surprised to see that it was only four o'clock. Katie and Rita were still at Josh's birthday party. It was hard to believe that she and Alan had left the house only seven hours ago. It seemed more like seven years.

"Do you want coffee?" she asked.

"No."

"I do." She headed for the kitchen, needing something to do with her hands, something to forestall the inevitable confrontation. In the kitchen she fussed with coffee, filters and the drip coffeemaker, knowing that at any moment he would ask.

Still, when the first question came, it shook her.

"So," he started, almost as if they were about to discuss what to watch on television that night, "where did you practice medicine?"

She froze, a sickness building in the pit of her stomach. For a brief moment her mind raced, sorting through all the possible answers, all the possible fabrications. But in the end she couldn't lie anymore. She was tired of lying. "I'm not a doctor."

"What are you then?" His voice remained deceptively quiet. "Or maybe I should ask, *who* are you?"

She heard the undercurrent of rage in his voice, but it was too late to avoid his anger and contempt. She'd crossed that line months ago.

"My name is Maura, not Maureen, and I'm a nurse."

"Maura?" The name sounded so familiar, yet so foreign on his lips.

"Yes." She poured water into the coffeemaker and flipped the switch. Turning to face him, she shoved trembling hands into the pockets of her jeans. "Maura Anderson."

He stood and looked at her, his expression demanding that she continue.

"I was born and raised in Chicago like I said...." She shrugged, a gesture of nonchalance, trying to convince him—or maybe herself—that this was nothing, that it meant nothing, this small lie she'd told. "But David and I moved to Miami about ten years ago." Again she paused, the sickness in her stomach becoming fear. "I was a trauma nurse at Miami General until..." Her voice broke, and for a moment she wasn't sure she could continue. But she had no choice. Bracing herself, she pushed on. "Until seven months ago."

Still he said nothing. His silence unnerved her more than a dozen direct questions. Her fear grew. She wanted him to say something, do something. When he didn't, she continued to speak, needing to fill the emptiness between them.

"Everything else I told you was true. David's dead, my father's—" She stopped herself, realizing that she rambled.

"Why?" he asked. The single word, spoken without expression, echoed through the room. She preferred his silence.

She shook her head, not yet ready to answer this biggest of all questions. She could see his pain, and it almost broke her. She'd never meant to hurt him. She'd never meant to hurt anyone. She'd only wanted to protect her daughter.

He took a step toward her. "Why the lies?"

She closed her eyes briefly, then opened them to meet his. "I had to."

His eyes were dark and accusing. "Why? What are you running from?"

She turned away from him, afraid to see the disdain in his eyes when she told him. "I'm..." The words stuck in her throat. She didn't know if she could say them aloud.

"Maureen...Maura?" There was a plea in his voice she couldn't ignore.

"I'm wanted for kidnapping."

Silence. Never had she known such devastating stillness. She could hear her heart beating too rapidly in her chest and the blood pounding behind her eyes. The silence forced her to turn around, to see for herself the effect of her words.

He looked as if he didn't believe her. "Katie?"

Nodding, she bit her bottom lip to hold back the tears.

"Katie's not yours? You kidnapped her?" He took a step back, away from her.

"No. It's not what you think." She started to move toward him, hand extended, but stopped herself when he took another step away from her. "She *is* my daughter. My adopted daughter...."

Alan shook his head, and she rushed on.

"David and I adopted her three years ago, when she was only two weeks old." The tears flowed now. There was no way she could stop them. "She was the answer to our prayers. We'd wanted children for years, but I couldn't..." She paused, pulling herself together, reigning in the emotions threatening to make her words and thoughts incoherent.

When she spoke again, she'd regained some control, although her voice remained shaky. "Last fall, Katie's birth mother sued for custody. She was only sixteen when Katie was born." She spread her hands, a gesture of frustration. "Now she wants Katie back."

Again the silence.

"Alan, please."

"Why didn't you tell me?" There was anger in his voice, but there was also pain. Pain she'd caused.

She shook her head again, no longer making any attempt to stop the tears, and turned away. "I couldn't."

He moved up behind her, close, but not touching. "Damn it, Maureen, you're wanted for kidnapping. That's a federal offense."

Maura closed her eyes and took a deep breath. *Courage,* she told herself, *he'll understand. He won't turn you in. He can't.* Opening her eyes, she turned back to face him. That's when she saw the danger in his eyes. She had to make him understand.

"I was afraid you wouldn't understand."

"Damn right I don't."

"They were going to take her away from me. They were going to give her to a stranger."

He flinched, and she hurried on, feeling time closing in on her. "I'm her mother, Alan. Surely you can understand that I couldn't lose her, that I just couldn't hand her back to them."

"You're not her mother—"

"Yes, I am. I'm the only mother she's ever known. I may not have given birth to her, but she's mine. We belong to each other. I raised her, loved her..."

Alan shook his head. "How could you do this?"

"How could they take her from me? How could I let them?" She moved toward him and placed a hand on his arm. "Please. Try and understand?"

"No!" he said, pulling his arm from her grasp.

Maura fell back as if he'd hit her. Her mind raced, wondering if she had time—time to gather Katie, time to run, time to get away before he turned them over to the authorities.

Alan backed farther away, a lone hand wandering to his head. "I need to think about this."

"Alan, please..."

"No." Instantly he lifted both hands in a defensive gesture. "Don't say anything more. I...I've got to go."

For long moments after the door slammed behind him, Maura couldn't move. She stood rooted to the floor, feeling as though her life were over. It had ended the moment he turned his back on her. As she'd always feared, he hated her for what she had done. How could she go on? Why would she even want to?

The grandfather clock in the front hall struck the hour, snapping her back to the present. There was still Katie. She had to protect Katie, and she had no time to lose. Katie and Rita would be home anytime now, and she needed to be ready. There was an eight o'clock bus out of Waiteville, and she and Katie would be on it.

ALAN COULDN'T GO back to his office—not with the anger and pain still surging through his blood. The temptation to pick up the phone and turn Maureen in would be too great. He needed time alone. Time to try to understand. Time to figure out what he was going to do.

So he drove.

Still, for a long time he couldn't think. Thoughts tumbled through his mind like wayward children. He tried to concentrate on the crime, on a woman stealing a child and running.

Instead, he heard laughter, Maureen's light, sexy laughter—the way it had been the day they stopped at Cliff's—and Katie's giggles as her mother bounced and tickled her all the way down the stairs. He remembered the two of them together the day they'd picnicked in the mountains, the sounds of their love mingling with the chatter of summer birds.

Frustrated, he wrenched his thoughts back to the present. She'd taken the law into her own hands. She had lied to him. For a second, he wasn't sure which angered him more. Certainly the crime was the bigger offense. Yet, deep inside, he knew it was the lies that really hurt.

What would he have done in her situation?

The thought struck him unawares, and he tried to turn it aside. This wasn't about him. This was about Maureen. Still, the question nagged at him. What would he have done in her place? There must have been an alternative to taking Katie and running. But what if there hadn't been another way? What if his only other choice had been to lose her? What would he have done?

He pulled the Jeep off to the side of the road and killed the engine. Leaning his head back against the seat, he shut his eyes. He thought of Katie, with her eyes the color of dark chocolate and just as sweet, always smiling, always laughing. He'd known her only a few months, yet she had captured his heart. What if she had been his since birth? What if he'd changed her diapers and walked with her at night when she couldn't sleep? Could he have handed her back to an indifferent legal system? To a stranger she didn't even know?

His thoughts shifted back to Maureen…Maura. He forced himself to say her real name aloud. "Maura." And then again. "Maura." A delicate, melancholy name. It fell from his lips softly but settled like a weight around his heart.

She loved Katie as deeply as any woman who had given birth. How had she felt, all alone, when they'd come to take her child away?

Suddenly he realized he'd been harboring secret dreams these past months. Making plans. He wanted them both, Maura and her bright-eyed little girl, as his own.

Now it looked as if he couldn't have either. And the pain of his loss tore at his gut.

IN THE BEDROOM she shared with Katie, Maura glanced around, trying to decide what to take. They had come here with so little, but over the last few months they'd accumulated so much. Her gaze fell on the big pink elephant Alan had won for Katie at the festival, and she almost lost control. Digging her nails into the palms of her hands, she forced the tears aside. This was no time to give in to hysterics.

Moving to the closet, she pulled out the small suitcase she'd found in the consignment shop. It wouldn't allow her to take everything, but it would hold more than the backpack they had arrived with. Of course, there was no room for the stuffed elephant, but Maura promised herself she would get Katie another one.

"Mommy!" Katie's excited voice, followed by the slamming of the front door, stopped Maura cold. She didn't want Katie to find her packing, so she headed out to intercept her.

They met in the front hallway. Maura swept her daughter into her arms and held her tight.

"Hi, sweetie," she said, suddenly desperate to hold this child. "I missed you." She showered kisses on Katie's soft cheeks, loving the scent of little girl mixed with the smell of sweets.

"Stop, Mommy." Katie squirmed out of her mother's tight embrace. "I went to a birthday party!"

Maura choked back her emotions and forced herself to smile. "I know. Did you have a good time?"

Katie nodded vigorously. "Uh-huh."

"Tell me about it." Maura set her down, then sat on the stairs so she would be at the child's eye level.

Katie leaned against her mother's knees, her eyes shining. "We had cake. And pink ice cream. Josh got lots of presents."

"He did?"

"He certainly did," Rita agreed, laughing, as she appeared in the hall. "Lots."

"Lots of presents!" repeated Katie. "Can I have a birthday party?"

The innocent question struck Maura square in the chest. She opened her mouth to answer, but no words escaped.

Katie didn't seem to notice. "I can even play 'Happy Birthday.'" Grabbing her mother's hand, she said, "Come see."

Maura tossed a quick glance at Rita as she let Katie lead her into the living room. Climbing up onto the piano bench, Katie patted the seat next to her. "Sit, Mommy."

Maura sat, and Katie turned her attention to the keyboard. The next thing Maura knew, her daughter was playing a one-fingered version of "Happy Birthday." When she was done, Maura once again choked back tears and smiled.

"Why, that was wonderful, sweetheart. Where did you learn it?"

"Aunt Rita taught me."

Maura threw another glance at Rita and saw the concern on the other woman's face. Evidently, Rita wasn't as oblivious to her emotional state as Katie.

"Mommy." Katie's voice brought her attention back to the child. "Can I have a birthday party, with pink ice cream and lots of presents? Can I?"

Maura reached out with trembling fingers and touched her daughter's dark curls. What could she say? Yes, sweetie, we'll have a party, just you and I. We'll have cake and pink ice cream if you want. But there won't be any laughing children or piles of presents. It will just be the two of us, because we're leaving tonight. You'll never see Aunt Rita or Josh or Uncle Alan again. They'll no longer be a part of our lives.

What was she thinking of?

With sudden, blinding clarity, Maura saw what she was doing to Katie's life. It hit her like a physical blow, and reeling from the impact, she dropped her hand away from Katie. All along she'd been thinking of herself, only herself, and how she couldn't lose Katie. Now she could see their lives as a series of places, temporary places, where they could be safe only for a while. She'd been telling herself she was saving Katie from an unstable home, when all the time she was creating just such an environment.

"We'll see," she finally managed to say. Struggling to her feet, she met Rita's gaze. *What am I going to do?*

"Come on, Katie," Rita said, moving to Katie and lifting her from the piano bench. "Let's take a short nap."

Katie protested, but Maura barely heard as Rita ushered the child out of the room and up the stairs.

When Rita came back, she sat next to Maura and took her hand. "I saw the suitcase."

Maura turned and met the other woman's gaze, unable to say anything. It was over. She couldn't run anymore. But she couldn't stay, either.

"You're leaving," Rita said.

Maura nodded, still unable to speak.

"Do you want to talk about it?" Rita's voice was gentle, concerned. "Maybe I can help."

Maura shook her head, but Rita ignored it. "Maureen, you can't just keep running away. Now tell me. Is this about Alan?"

Maura burst into tears and Rita instantly wrapped her arms around her, rocking her the way she so often rocked Katie.

It was some time before Maura could speak. But when she did, the story stumbled from her lips. She couldn't look at Rita, but she didn't hold anything back, either. She needed to tell everything, to rid herself of the poison that had been growing in her since the night she'd fled with Katie. She needed to cleanse herself of the lies. She needed everything to be out in the open.

When she finished, Rita handed her tissues and squeezed her hand. "Do you feel better now?"

Maura nodded and forced herself to meet the older woman's gaze. What she saw surprised and warmed her. Rita looked at her with compassion and love.

"Tell me, Maura," she asked, "how could this happen? If you and your husband legally adopted Katie, why is there any question about custody?"

Maura rested her head against the back of the couch and sighed. "It's because of Katie's grandparents. They didn't know about Katie until very recently. Evidently they were out of the country when she was born, and their daughter never told them about her pregnancy. Until now. *They* claim she was too young to make a decision like that, and the state should never have allowed it."

"But can they get away with that?"

"They're very wealthy and influential." Maura turned her head and looked at Rita. "The court seemed very impressed with the fact that they could offer Katie much more than a single working mother."

"It just doesn't seem fair."

"No. It doesn't." Maura closed her eyes, and silence fell between them for a few moments. Then, taking a deep breath, she added, "But there's something else, as well. Something that makes their case even stronger.

"The lawyer who handled the adoption has been indicted for bribing officials and paying off expectant mothers." Her voice broke, but she steeled herself and went on. "And there's evidence that David, my husband, knew about it."

"Oh dear."

"So there's not only the question of whether Katie's grandparents are entitled to custody, but of whether the adoption was ever legal to begin with."

"*Was* your husband involved?" Rita asked gently.

Maura closed her eyes and sighed. "I don't know. It's possible. He wasn't very strong. And I wanted a baby so much. He could have..." She let her voice trail off, then turned to look at the other woman. "But I swear *I* had no idea." Neither spoke for a few moments, then Maura added, "I'm so sorry, Rita."

"For what?" Rita smiled sadly and reached up to brush a strand of hair away from Maura's cheek. "For bringing a little sunshine into this old house? For bringing friendship to a lonely little boy? Or for bringing love into my nephew's heart...."

"He doesn't love me."

"Of course he loves you. Why do you think he's so angry?"

Maura shook her head. Of all her regrets, this was the greatest. "Even if he felt something for me, it's gone now. I lied to him."

"Yes. And when someone you love lies to you, it's painful." Rita took her hand again. "Right now he's hurting. He'll get past it."

Maura shook her head again. "I never meant to hurt him. I love him."

"I know." Rita squeezed her hand and smiled softly. "Did you tell him?"

"No." Maura looked down at her hands. "I couldn't."

"Why?"

Maura sighed. "We're so different. What I did, defying the law... he never would have done it."

"Are you so sure?"

Maura met her gaze again, suddenly unsure in the face of this woman who knew Alan so well. "Maybe if I'd told him the truth sooner..."

"He's had a shock, dear. Give him a chance to get over it."

Maura looked away and considered Rita's words. Would Alan come to understand what she'd done? Would he forgive her? Her heart soared at the possibility. Then she remembered the look on his face when he'd stormed out of the house. There had been more than anger and pain, there had been contempt. He hadn't even wanted her to touch him.

No, this wasn't something he would get over.

"It's too late," she said finally. She rose from the couch and moved away, putting distance between herself and Rita's silent pleas.

Rita started to say something else but stopped. Instead, for several long moments she let silence settle between them. Then she asked, "What are you going to do now?"

"Katie deserves a home." Maura hesitated, then added, "I have to take her back to Miami."

HOURS LATER, Alan returned to town. Still unsure what to do, he drove back by Rita's. It was after dark, and the lights were on inside the house. He stopped for a moment and sat staring at the windows, at the silhouettes behind the drapes.

What was she thinking in there? What was she doing?

He considered going in. He wanted to talk to her, to tell her he loved her. But he couldn't. Not yet. He wasn't ready. His pain and anger hovered too close to the surface. He might say or do something he would regret later. So he started the car and headed downtown.

At the station he went directly to his office, pausing only long enough to tell Jake he wasn't to be disturbed. Inside he closed his door and, not bothering to turn on the lights, collapsed in the chair behind his desk. Resting his head on his arms, he tried shutting down his thoughts and letting his mind drift.

He loved her.

Despite everything that had happened, despite everything he had learned about her, he loved her. Over the last few months she had crept into his life... and into his heart.

The ironic part was that the traits that made him love her, her strength and will, were the very things that would take her away from him. How many people would have had the courage to do what she had done, to give up everything to protect someone they loved? He couldn't help but admire her, even while he condemned her actions.

"Sheriff—"

Alan lifted his head to see Jake standing in the doorway. "I told you I didn't want to be disturbed."

"I know, Sheriff." Jake fidgeted. "Bud Simmons is out front. He said it was important."

Alan straightened in his chair. "Is Tommy all right?"

"Yes, sir. It's just Bud. He's being pretty insistent."

Alan hesitated, not knowing if he was up to dealing with Simmons tonight. But did he have a choice? "Okay," he finally said. "Send him in."

Bud surprised him. For some reason, Alan hadn't expected him to walk in as his usual surly self, although a contrite Bud Simmons, hat in hand, was probably too much to ask for.

"What can I do for you, Bud?"

The big man glanced around at the dark office. "Got problems with the lights? Didn't you pay your electric bill?"

Alan sighed and shook his head. "It's been a long day, Bud. Why don't you state your business and be done with it."

Bud glanced away and then walked over to stare out the window. For a long time he said nothing, then in a flat voice he stated, "You know about the hunting."

"Yes," Alan answered, somewhat surprised that Bud would bring up the subject. "I know about it."

"So." He paused. "What are you gonna do about it?"

Alan leaned back in his chair, crossing one long leg over the other. To be honest, he hadn't really thought much about Bud and his illegal hunting activities since... since Friday night. His mind had been so tied up with Maura, he'd hardly given Bud a second thought.

So, what *was* he going to do about it? Arrest him? And then what? What about Joey, and Tommy lying hurt in the hospital? Hell, he just didn't know what was right anymore.

"Well, Bud," he finally answered, in a voice sounding weary even to his own ears, "I guess it all depends on what you plan to do about it."

Bud didn't say anything at first but just stood there, his eyes focused on the dark street beyond the plate glass window.

"If I told you it'll stop, would you believe me?" Bud asked.

"I might."

Bud turned and met Alan's gaze, and for the briefest moment Alan thought he saw a silent plea in the other man's eyes. Then they turned hard and indifferent again. "Well," Bud said, "you let me know what you decide."

"Yeah. I'll do that."

He thought Bud would leave then. He wanted the quiet, dark office returned to him. But Bud stayed put, turning back to the window.

Alan sighed. "I'm not going to arrest you, Bud."

Bud didn't seem to hear him. Instead, he asked, "Did you really go to Seattle, like you said, and check out that place?"

"You mean the alcohol rehabilitation center?" Two surprises from Bud Simmons in one night were almost more than Alan could handle.

Bud kept his back to him. "Yeah."

"Yes, I did."

Alan uncrossed his legs and came forward in his chair, wondering at the workings of fate. He'd mentioned the center to Bud the day he and Maura had driven to Seattle. Bud had grown angry at Alan's suggestion. Could some good come from Tommy's injury? "Do you want the information I picked up?"

Bud hesitated, and Alan sensed the battle raging within the other man. This was probably one of the hardest things he'd ever faced. Alan pulled a large envelope out of a drawer and tossed it on the desk. "You're welcome to it."

"Well, I thought I'd check it out." Bud shrugged and turned, picking up the packet. "That is, after Tommy gets out of the hospital."

Alan hesitated, carefully weighing his next words. "You got two fine boys there, Bud."

Bud met his gaze for a moment and nodded. Then he slipped the envelope into an inside pocket of his jacket and without another word left the office.

Once Bud had left, Alan sat staring at the closed door. Suddenly he knew what he had to do. Grabbing his hat, he headed for the door.

IT WAS a long, quiet drive to Seattle.

Katie had cried when Maura told her they were going back to Miami. She didn't want to leave. It tore at Maura's already shredded heart to see Katie so upset, but there was nothing to be done about it. Her only comfort was in knowing that, this time, she was doing the right thing. The motion of the car finally soothed Katie, and she settled down and fell asleep on her mother's lap.

Silence permeated the night.

Maura felt talked out. Everything that needed to be said had been discussed back at the house. The hour after she'd cried on Rita's shoulder had gone quickly. Then, before they'd left, she had called her father. The conversation had been strained at best.

It was after midnight in Chicago, but her father had been wide-awake. "Yes," he answered in his usual cool voice.

"Father," she said tentatively, reverting to the formal address she used whenever she felt unsure of his reaction.

There was a pause on the other end of the line, and for a moment Maura thought he would hang up. She was just about to say something, apologize, tell him she'd gotten his note, anything to keep him on the phone, when he spoke. "Maura?"

Tears of relief flooded her eyes. "Yes. It's me."

"Thank God." If she hadn't known her father so well, she would have sworn she heard emotion in his voice. "Where are you?"

"I'm still in Waiteville." Funny how quickly she'd come to accept his knowledge of her location. "I need your help."

"Yes. I know. But you have to turn yourself in."

"That's why I called." She hesitated, knowing once she said the words there would be no turning back. "I'm going back to Miami."

She heard his sigh across the miles. "That's good. I'll meet you there. No guarantees, but I think I can help you. You've been charged with contempt of court. But if you turn yourself in..."

"Contempt of court? Not kidnapping?"

"No. You're still Katie's legal guardian, and the charges against David have been unsubstantiated. However..." He paused, and Maura felt the room closing in around her. "You're probably going to lose the child."

Maura bit her lip to hold back her tears. She knew this. She had known it all along. She'd sat in that courtroom all those months ago and listened to the allegations against her husband and the lawyer he had used to adopt Katie. When she'd heard that the lawyer had been indicted, she had known they would take Katie away from her. That's why she'd run.

Now, even with her father's help, she knew it was a lost cause. If she returned to Miami, she would lose her daughter. Yet Maura also knew she had to go back so that Katie could win. So that she would have a chance at a normal life.

"Yes," she finally said. "I know."

After that her father's demeanor returned to the polished efficiency she was used to. Maura listened numbly. If she could get to the Seattle airport, he would arrange to have tickets waiting for her and Katie. Someone would meet them in Miami, and he would have a place for them to stay.

Rita had agreed to drive them to Seattle but begged Maura to wait for Alan. But she couldn't face him. She'd left him a note instead, even though it had nearly killed her to write it. She had wanted to say so much, to tell him she loved him and that she was sorry for hurting him. She longed to say so many things, to talk of all he had given her, all he had taught her. But in the end she'd been unable to say anything except that she was sorry and that she was going back to Miami.

Now there was nothing left but the long dark road to Seattle and the airport waiting at the other end. After the airport there was Miami, and the people who would take Katie away from her.

When they arrived at the airport, Maura suggested that Rita drop them off and head home, but she refused. Instead, she parked her car and walked them in, helping with Katie as Maura got their tickets and checked their single bag. Still she refused to leave. She accompanied them to the gate area and sat while they waited for their departure time.

Rita held Katie while Maura rested her tearstained eyes. Even though she'd suggested that Rita go home, she was grateful for the other woman's presence. She wasn't sure if she would have been able to go through with this without Rita's quiet support.

In Miami she would have her father with her, and for once she felt grateful for the strength she knew he would provide. But it wouldn't be enough. She wondered if anything would ever be enough again.

Her days yawned before her like a deep, desolate pit where no sun dared reach. Without Alan, without Katie, she might as well be left alone at its bottom without even a candle to light her way.

When Rita touched her arm, she turned and forced a weary smile for the other woman. Rita smiled back and gestured for Maura to look up. When she did, her breath caught in her throat. Alan stood across the waiting area, holding an oversize pink elephant.

"I think I'll take Katie to the ladies' room," Rita said, standing with the sleeping child still in her arms. "We'll be back in a few minutes."

Nervously Maura stood and glanced at Rita, who smiled and said, "It will be okay, Maura. Talk to him."

When she looked back at Alan, he walked toward her, stopping just out of reach. She studied his face. There was sadness and longing there, and something else she couldn't read.

"You forgot something," he said, depositing the elephant in the chair next to Maura. Then, turning slightly, he glanced at the destination written above the check-in desk. "You're going back to Miami."

Something large lodged in Maura's throat, blocking her attempt to speak. She nodded.

"Do they know you're coming?"

"I called my father," she answered in a voice that only vaguely resembled her own. "He's going to meet us. I... suppose he'll notify the authorities."

Alan shoved his hands into the pockets of his jeans and took a deep breath. "You should have said goodbye."

"I thought..." Her voice broke, but she gathered herself together. "I thought everything had been said."

He looked at her then, and she saw the pain she had caused fill his eyes. "Not everything."

"I left you a note."

"Yes." He sighed and let his gaze drift to the floor in front of him. "A note."

"I'm sorry, Alan. I didn't think you'd want to see me again. I didn't think it mattered."

He lifted his eyes back to her. "It matters."

For a moment the world stopped. All she could see, all she knew, was this man standing in front of her. His eyes, filled with longing, captured her, making her want nothing more than to crawl into his arms and stay there forever.

"I love you," he said. The three words, spoken quietly in a crowded airport, brought fresh tears to her eyes.

"I'm sorry," she said again. She wished things were different. That they'd met some other time, some other place. Again she fought the desire to step into his arms and take what comfort he would offer.

"Forget Miami," he said. "My Jeep is outside. Get Katie and we'll leave." Maura shook her head, but he kept talking. "We can be in Canada within a couple of hours. We'll make a life for ourselves there."

Maura shook her head again. "No. I can't hurt either of you like that anymore."

"I want it. I want you."

"What kind of life could we have?"

"A good one. As long as we're together. The three of us."

"No," she repeated. "I thought that way, too. But I was wrong. We'd spend our lives looking over our shoulders. And soon you'd come to resent me for taking you away from the people and places that you love. And Katie, she'd wonder..."

"I love *you*. And Katie."

She closed her eyes and nodded. "Yes. And I love you."

He reached out and touched her and she could no longer resist him. She melted into his arms, resting her head against his chest, where she could hear the beating of his heart through the fabric of his shirt. It was the same shirt he had worn that first night at Rita's. That time seemed so long ago, so very far away.

"I have to go back," she said, wishing it wasn't true.

"Then I'll go with you."

She pulled back, searching his face. "I can't let you do that."

"You don't have a choice." He reached behind him and pulled a long airline envelope out of his back pocket. "I've already bought the ticket. I figured if you wouldn't let me take you to Canada, I'd go with you to Miami."

She couldn't let him make this sacrifice for her. "No, Alan, I was wrong—"

He placed a finger against her lips. "We were both wrong. You for taking on the law alone. Me for being too bullheaded to see beyond my black-and-white world." He leaned down and pressed a brief kiss to her lips. "But I don't intend for either of us to spend the rest of our lives paying for our mistakes."

"Alan..." Her resolve weakened.

"Hush." His hands found her face and gently lifted it to his. Soft caramel-colored eyes, filled with love, bored into her soul, beckoning her. "I'm going with you. I'm going to help you fight for Katie."

"And your job?" She was desperate, knowing he should stay, yet wanting him to come with her. "What about Waiteville?"

He brushed her lips with his, tempting her, pleading with her. "Waiteville will be here when we get back. And so will my job."

"When we get back?"

"Yes," he whispered. "When *we* get back. You see, I plan to marry you. And we're going to go through this together."

For long moments she stood in his arms, not knowing what to do. There was nothing she wanted more than to accept what he offered. It seemed a miracle that he was even here. But he was. Strong and warm, holding her within his arms, he gave her the comfort and support she longed for. And she loved him, more than she had ever thought herself capable of loving a man.

With a sigh of resignation, she rested her head back on his chest. "I love you."

"Say it again," he whispered against her hair. "And then keep on saying it for the rest of our lives."

"I love you."

CHAPTER SIXTEEN

THE FLIGHT TO MIAMI was both the longest and shortest Alan had ever known. On one hand he was anxious, wanting to get there and face whatever lay ahead. There would be no life for the three of them until they got through the next few weeks. And more than anything, he wanted a life with Maura and Katie.

On the other hand, he wished he could stop the clock. He didn't know how long he would have either of them with him once they landed. When the authorities were notified, Maura would most likely be arrested, and Katie... He couldn't bear to think of Katie handed over to the child welfare people.

Fortunately it was late, and the plane was half-empty. After takeoff, he removed the armrest from between two seats and laid Katie down. With a pillow and a blanket tucked around her, the child fell instantly to sleep. Then, in his seat across the aisle, Alan gathered Maura close. She rested her head against his shoulder and spoke to him of all the things she'd never dared to speak of before.

It was like a dam giving way.

She told him about her father and the note she'd received from him. She relayed the conversation she had had with him a few hours ago and said that he would meet them in Miami. Then she talked about his practice and his unique skill in the courtroom, and how she hoped it wasn't too late.

"So why didn't you go to him about Katie in the first place?" Alan asked.

Maura sighed. "I didn't think he'd help me."

Alan shifted away from her just enough to see the expression on her face. "He's your father. Why wouldn't he help you?"

She shook her head. "It's a long story."

"It's a long flight." Alan settled her back against his side. "We've got time."

Maura paused as if gathering her thoughts. "You know that my father raised me."

"Yes."

"Well, we clashed the entire time I was growing up." She idly picked up the cocktail napkin that had been sitting under the soda she'd had earlier. She toyed with it for a moment, folding it and then unfolding it before dropping it on her lap. "It seemed we could never agree on anything, and neither one of us was willing to give an inch. He'd want one thing, so I'd do the opposite."

"On purpose?"

Maura nodded. "Sometimes."

She picked up the napkin again, creasing the fold sharply between her fingers. "He would have preferred a docile, obedient daughter. Not a strong-willed female who wanted her own way as much as he wanted his. And I would have preferred..." She paused and shrugged. "I don't know. Maybe I would have been independent and rebellious no matter what kind of father I had."

Alan chuckled softly. "You? Independent?"

Maura smiled slightly and gave him a gentle jab in the ribs. "You're supposed to be on my side."

"Oh, I am." He kissed the top of her head. "Go on."

"Anyway..." She tossed the napkin aside once again. "Growing up with him was one fight after the other. But the confrontations turned into a major battle when I refused to go to law school." She carefully folded her hands in her lap as if trying to still their wanderings. "He wanted me to take my place at his side, and of course I wanted nothing to do with the law."

"So you had a falling-out over careers." Alan reached over and slipped his hand between her entwined fingers. "That's not unusual."

"Don't defend him." Maura glanced at him and shook her head. "He does that very well all by himself. Besides—" she turned back to look straight ahead "—that's not why I didn't go to him." She hesitated for a moment before going on. "As for my career, he probably figured I'd eventually come to my senses, forget nursing and go to law school. Then I met David."

Alan tightened his hold on her hand. "And he didn't approve."

"Hardly. Dad and I had a knock-down-drag-out fight. That is, he fixed me one of the infamous Jacob Anderson expressions of disappointment, while I screamed and cried." She paused, taking a deep breath. "I married David anyway, and Dad refused to come to the wedding. He sent legal papers instead, disowning me."

She sat for a few moments without speaking, and then added, "I'm not sure at the time whether I didn't believe him or I just didn't care. Anyway, I thought he would eventually come around."

Alan pulled her a little closer, offering silent comfort. Maura acknowledged the gesture with a smile and, after a few seconds of silence, continued with her story.

"David and I moved to Miami, and we didn't have much contact with Dad for a few years. Then when I found out that I couldn't..." Her voice broke, but she took another deep breath and went on. "When I found out I couldn't have children, I went to him and asked if he'd help us adopt. That's when I found out just how serious he was about disowning me."

She pulled away from Alan then, sitting upright in her seat while slipping her hands from his. "He refused my call," she said in a stoic voice that defied the strong emotions Alan heard in her words. "Not once, but several times. I tried him at his office and at home. Finally, his secretary asked me to stop bothering them. I didn't call again."

She didn't say anything else for a few moments, and Alan sensed the pain in her silence. He suspected her father had hurt her deeply. Despite her talk about their disagreements, all her brave words about how she'd defied him, Alan guessed that she loved the older man more than she would care to admit. When he'd refused to help her, it must have broken her apart.

"Anyway," Maura said, interrupting his thoughts. "That's why I didn't call him when Katie's birth mother sued for custody. I thought he'd refuse me again, and I couldn't..." She didn't finish her sentence, but Alan heard the words she didn't say. She couldn't handle another rejection from her father, a man she obviously loved deeply, so she hadn't even called him.

Alan pulled Maura back against him, pressing her head down on his shoulder. She didn't resist. She remained silent after that, her words obviously dried up. After a while she fell into a restless slumber.

Alan couldn't sleep. Not at first.

His thoughts stayed with Jacob Anderson. Anger built inside him as he considered what Maura had told him about her father. Alan wanted to throttle the man for hurting her, but he pushed the pointless emotion aside. Anger wouldn't do them any good. He had a fair idea what lay ahead of them in Miami and knew it could get rough. And as much as he wanted to protect Maura and Katie, there would be little he could do. Unfortunately, their fate rested in the hands of Jacob Anderson and his skill at negotiating the legal system. Still, Alan wasn't at all sure they could trust the man. And he sure as hell didn't like him.

He shifted in his seat, and Maura murmured sleepily against his chest. He touched her cheek gently with his free hand and kissed the top of her head. With a sigh, he leaned his head back against the headrest and closed his eyes.

He couldn't lose her.

As the plane headed east into the rising sun, Alan slept fitfully. He dreamed of cold, impersonal courtrooms and a tall thin stranger with hawk eyes and silver-tipped hair. His head dropped forward and he woke with a start, relieved that he still sat on the plane, with Maura tucked against him. Then he fell again into a light slumber, and he was back in that courtroom, searching for Katie, hearing her cries but unable to find her in the crowd of people, all with blank gray eyes and hard faces.

Both he and Maura awoke as the pilot announced their final descent into Miami. Maura moved over to sit next to Katie for the landing. Once they were on the ground, Alan set Katie on his lap, and the three of them waited for the rest of the passengers to disembark. When everyone was off, Maura met his gaze and there was no mistaking the fear in her eyes.

Neither of them knew for sure what lay at the other end of the jetway. Would there be child welfare people waiting to take Katie away from them? Would the police be waiting to arrest Maura? Or would there just be Jacob Anderson?

Alan reached over and took Maura's hand. "Whatever happens," he tried to reassure her, "we're in this together."

She nodded, but he could see the effort it cost her to keep her fear under control. "Promise me you'll make sure Katie's okay," she said. "Don't let them put her just anywhere."

"She'll be fine."

"Promise me." She squeezed his hand tight to emphasize her words. "I might not be in any position..."

"Hush..." He leaned forward and kissed her lightly on the cheek. "It will be all right. I promise. " With Katie balanced against his chest and Maura's hand still in his, he stood. "Come on, we've got to go now."

Maura closed her eyes and took a deep breath. Then she nodded and let him lead her off the plane. They walked silently down the jetway, hand in hand, and came to a halt as they stepped inside the terminal building.

The gate area was almost empty of the plane's other passengers and those waiting to meet them. And there were no police or officials waving legal papers in their faces. There was only one man, tall, blond, muscularly built, that Alan recognized immediately. Wrapping his free arm about Maura's shoulders, he maneuvered her toward the other man.

"Cooper," Alan said. "I guess I shouldn't be surprised to find you here."

"No more than I am to see you." Cooper met his gaze for a moment, then turned to Maura. Alan instinctively tightened his hold on her. "The name's Sam Cooper, ma'am. Your father sent me to fetch you."

Maura glanced quickly at Alan, then turned back to the other man. "Where is he?"

"Taking care of some legal matters." Cooper smiled knowingly. Then, reaching over, he relieved Maura of her suitcase, leaving her to carry Katie's stuffed elephant. "Now, if you'll come with me..." With a gesture for them to follow, he turned and started down the concourse.

Alan hesitated only a second before saying to Maura, "It's okay. We've met before. Let's see where he takes us." Releasing his hold on her, Alan adjusted Katie in his arms as they started walking.

When they caught up to Cooper, Maura asked, "Where are we going?"

"Your father's arranged a place for you to stay." Then, with a quick glance at Alan, he added, "But I don't think he was counting on your friend here."

"I guess he's in for a surprise then," Alan said.

Cooper chuckled softly. "Can't wait."

By the time Cooper loaded the three of them into a waiting limo, Maura felt ready to collapse.

They drove north.

Maura wanted to close her eyes, but fear and uncertainty wouldn't allow it. Not to mention Katie, who had come fully awake as they made their way through the Miami airport. First she explored the inside of the limo with all its various buttons and compartments. Then she discovered a new audience in Sam Cooper. She happily scrambled from one window to the other, from Maura's lap to Alan's, just to see Cooper's response. To Maura's surprise, Sam Cooper didn't let the little girl down. He laughed and talked to her while pointing out sights the child couldn't possibly understand. And Katie would ooh and aah and giggle, and Sam would laugh with her.

Maura suspected that Cooper was the man who had delivered her father's note to Rita. Possibly he was responsible for finding her. She knew her father often employed an assortment of nontraditional individuals to assist with his cases. Men with unique skills. She'd never met any of them, but she would have pictured them much differently than Sam Cooper. She would have thought them harder, more remote. And she never would have imagined one of them enjoying the company of a child.

Along with her surprise at Cooper, the sight and sounds of her daughter's happiness did strange things to Maura. She knew she should be enjoying this time with Katie. Yet the thought that Katie might soon be taken from her was a weight about her heart.

Forty-five minutes later, the limo pulled up to the guard gate of one of Miami's more exclusive neighborhoods. The driver lowered his window and nodded to the guard. The gate opened immediately.

"Your father doesn't mess around," Alan commented, taking Maura's hand in his.

Maura shot him a shaky grin, but it was Cooper who answered. "The man has a way about him."

Leave it to her father to put them up in an estate, Maura thought a little bitterly. No hotel room or small apartment for Jacob Anderson. He'd rented a million-dollar showplace right on the Intracoastal Waterway.

It didn't take long, however, for Maura to forget her disgruntled thoughts about her father. The house offered cool refuge from the thick Florida heat and a welcoming housekeeper, Mrs. Berd, who took immediate charge of Maura's energetic three-year-old. Then Maura caught sight of the large bed in the room made ready for her and wanted nothing more than a few hours of uninterrupted sleep. She knew it would work wonders for the way she saw the world.

After making sure Katie would be properly fed and looked after, Maura retreated to her bedroom and collapsed on the bed. It felt like heaven. Even so, at first she thought she wouldn't be able to shut off her thoughts and fears. But her exhaustion, the comfortable bed and the soft hum of the air conditioner combined to prove her wrong. It only took a few moments for her to fall into a deep sleep.

HOURS LATER, Maura awoke slowly to the feel of a hard thigh pressed against her side. Gentle fingers caressed her cheek. Opening her eyes, she warmed to the love reflected in Alan's features.

"Hi," she said shyly.

He answered her with the lightest brushing of his lips against hers. "Feel better?" he asked softly.

"I do now." She lifted her hands to his face and deepened the kiss, wishing the moment could last forever. But the tendrils of reality crept back into her thoughts even before their lips parted.

"Where's Katie?" she asked.

"In the living room. With your father."

Maura pulled herself to a sitting position. "He's here?"

Alan nodded. She glanced toward the door and then back to Alan. "It's okay," he said.

Maura swung her legs off the bed. "I need a few minutes to get cleaned up."

"Sure." Alan stood and headed for the door. Then he stopped and seemed to study her before asking, "Are you all right?"

Maura forced a smile. "Sure. I'm fine."

"Okay." He hesitated a moment longer before opening the door. "I'll be in the other room if you need me."

Maura waited until he'd closed the door before dragging herself to her feet. Catching sight of herself in the vanity mirror, she almost moaned out loud. She quickly grabbed a brush out of her purse and ran it through her short dark hair.

What would her father think when he saw her? What would he say about her hair? Shaking her head, she turned away from the mirror. Funny—after all they'd been through and all that lay ahead of them—she still cared about her father's opinion. The thought irritated her for reasons she didn't bother to dissect, and she tossed the brush back into her purse.

It took her a few more minutes to freshen up. At the door to the room she stopped, suddenly unsure of what she would find on the other side. It had been ten years since she'd seen her father. Nearly five since she'd spoken to him. Bracing herself, she turned the knob and stepped into the hallway.

She followed the sounds of voices until she came to the living room. For a moment she stood on the threshold, watching. Alan saw her first. He stood with his back to the room, staring out a set of sliding glass doors that opened onto a lush pool area. Evidently sensing her presence, he turned and met her gaze. He offered so much with just a look. Love. Compassion. And strength. She smiled softly, gratefully acknowledging his gifts. Then, in silent communication, they both shifted their attention to Katie and Jacob Anderson.

Jacob had Katie on his lap, an open picture book in front of them. Maura experienced a tinge of jealousy. She couldn't remember her father ever reading to her when she was a child. He'd always been too busy. There had been a string of nannies, and then, when she was older, governesses. But here he sat with his granddaughter, attempting to entertain her in a way he knew nothing about. Her jealousy vanished. He was trying, and she'd never known him to do even that before.

He looked up and met her gaze. "Maura."

In that one word she heard so much. Or was it in his eyes? There was love and sorrow, pain and apology. Could her father have really changed so much?

"Mommy, you're awake."

Katie's words diverted Maura's attention. She smiled and laughed lightly. "It looks like you've been kept busy enough."

Katie smiled in return, and Jacob stood, setting her on the floor. The child carried the picture book over to Maura, who squatted down to look at it.

"Look what Grandpa Jacob bought me," Katie said, showing her mother the book. "He's been reading it to me, too."

"Wow. That was really nice of him. Did you thank him?"

"Uh-huh." Katie nodded.

"Good girl." Maura pulled the child into her arms and gave her a hug. Then she looked up and met her father's gaze. He still stood across the room, in front of the chair where he'd been holding her daughter. There was an uncertainty in his eyes and stance that she'd never seen before.

Rising, she took a single step in his direction—unsure herself of how best to greet him. Then suddenly, without knowing who had moved first, she was in his arms. For a few moments, she forgot why he was here and what they faced in the weeks to come. She only knew that she finally had her father back.

A SHORT TIME LATER, the four of them sat around a patio table while the housekeeper served lunch. In silent agreement the adults had put off talking about the events that brought them all together. Mostly they let Katie lead the conversation. She chattered and giggled, making it easy for them to forget the real reason they were all here.

Maura loved watching Alan with Katie. Her father tried, but it was pretty obvious that being around a three-year-old was a new experience for him. But Katie and Alan were easy with each other, and the child didn't seem to suspect anything was amiss.

Then Katie threw them all, bringing their problems into sharp focus with a simple question.

"Are you my *real* grandpa?" she asked Jacob.

"Well, I..." Jacob glanced at Maura before turning his attention back to Katie. Then, shifting in his seat, he said, "Actually, I'm your adopted grandfather."

"What's that?"

Jacob turned to Maura again, a question in his eyes.

"Adopted means special," Maura said, coming to her father's rescue. She'd planned on explaining Katie's adoption to her someday, but this wasn't exactly how she'd foreseen their first conversation on the topic.

"Am I adopted?" Katie asked.

Maura took a deep breath. "Yes. Which is very special, because of all the children in the world, your daddy and I picked you to be our little girl. Because we loved you very much."

"But what about Grandpa Jacob?" Katie obviously wasn't the least concerned about her relation to Maura. It was Jacob who had her confused. "Did he pick me, too?"

"Well..." Maura met her father's gaze across the table. "Yes, he did."

"So he's a pretend grandpa. Like Aunt Rita." Katie seemed satisfied that she had it all figured out.

"Like Aunt Rita?" Jacob questioned, looking at Maura again. He obviously wasn't used to a child's logic.

"Rita is Alan's aunt," Maura explained. "Katie and I lived with her in Waiteville."

"And she said we could pretend that she was my grandma," Katie added. "She said if we pretended long enough it might come true."

A hush fell over the group. Maura sensed there was more to come. Jacob broke the silence.

"Katie," he said, "would you like to meet your real grandma and grandpa?"

No. Maura mouthed the word, but before any sound escaped, Alan grabbed her hand.

"I guess," Katie said thoughtfully. "Are they nice?"

"Very nice. And they want to meet you," Jacob continued. "They live in a really big house, right on the beach."

Maura gripped Alan's hand, waiting to hear Katie's answer. But Katie had already put aside questions about grandparents and adoptions. "Maybe tomorrow," she said. "I want to go in the pool today."

Jacob obviously didn't know what to say. Maura figured he'd probably never been so summarily dismissed in his life.

"Come on, princess," Alan said, standing and pulling Katie out of her chair. "We'll let your mommy and Grandpa Jacob talk. We'll go see if Mrs. Berd can find us a couple of swimming suits so we can go in the water."

Katie squealed her approval, and Alan lifted her onto his shoulders and headed into the house.

Without the buffer of Katie and Alan, silence fell heavily between Maura and her father. Maura listened to the sounds of her daughter and Alan inside the house, wishing she could join them. She didn't want to be alone with her father. She didn't want to have the conversation she knew was inevitable.

"It's time," Jacob said, as if reading her thoughts. "We need to talk."

Maura turned to meet his gaze, then nodded slowly. "Okay. But not here. Alan and Katie..."

"Come on." Jacob rose from his chair and offered her his hand. "Let's go into the den."

Maura put her hand in his and followed him inside. Once the door was closed behind them, she asked the question foremost in her mind. "Does Katie have to go to them? To her grandparents?"

"Yes." Jacob nodded and lowered himself into an armchair. "I spent the morning dealing with the district attorney's office. They've agreed to let Katie stay with her maternal grandparents until all this is settled."

"Why can't she stay here?" But she knew the answer to the question even before she asked it. The authorities didn't trust her not to run again.

"I'm sorry." Jacob smiled sadly at his daughter. "They're good people, Maura. They'll take care of her. And we'll do everything we can to get her back."

Maura bit her lip and sat in the chair across from him. "When?"

"This evening."

"So soon?" Maura clenched her hands in her lap, trying to still their sudden trembling.

"Would it make it easier if we put it off?"

For a moment she just stared at him, and then she shook her head. "No. Time won't make it easier."

"That's what I thought."

Maura closed her eyes and leaned back against the chair.

"We'll take Katie over there after dinner," Jacob said. "And tomorrow we'll go downtown."

Maura opened her eyes. "What are my chances?"

"The fact you came in voluntarily will help you a great deal. You'll end up with community service for the contempt of court charge..."

"No," Maura interrupted. "That's not what I meant. What are my chances of keeping Katie?"

Jacob sighed and ran a hand through his hair. "I wish I could say they were good. But I don't know yet. Cooper's looking into a few things for me. Let's see what he can find out."

THEY TOOK THE LIMO that evening to deliver Katie to her grandparents. Jacob had to give Maura credit. She'd talked the visit up to Katie so that the child was willing and even excited to meet her "real" grandparents. He knew Maura was in pain, but for the child's sake, she'd hidden her own feelings.

And then there was the man. Alan Parks.

Jacob watched him with Maura and Katie. It was obvious the three not only cared for one another, but were comfortable together. If Jacob believed in such things, he might have even said they belonged together. He had to admit that at first he'd been unhappy about the relationship between his daughter and Waiteville's sheriff. Now he wasn't so sure. Parks possessed none of the weaknesses of Maura's deceased husband, David. And in fact, Jacob had developed a grudging respect for Parks at their very first meeting.

Jacob smiled to himself as he remembered waltzing into the house looking for Maura and finding the grim-faced Parks instead. Remembering his last telephone conversation with Cooper, Jacob knew immediately that this was Waiteville's sheriff.

"Where's Maura?" Jacob asked.

"Sleeping."

Jacob started to suggest they wake her, but something in Parks's expression stopped him. "I'm Jacob Anderson," he said instead. "Maura's father."

"I know."

"And you're the sheriff."

"Alan Parks." The man didn't offer a handshake or even a smile. But Jacob met his gaze, refusing to flinch under the iron scrutiny.

"I've got a question for you," Parks said. "I'll ask only once, but I strongly suggest you answer truthfully."

Jacob bristled at the other man's tone, even as he appreciated Parks's direct manner. "And just what question is that?"

"Are you going to help her this time?"

Jacob sighed, suddenly more tired than he'd ever been in his life. He didn't answer immediately but dropped the package he'd been carrying onto the coffee table and lowered himself into the nearby chair. Then he looked back at Parks, steadily meeting his gaze. "Yes," he answered. "I'll do everything I can for both her and the child."

Parks seemed to consider his answer for a moment and then nodded. It had been their first and last conversation. From then on, there was always someone else around, Maura or the child—both of whom Parks seemed determined to protect.

Jacob shook off his thoughts as the driver turned off the road onto a long driveway leading to the Sanchezes' home.

The house was a veritable showplace, no less than Jacob had expected. He'd done some checking on Mr. and Mrs. Roberto Sanchez, Katie's maternal grandparents. They'd come to Miami just before the Castro regime in Cuba, managing to bring a good deal of their wealth along with them. Now they were model American citizens, and he could hardly blame them for wanting their granddaughter.

He glanced at Maura and saw the fear in her eyes. Parks must have sensed it, as well, because he took her hand even as he continued talking to Katie. In front of the house, Parks helped Maura out of the limo, taking the little girl from her as easily as if Katie belonged to him. If nothing else, the man obviously cared for both mother and child.

They approached the house and the door opened before they reached it. Maura stopped, and for a second Jacob thought she would bolt. He started to move toward her, to offer his support, but Parks beat him to it. The man put a protective arm about her shoulders and the three of them moved through the door.

Jacob followed behind.

Alan kept a close eye on Maura while at the Sanchezes' home. She held up surprisingly well. She smiled and spoke courteously to Mr. and Mrs. Sanchez, Katie's grandparents. If she hugged and kissed Katie a little too fiercely, it was to be expected. If her smile was a little too bright, too forced, no one said anything or probably even noticed, except Alan himself. And when the young woman, Roberta, entered the room, dark and sullen as teenagers often are, Mrs. Sanchez introduced her daughter. Alan saw a flash of compassion spark Maura's blue eyes, and she smiled kindly at the girl who had given Katie life.

Then they left, leaving Katie behind, and Maura's control crumbled. The moment the limo's doors closed behind them, she fell into Alan's arms, great gulping sobs racking her body. He held her close, wishing there was some way to comfort her, but knowing there was none.

Later that night they made love. And there was a desperation between them. A need to hold, love and be loved, as if they might lose each other as well as Katie. It left Alan sated but saddened, because through it all, he suspected Maura held a piece of herself back. And he wondered if things would ever be the same between them without Katie.

THE WEEKS THAT FOLLOWED were merciless.

Maura moved through Jacob's rented house like a wraith. Alan was always there for her, and at times he broke through her misery. For a little while she would actually smile or even laugh at some joke or anecdote he told. But her happiness was always short-lived.

They made love frequently and fervently, but it never seemed enough. It never totally blocked out the pain of Katie's absence. Maura wanted desperately to close her eyes just once without seeing her daughter's face or hearing her laughter. She wanted to sleep without dreaming of dark eyes, dark curls and a bewitching three-year-old's smile. But nothing gave her the relief she sought.

Some nights she would remain sleepless, listening to the night sounds of the house, knowing that Alan was also awake. On those nights, she knew she was losing him, and that there was no one to blame but herself. She would turn and bury her tear-streaked face against his shoulder, wanting to hold on to him. And for a few hours, she'd think she had succeeded. And then dawn would come, and she would lose herself again in the black hole of despair.

Every few days they visited Katie. At first the child was her usual bright self, and Maura delighted in being around her. But as time passed, the visits became more difficult.

"Mommy, I wanna go home," Katie said one day as she and Maura walked along the beach behind the Sanchezes' house. "I don't want to stay here anymore."

Maura stopped and squatted down next to her daughter, taking the little girl's hands in hers. "But aren't you having fun with your grandparents?" she asked. It took all her strength to keep smiling. "Don't you like swimming in the ocean and building sand castles?"

Katie looked down at the ground, her bottom lip trembling slightly, and shrugged. "Yeah."

"You know they love you very much." Maura tried putting enthusiasm into her voice. "And they want to get to know you better."

"Don't you love me anymore?"

The question tore through Maura's heart, and she nearly lost her resolve to be strong. Pulling Katie into her arms, she blinked furiously to hold back her tears. "Of course I love you, sweetie. I'll always love you." Then with a strength she didn't know she possessed, she pulled away and forced the child to look at her. "But so do your grandparents, and they deserve to spend a little time with you. Can you stay with them for just a little longer?"

Katie shrugged again and nudged the sand with her toe. "I guess."

"Good girl," Maura answered, still fighting her own internal battle for control. She held Katie close a while longer, wondering how many more of these conversations she could get through. But as she started to rise, Katie burst into tears.

"I wanna go with you," she cried, throwing herself against her mother. Maura wrapped her arms around the small body while the child clung tightly. "I don't wanna stay," Katie repeated over and over between her sobs.

Maura held her for what seemed an eternity, murmuring soothing words. She no longer made any attempt to stop her own tears. It would have been a wasted effort, anyway. Katie was hurting, and though it tore Maura apart inside, there was nothing she could do about it. Finally Katie's crying slowed, and Maura lifted the worn-out child to carry her back to the house. By the time they arrived, Katie had fallen asleep in her arms.

MEANWHILE JACOB carried on with his legal machinations. Maura pleaded guilty to contempt of court and was sentenced to two hundred hours of community service. In a sense it was a lifesaver. She volunteered at a local women's clinic, and for a few hours a day, at least, the work kept her from dwelling on Katie.

Still, the custody battle raged on.

Their first break came the day the court granted Jacob's request for a psychological evaluation of Roberta Sanchez, Katie's birth mother.

"It's what I've been hoping for," Jacob explained to Maura and Alan. "Hopefully the findings will substantiate the fact that Roberta is too immature to be a mother to Katie."

Maura threw a glance at Alan, strangely disturbed by her father's revelation. But Jacob didn't give her time to evaluate her reaction. The same excitement was in his voice that Maura had heard before, when he thought he was about to wrap up a case.

"Roberta's been in and out of counseling since she was twelve years old," he said. "And her parents still have difficulty controlling her. Several nights ago she was arrested during a drug raid at a party that got out of hand. Roberta herself was clean, but just being at the location hurts her bid for custody."

Maura smiled and hugged both her father and Alan, accepting the news with renewed hope that she would regain custody of Katie. But later that afternoon, she sat on the patio thinking about what her father had said. Alan joined her and gently kissed her on the cheek as he sat in a lawn chair next to hers.

"Arc you okay?" he asked.

Maura turned to him and smiled sadly. "It seems you've had to ask me that a lot lately."

Alan took her hand. "I've been worried about you."

"Yes, I know." Maura wove her finger through his. "I know I've been a burden, moping around here..."

"You have a right."

"Do I?" For the first time since she'd turned Katie over to the Sanchezes', Maura believed she saw things clearly. "Mr. and Mrs. Sanchez love Katie, too."

"Yes, they do." Alan nodded. "But they're her grandparents, not her parents."

"And what about Roberta?" Maura asked. "No matter how badly I want Katie back, I can't help feeling sorry for Roberta. And I don't like trying to prove her an unfit mother."

"You've seen how she acts around Katie," Alan said gently. "She hardly acknowledges the child's existence."

Maura sighed, knowing it was true. "She's a child herself."

"Exactly." Alan lifted a hand to run a finger down Maura's cheek. "And Katie needs a mother."

Maura turned and met his gaze, seeing a world of caring in his eyes. "I love you," she said. "I don't know how I would have gotten through all this without you."

"You would have managed."

Maura shook her head. "I don't think so."

Alan smiled and dropped his hand. They sat quietly for a while as the light faded around them.

"Alan," Maura said, breaking the silence, "I want you to know that whatever happens with Katie..."

Alan squeezed her hand. "It's okay, you don't have to say anything."

Maura turned in her chair to face him. "Yes, I do. I want you to know that I'm going to be all right. When this is all over..."

"When this is all over, I'll be here for you, no matter what happens."

"Yes," she said. "I know. And whatever happens, I'll always love you."

AFTER WEEKS OF frustration, events took on a new momentum. With each passing day, Maura's hopes of regaining custody of Katie looked better. Roberta's lawyer had objected strenuously to the psychological evaluation, but to no avail.

Then the report came back, and all of Jacob's claims proved true. Not only was Roberta too immature to raise a child, but according to the report, she'd actually told the psychologist that she wanted nothing to do with Katie. She considered the child a burden, and it had been her parents' idea all along to sue for custody.

That might have been the end of it right there if it hadn't been for the Sanchezes' influence and money. As it was, their lawyer only managed to drag the decision out another week. The judge demanded a closed session with Roberta Sanchez to make his own evaluation. And when he came out, he dismissed the case.

Maura Anderson maintained custody of her adopted daughter.

THE MORNING they brought Katie back was the happiest day of Maura's life. She stood at the window watching, waiting to see the car that would bring her daughter back to her. Alan seemed as anxious as she was. It was almost as if now that the crisis was past, now that he no longer needed to be the strong one, he could release his own emotions.

When the car pulled up outside, they were out the front door before the engine had been shut off. Mrs. Sanchez opened the car door and Katie sprang out.

"Mommy!" she yelled, and threw herself into her mother's waiting arms. Maura cried and laughed as the child planted mushy kisses all over her face.

"I missed you so much," Maura said through her tears of joy. "So much."

Katie giggled and gave her mother one final hug before squirming sideways to climb into Alan's arms. She wrapped her arms around his neck and buried her head against him. Closing his eyes, Alan held her tight, and when he opened them, Maura saw the soft shine of dampness in his eyes. She stepped into his arms and he drew her into a three-way embrace.

"Can we go home now?" Katie asked.

Maura and Alan laughed. "Where do you mean, sweetie?" Maura asked, not sure where her daughter considered home. "Back to our old house where we lived with your daddy?"

Katie shook her head. "No, back to Aunt Rita and Josh."

"Well, I don't know," Alan said. "I was hoping you and your mom would come live with me. I have a house just a little ways from Aunt Rita and Josh."

Katie seemed to consider this new situation for a moment. "Would you be my new daddy, then?"

"I think that could be arranged." Alan met Maura's gaze and smiled. "What do you say, Mom?"

Maura laughed out loud. "It sounds like a great idea to me."

"Then let's go home." Alan leaned over and kissed her gently. Then, turning to Katie, he added, "What do you say, princess? Are you ready?"

Katie nodded vigorously and hugged his neck. "Yeah. Let's go home."

EPILOGUE

THE DOORBELL RANG, and Maura slipped away from the noisy group of children to answer it. When she saw who was outside, she smiled. Tommy Simmons stood on the porch holding a square box wrapped in bright pink paper.

"Howdy, Mrs. Parks."

"Tommy, what a nice surprise." She moved back to allow him to step inside. "Katie will be thrilled that you're here."

"I can't stay," he said, tossing a glance over his shoulder at the truck that waited outside. "I promised Joey I'd help him make his deliveries today. But I wanted to bring this by for Katie."

"Wait a minute. I'll get her." Maura returned a few minutes later with Alan and Katie in tow.

"What is it?" Katie sprang toward the box that Tommy had set on the floor.

"Open it and see, silly." Tommy crouched down on the floor next to the little girl.

Katie turned, wide-eyed, to her mother, enjoying the drama of the unexpected present. "What could it be?"

A soft scratching brought her attention back to the box, and she quickly untied the ribbon. When she lifted the lid, a wet brown nose inched over the top.

"For me?" Katie leaned down and pulled the small brown bundle into her arms. The puppy squirmed and licked her face.

"Since you're five now, I figured it was time you learned how to take care of something," Tommy said. "That is, if it's okay with your mom."

Katie turned pleading eyes toward her mother. "Can I, Mommy? Please."

Maura pursed her lips and pretended to think about it. "I don't know. What do you think, Dad?"

Alan dropped an arm around his wife's shoulders and leveled a serious look at his daughter. "You'll have to feed her."

"I will."

"And take her for walks."

"I promise."

"She'll be your responsibility."

"I know. Oh, please. I'll take real good care of her. I promise."

"Well..." Alan paused before giving in to the huge grin he'd been holding back. "Sure, she's all yours."

Katie let out an excited screech, and with the puppy still caught in one arm, she threw her other arm around Tommy's neck. The boy turned beet red and nearly lost his balance. They all laughed, and Katie took off for the back porch to show off her latest and favorite gift.

"I think you made a hit," Maura said to Tommy, who was just recovering his composure.

Alan planted a hand on the boy's shoulder. "It was a great idea. And you picked out a good one." Tommy had approached Alan last week about the puppy, and Alan had assured him that Katie would be delighted.

Tommy grinned. "She really liked it, didn't she."

"She sure did," Alan agreed. As they walked toward the front door, he asked, "How's your pa doing?" Bud Simmons had spent six months in an alcoholic rehabilitation center in Seattle. It had evidently been a long haul, but he'd come home a sober man.

"Real good. He and Mrs. Cellar sure have been spending a lot of time together."

Alan chuckled. "If the rumors around town are true, looks like you and Joey might have a new mom soon."

Tommy grinned from ear to ear. "I sure wouldn't mind." While Bud had been in Seattle, Tommy and Joey had stayed with Jean Cellar. "Mrs. Cellar sure can cook a whole lot better than Joey."

Alan laughed again, and Maura gave Tommy a quick hug before letting him out the door. Once again he blushed, but allowed the gesture. Then he hurried out the door, turning to give them a quick wave as he climbed into his brother's truck.

Maura sighed and closed the door behind him.

It seemed like ages since she and Alan had taken Katie back to Miami. In fact, it had only been thirteen months. So much had happened. So much that she was grateful for.

Alan moved up behind her and circled her waist with his arms. "How about if we sneak upstairs?"

"Mmm." Maura folded her arms over his and bent her head sideways, giving him access to her neck. "You don't think a backyard full of five-year-olds is a little much for your aunt?"

Alan found skin beneath her soft blond curls and planted tempting kisses along her nape. "Rita loves kids."

"Not that much."

"The Sanchezes will help."

"You want to bet?" Maura laughed, thinking of Katie's sophisticated grandparents, who had flown in from Miami for the birthday party.

"Okay, so they're not exactly used to a bunch of savages," Alan agreed. "What about Roberta?"

"And risk getting those fine linen slacks dirty? I don't think so."

Alan moaned. "We could make it quick."

Maura laughed and turned in his arms. "It's never that quick." She found his lips and let herself be drawn deeper into his embrace.

When she pulled away, he said, "You're a tease."

"Yes," she answered, "but a very, very lucky tease."

"Oh? How so?"

Maura slipped her arms around his neck and nuzzled his cheek. "I can't imagine. Unless it's having a beautiful five-year-old daughter and the best husband in the whole world."

"Mmm." Alan buried his face in her hair. Even after all these months, he couldn't get used to it, the soft texture, the pale color, the way it fitted perfectly with her fair skin and bright blue eyes. "And the most handsome."

Maura laughed. "That goes without saying."

"Did I ever tell you how I love your hair?"

"At least a million times."

"Dyeing your hair back to its natural color was one of your father's better ideas."

"Oh yeah?" Maura said, snuggling deeper into her husband's arms. "You didn't like me as a brunette?"

"Well, maybe." Alan let his hands roam to her soft bottom, amazed that he still couldn't get enough of her. He pulled her tight against his arousal, showing her just how much he needed her. "Are you sure we can't go upstairs?"

"Later." She gave him a final kiss and, taking his hand, stepped out of his arms. "Come on, we've got a party to go to."

Alan stood still, not letting her draw him toward the sounds of noisy children. "Later you have to go to the clinic."

"Ah," she smiled seductively. "You remembered."

"How could I forget?" Then, with an exaggerated sigh, he pulled his wife back into his arms. Shortly after returning to Waiteville, Maura had gone to work for Doc Readon at his clinic. "All work and no play makes Maura a very dull girl."

Maura rubbed herself against him while brushing her lips across his. "Am I getting too dull for you?"

Alan moaned aloud. "Say it."

"Say what?"

"You know. Say it."

"You mean..." Maura rose on tiptoe and whispered into his ear, "I love you."

"Yeah." Once again he buried his face in her soft cloud of hair. "My three favorite words."

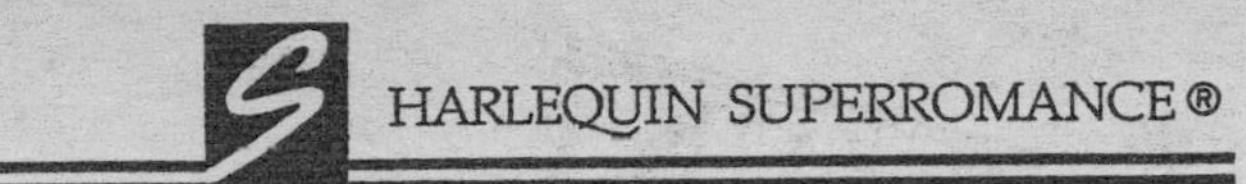

COMING NEXT MONTH

#594 THE PRINCESS AND THE PAUPER • Tracy Hughes

Jessica Hartman's beloved father was gone, leaving maddening instructions in his will. In order to inherit her share of the ailing company that bore her name, she would have to work side by side with her estranged half-brother. Like it or not, she would have to confront the forbidden feelings Cade ignited in her.

#595 NOT QUITE AN ANGEL • Bobby Hutchinson

Sometimes private investigator Adam Hawkins thought Sameh Smith was from another planet. In her endearingly clumsy way she helped derelicts, street kids and prostitutes. But she was also a mystery. She had no personal history prior to April 1994, and Adam was determined to find out why.

#596 DANCING IN THE DARK • Lynn Erickson

Alexandra St. Clair Costidos wanted her son back. His influential father had spirited him away to an impregnable Greek island to punish her for leaving him, and the law could do nothing. It was time for drastic measures. Alex hired mercenary John Smith to help her, but even if she regained her son, she was in danger of losing her heart.

#597 THE YANQUI PRINCE • Janice Kaiser

Reporter Michaela Emory thought it was time to take some risks. How else could she have wild adventures and meet the man of her dreams? Suddenly, she got the chance to do both when she flew to South America to interview the legendary Yanqui Prince. A modern-day Robin Hood, Reed Lakesly was renowned for his courage and charisma. Suddenly Michaela had more adventure and passion than she'd bargained for....

AVAILABLE NOW:

#590 KEEPING KATIE
Patricia Keelyn

#591 TWILIGHT WHISPERS
Morgan Hayes

#592 BRIDGE OVER TIME
Brenda Hiatt

#593 GHOST TIGER
Janice Carter

INDULGE A LITTLE 6947 SWEEPSTAKES
NO PURCHASE NECESSARY

HERE'S HOW THE SWEEPSTAKES WORKS:
The Harlequin Reader Service shipments for January, February and March 1994 will contain, respectively, coupons for entry into three prize drawings: a trip for two to San Francisco, an Alaskan cruise for two and a trip for two to Hawaii. To be eligible for any drawing using an Entry Coupon, simply complete and mail according to directions.

There is no obligation to continue as a Reader Service subscriber to enter and be eligible for any prize drawing. You may also enter any drawing by hand printing your name and address on a 3" x 5" card and the destination of the prize you wish that entry to be considered for (i.e., San Francisco trip, Alaskan cruise or Hawaiian trip). Send your 3" x 5" entries to: Indulge a Little 6947 Sweepstakes, c/o Prize Destination you wish that entry to be considered for, P.O. Box 1315, Buffalo, NY 14269-1315, U.S.A. or Indulge a Little 6947 Sweepstakes, P.O. Box 610, Fort Erie, Ontario L2A 5X3, Canada.

To be eligible for the San Francisco trip, entries must be received by 4/30/94; for the Alaskan cruise, 5/31/94; and the Hawaiian trip, 6/30/94. No responsibility is assumed for lost, late or misdirected mail. Sweepstakes open to residents of the U.S. (except Puerto Rico) and Canada, 18 years of age or older. All applicable laws and regulations apply. Sweepstakes void wherever prohibited.

For a copy of the Official Rules, send a self-addressed, stamped envelope (WA residents need not affix return postage) to: Indulge a Little 6947 Rules, P.O. Box 4631, Blair, NE 68009, U.S.A.

INDR93

- - - - - - - - - - - - - - - - - - - -

INDULGE A LITTLE 6947 SWEEPSTAKES
NO PURCHASE NECESSARY

HERE'S HOW THE SWEEPSTAKES WORKS:
The Harlequin Reader Service shipments for January, February and March 1994 will contain, respectively, coupons for entry into three prize drawings: a trip for two to San Francisco, an Alaskan cruise for two and a trip for two to Hawaii. To be eligible for any drawing using an Entry Coupon, simply complete and mail according to directions.

There is no obligation to continue as a Reader Service subscriber to enter and be eligible for any prize drawing. You may also enter any drawing by hand printing your name and address on a 3" x 5" card and the destination of the prize you wish that entry to be considered for (i.e., San Francisco trip, Alaskan cruise or Hawaiian trip). Send your 3" x 5" entries to: Indulge a Little 6947 Sweepstakes, c/o Prize Destination you wish that entry to be considered for, P.O. Box 1315, Buffalo, NY 14269-1315, U.S.A. or Indulge a Little 6947 Sweepstakes, P.O. Box 610, Fort Erie, Ontario L2A 5X3, Canada.

To be eligible for the San Francisco trip, entries must be received by 4/30/94; for the Alaskan cruise, 5/31/94; and the Hawaiian trip, 6/30/94. No responsibility is assumed for lost, late or misdirected mail. Sweepstakes open to residents of the U.S. (except Puerto Rico) and Canada, 18 years of age or older. All applicable laws and regulations apply. Sweepstakes void wherever prohibited.

For a copy of the Official Rules, send a self-addressed, stamped envelope (WA residents need not affix return postage) to: Indulge a Little 6947 Rules, P.O. Box 4631, Blair, NE 68009, U.S.A.

INDR93

INDULGE A LITTLE
SWEEPSTAKES

OFFICIAL ENTRY COUPON

This entry must be received by: MAY 31, 1994
This month's winner will be notified by: JUNE 15, 1994
Trip must be taken between: JULY 31, 1994-JULY 31, 1995

YES, I want to win the Alaskan Cruise vacation for two. I understand that the prize includes round-trip airfare, one-week cruise including private cabin, all meals and pocket money as revealed on the "wallet" scratch-off card.

Name____________________________________

Address ________________________ Apt. ____________

City____________________________________

State/Prov.__________________ Zip/Postal Code____________

Daytime phone number____________________________
(Area Code)

Account #____________________________________

Return entries with invoice in envelope provided. Each book in this shipment has two entry coupons—and the more coupons you enter, the better your chances of winning!

INDULGE A LITTLE
SWEEPSTAKES

OFFICIAL ENTRY COUPON

This entry must be received by: MAY 31, 1994
This month's winner will be notified by: JUNE 15, 1994
Trip must be taken between: JULY 31, 1994-JULY 31, 1995

YES, I want to win the Alaskan Cruise vacation for two. I understand that the prize includes round-trip airfare, one-week cruise including private cabin, all meals and pocket money as revealed on the "wallet" scratch-off card.

Name____________________________________

Address ________________________ Apt. ____________

City____________________________________

State/Prov.__________________ Zip/Postal Code____________

Daytime phone number____________________________
(Area Code)

Account #____________________________________

Return entries with invoice in envelope provided. Each book in this shipment has two entry coupons—and the more coupons you enter, the better your chances of winning!

© 1993 HARLEQUIN ENTERPRISES LTD. MONTH2